The
LIGHTHOUSE
S★CIETY

JERRY GRAFFAM

Dear Nathan,

I hope to see you back in Maine soon and angrateful for all your support!

Best Wishes!

Jerry L. Griffam

The Lighthouse Society / Jerry Graffam
First Edition Paperback: May 2012
ISBN 13: 978-1-936185-68-9
ISBN 10: 1-936185-68-7

Editor: Reba Hilbert
Interior Design: Susan Veach
Cover Design: Laurie McAdams

Readers may contact the author at: www.jerrygraffam.com

Published by Charles River Press, LLC
www.CharlesRiverPress.com

Dedicated to my parents,
Ward & Linda Graffam.
Your love and support have
guided and inspired me.
I love you both!

Very Special Thanks to Jerry Fisher,
my friend and the first editor to believe in
me and this story.

To those who have supported me
throughout this project:

My wife, Julie, Kristen & Dan King,
Ward & Kristin Graffam,

Bill & Linda Nickerson,
Genie Boone, and Jennifer Jermann Varney.

Chapter One

At the tender age of twelve, Jack Chandler was far too young to understand the underlying tension often involved in adult arguments. The whole ride from Portland to the ferry terminal in Rockland, his parents argued whether or not they should try and catch the last ferry to Carroll Island or get a hotel room on the mainland while the fierce nor'easter pounded Penobscot Bay and its islands. And while most twelve-year-olds lacked the intuition to give it any more thought, Jack knew there was something else driving the discussion. He could tell his father wanted to be on that ferry, storm or no storm. As he did in most of the family arguments, his father won this round.

With his bright blue CB Sports parka practically stretched over a turtleneck, a heavy wool sweater, and a hand-knit scarf wrapped twice around his neck, Jack felt as if he had on a child-sized straightjacket. He could move his head far enough to see the deckhands coiling frozen lines at the stern of the ferry, but he never let his peripheral vision drift away from the cabin door leading to the bridge.

Timothy Chandler had gone up to confront Captain Davidson about a beer bottle being tossed out the pilothouse window, but Jack hadn't seen the bottle. He often heard his parents talk about Davidson being a drunk, but the look of rage in his father's eyes made him think there was something else he went to confront him about. Perhaps the beer bottle was a trigger, but that look was all too familiar to Jack. It was the look his father got just before he was going to put Jack over his knee and spank him for staying out after dark or going out on his skiff with Jimmy Reynolds after a dense fog rolled in over Carroll Island's rocky shore.

With a half-inch of newly fallen snow resting on his puffy shoulders, Jack stood silent, his eyes again glued on the door. His ears, while muffled by his ski hat, were tuned in to every sound.

"Jack, honey," his mother said, gently tugging at his parka sleeve. "Let's go inside and get you warm. You're going to catch your death out here."

Jack struggled to turn his head just enough to catch a glimpse of his mother. While all the layers of clothing made him feel constrained, he couldn't understand why her tall, wiry frame was covered by nothing more than an overcoat and leather gloves. Her long brown hair—speckled with large flakes of fresh snow—floated in the gusts of wind, which swirled around the iron-grated deck. Little tornado-shaped plumes of newly fallen snow danced around the parked cars. Laura Chandler's face didn't have the sense of urgency that Jack felt in the pit of his stomach.

His mother stepped in front of him and crouched down. Her cheeks were bright red from the cold as she tried to block the driving snow from her face with her hand. "Jack Chandler, I'm not going to ask you again."

"I want to wait out here for Dad," Jack replied.

"Jack, your father will be down shortly." Her tone had gone from motherly to angry, but Jack didn't budge. "Why must you always be so stubborn, young—"

"Mom, what's that flashing red light?" Jack pointed just off the port side of the bow.

Laura Chandler turned, saw the beacon, and grabbed Jack's sleeve.

Jack fell forward from the jolt of his mother's forceful tug. He knew this wasn't about getting warm. The flashing light was too far away to be on the ferry, but close enough that it scared his mother. "Shouldn't we get Dad?"

"Jack, we have to get—"

Laura Chandler's command was interrupted by the deafening sound of the ferry's foghorn followed by static coming from the PA system. "Ladies and gentlemen, we have an emergency." The voice was not Captain Davidson's. "Deckhands, secure the cabins. I think we're…"

The force of the ferry's hull striking the rocky ocean floor threw Jack and his mother to the deck. The PA system went silent and the cabin lights flickered before going out completely.

Jack looked up and saw his mother clenching the metal grate with one hand while reaching for him with the other. The sound of the steel hull being crushed by the granite ledge was piercing. "Mom, what's happening?" Jack cried out, trying to reach her hand.

Having collided with a ledge, the ferry's forward momentum had stopped in its track, but the brute hydraulic force of the ocean swells lifted the bow of the ferry before dropping it back down on the sea-covered mass of rock.

Each time the ferry rose then fell back to the surface, Jack could feel his whole body pound against the deck. The horrific screeching sound of metal and rock colliding faded a little with each crash. Jack could feel his grip loosening from the grate; his strength was being sucked out of him, and he was overcome with fear.

The sound of his mother's screaming voice was the last thing he heard as he again bounced up from the deck and landed, this time on his head. His vision quickly blurred, and he felt a cold, numbing sensation.

* * *

The next thing Jack heard was the sound of his grandparents' voices as they hovered over him. For days he had been in a coma after the ferry sank and he was found along the shore near Tenants Harbor. When he awoke, he had no idea where he was, but he knew that his parents weren't there with him.

Jack's grandparents smiled at him and held his hand, but he couldn't make out a word they were saying. His head pounded with a headache like no other before. He wanted to talk, but couldn't. He wanted to cry, but that too was impossible. Fear was the only thing he could remember. Jack had absolutely no idea what had happened.

Chapter Two

Working in the insurance industry was not something Jack had ever imagined while in college. He had spent long nights studying European literary theorists and writing short stories. His quirky, almost opinionated fiction won him praise from professors and fellow students at the University of Maine. Mentors lauded his use of prose, and some went so far as to say that he would be one of the great young literary writers to come out of the state. Jack was ambivalent to the idea. He was fully aware of the constant battle between those who wrote and followed literary fiction as opposed to those who wrote commercial fiction.

"Jack Chandler's prose sings," one columnist wrote. Whether it be naivety or indifference, Jack hadn't a clue what that meant. He chose to study English because it enabled him to escape what he perceived as a deeply flawed world through the use of his imagination.

While it was an honor to see his work published in magazines and literary journals, Jack had never bought into the idea that the only good fiction was literary fiction. Wasn't the point of fiction to entertain? And if that was the case, why did so many writers turn their noses up at those names that lined the bestseller lists? Jack had plenty of experience with jealousy and decided he wanted nothing to do with it.

And so Jack found himself in a six-by-six-foot cubicle at the Maine Life & Trust insurance company. Hundreds of miles from the cutthroat literary houses of New York City and five years removed from writing of any sort, Jack again found himself lost. Like so many times since his parents' untimely and tragic deaths, Jack was uneasy with his role in life. He chose insurance because he had found it interesting, but after years of paying long-term disability and life claims, he realized that he had spent far too much time helping others and little time focusing on himself.

* * *

As Jack sifted through all the new claims he'd received that Monday morning, he had absolutely no idea that the proverbial straw that broke the camel's back was staring him right in the face. At first glance it was nothing more than a term life claim for a hundred thousand dollars. *Pretty good coverage*, he thought. *Why the hell am I getting this? Just pay the damned thing, Lindsay.*

Jack typed the deceased's policy number into his computer and quickly read through the provisions as he reached for the phone and dialed.

"Thank you for calling Maine Life," a tired female voice answered. "This is Lindsay Porter."

Jack could hear the stress in her voice. "Hey Lindsay, what's wrong?"

"Besides it being Monday morning?"

"Did you bring me a life claim for a..." Jack flipped back to the first page. "George Watson?"

"Yes. You know I can't pay that claim, Jack. Take a look at the death certificate. The guy died over two years ago," she replied.

"Why can't you pay a two-year-old claim?" Jack sighed and looked over the death certificate. "You gotta be kidding me. No body?"

Jack nearly dropped the phone as his mind was immediately filled with faint images of his parents. It had been sixteen years, but he could still see the horrified look on his mother's face after the ferry crashed into the rocks. Jack's throat constricted and his heart began to pound like a drum.

"Jack, you there? You okay?"

Jack hung up the receiver and stared at the small piece of paper. He was actually jealous of this person's family. Jealous that a medical examiner had made a determination that after two years the man could finally be declared dead. The Watson family could get on with their lives.

Jack never got that closure. Timothy and Laura Chandler's bodies were never found. There were never death certificates issued for them. For all intents and purposes, they were still missing persons.

Jack knew that if he pushed hard enough, he could get those pieces of paper, but those certificates would never fill the empty void inside of Jack.

Chapter Three

Kendra Davids paced back and forth in the kitchen, nervous in anticipation. As a trial lawyer, she had watched hundreds of stone-faced jurors ponder the fates of the clients she defended. She exuded an air of confidence in the courtroom that overshadowed any amount of anxiety. She thrived on pressure.

Jack was the only person who'd ever perplexed Kendra. What began as a college romance had flourished into an engagement just six months ago. And although Kendra knew she wanted to spend the rest of her life with him, she couldn't help but feel that there was still so much to learn about him.

Kendra knew Jack would never keep something from her, but there were times when he just seemed distant. That afternoon Jack had seemed distant when he called. He told her he had big news he wanted to discuss with her over dinner. *What big news?* Kendra wondered. The two lived fairly normal, if not boring lives, and Jack hadn't mentioned anything that could clue her in to what he was alluding to.

Jack never seemed to have big news. He was the sort of mild-mannered guy that went with the flow. He went to work every day because he was interested in helping others, just like her. The big difference between the two was that Jack didn't have to work. When Jack's parents died sixteen years ago, he had become the wealthiest twelve-year-old in Maine. Kendra was thankful that he had loving grandparents who had been able to love and guide him through those tumultuous times and groom him into an honorable young man.

Kendra had only known Jack for about a year when his grandmother passed away, and then his grandfather, only months later. It was then she noticed a shift in his outward personality. The once boisterous and outgoing frat boy assumed a quiet demeanor.

* * *

The echo of a car door slamming shut in the garage startled Kendra. *My lord. I'm actually on edge,* she thought as she lightly sprayed some perfume on her wrists. She felt like she was on a first date, yet she and Jack had been living together for the better part of five years.

"Hey, sweetie," Jack said as he walked through the basement door. He had a dark blue portfolio in his right hand. The corners were somewhat worn and the color looked as though it had dulled.

Kendra had never seen it before, and it couldn't have been new. Maybe the surprise he spoke of was inside?

Jack grasped a bouquet of lavender-colored flowers in his left hand and held them out to her as he approached. "Obviously not fresh from the garden," he said, "but the florist assured me they came in this morning."

Kendra held the bouquet up to her nose and inhaled deeply. She smiled softly. "They smell wonderful," she said. "You always seem to know when I've had a tough day."

Kendra knew the flowers had nothing to do with her day, but

didn't want to bring up his surprise. She could tell he was trying to soften her up and decided to play along.

Jack set the portfolio on the brick hearth next to the woodstove. "What was so bad about your day?"

"Oh, nothing really," she replied. "The boss being the boss. Same old stuff really. Nothing I can't handle." Kendra always felt comfortable venting her professional frustrations to Jack, yet she held back now. She sensed he had something on his mind that was more important than her ongoing dispute with her boss.

Jack shrugged nonchalantly. "Okay, but if you decide you want to talk about it, I'm all ears."

Kendra got out a tall crystal vase from an overhead cupboard and dropped a penny into it. Her mother always told her that a penny and a spot of 7-UP mixed with the water kept the flowers alive longer. She had no idea if it was true, but followed the routine every time she got flowers.

Kendra walked over to the sink, turned on the faucet, and ran her small fingers through the water, waiting for it to get cool enough for the flowers. She looked back over to Jack and noticed there was something different about him. He didn't have on his normal work attire—khaki pants, loafers, and a solid-colored oxford. He wore an old suede jacket over a blue navy t-shirt. His thinning chestnut hair was messy.

"Smells great. What did you cook?" he asked.

"Just stir-fry," she replied. "I didn't have too much time after work. Henning kept me late again. Seems I have to consult on every case these days. I want a raise—a big raise. Either that or I'm outta there." Her tone was somewhat playful, but she actually meant it. She had had enough of her male chauvinist boss. In fact, she was sick of being a lawyer altogether. Although she would never admit it, if she had the kind of inheritance that Jack had, she'd leave the sixty-hour workweeks behind and focus on her true love—painting.

Kendra turned to the stovetop, stirred the small pot of white rice, and spooned a portion onto each plate. She looked down at the portfolio and said, "Since when do you bring work home with you?"

Jack picked the portfolio up off the floor and looked up at her with a coy smile. It was as though he had a bag of tricks in his hand. "This isn't from work, honey," he replied. "I left work around noon and came home to look for this. I spent nearly two hours sifting through all the boxes in the attic before I found it."

Kendra sensed giddiness in Jack's expression. It was more than just the way he was dressed. Jack was generally happy. And then it dawned on her. How could she be so stupid? Of course she had seen the portfolio before, but it seemed like forever. "Jack, is that your novel?"

"I don't know as though you could really call it a novel," he replied, "but it's the last piece of writing I worked on."

Kendra slipped her red apron from around her waist and tossed it into the corner. *This must be the surprise,* she thought. She never wanted Jack to stop writing in the first place. She had found it hard to believe that someone with such recognizable talent would just stop doing it, but respected his decision. Although she had never sold one of her paintings, she knew that there was a similar divide in the art community as there was in the literary world. The only difference was that she couldn't care less about what others thought of her work. Deep down, she knew Jack felt the same way.

"So where did you go after you found the novel?" she asked, glancing at his wardrobe again. "I assume you didn't go back to the office."

"I went out to the Cape to read."

Kendra set a plate down in front of him and sat across the table. "What's on your mind, Jack? Don't get me wrong, I'm happy you're taking an interest in your writing again, but you're acting a little strange. Sort of like you're going through a midlife crisis or something. You didn't go out and buy a new car, did you?"

Jack laughed. "I'm only twenty-eight years old for Christ's sake. I don't think one can have a midlife crisis at twenty-eight. And no, I didn't buy a new car."

Kendra truly didn't want to push, but she could tell Jack was in a good mood. "Something at work bothering you?" she asked. "We could compare horror stories over stir-fry. Pretty romantic if you ask me."

Jack's smile disappeared. "I don't know what it is really. I mean I really do like work and all, but it's just not as satisfying as it used to be."

"I know how you feel," Kendra said, rolling her eyes. "For me, it's like every day is the same."

"Exactly. Yet today I was going over some new claims and one came across my desk that sort of freaked me out. And to be perfectly honest, it shouldn't have, except..."

"Except what? Was it a life claim?"

"I review life claims every day, but this one... This one was a claim with no body."

Kendra suddenly felt like she was shrinking in her chair. She knew

Jack's parents' bodies had never been found.

"And for a moment I was actually jealous of the beneficiaries." Jack paused. "I honestly felt jealous because these people had closure and I never did."

Kendra was puzzled. "Why did they have closure?"

"Because there was a death certificate. The body was never found, but after a two-year search, the American Embassy in Turkey certified that the person was dead. I realize it's not the same as finding the body, but I would assume it could provide some finality."

One of the reasons Kendra was a good trial lawyer was because she had a response for anything the judge or the other counsel could throw at her. She was prepared for any scenario. Yet she sat there silent, having not a clue what to say to comfort Jack.

Jack rubbed the corners of his eyes with his palms and then perked up in his chair.

"So I just got up and left," he said. "I came back here with absolutely no idea what I was doing, but I had to find that book."

"Because it's based on someone losing their parents?" Kendra asked.

Jack shook his head and inhaled deeply. "No… no, I had to find it because it's unfinished. The story doesn't have closure."

Chapter Four

While Henry McKay hadn't been close with either Timothy or Laura Chandler, it was the Chandler family business that had provided the means for his success in life. And as his eyes panned around from the porch of the lightkeeper's house, with a chilly southwesterly wind numbing his aging face, he couldn't help but feel remorse for his role in the cover-up of their deaths sixteen years ago.

Through the tall spruce and pine trees that lined the northwestern shore of the island, he could see the lights of the village and the smoke wafting from the chimneys of the islanders' homes. The view wasn't any different now than it was that night in 1994, yet he knew—as well as anyone—it was that stormy winter night that had changed the island forever.

Henry McKay wasn't even a member of the Society then, but remembered that it was his aspiration to be named to the secret governing society that had allowed his better judgment to be clouded—to let those two people die in vain. It would have been easy to just come forth and present the truth to the authorities, yet he was given an option he couldn't ignore. The option of keeping the island's innocence intact or helping the others cover up what he thought at the time was an accident. The latter would not only lead to financial gain, but made room for a new person in the five-man society.

Henry knew he could listen to Kyle Foster, cooperate with the authorities, and do what was morally right, or he could side with the others, plead ignorance, and relish their promises for his future. As he helped bury the dead bodies that blistery February night, in a wooded plot of land near the lighthouse, he had clearly made his choice.

Henry waited patiently on the porch. The night was cold and dark, the only light coming from the quarter-moon above and the intermittent beam making its circular rotation, which emanated from the lamp atop the lighthouse tower.

He looked down at his silver wristwatch. It was a minute before eight o'clock and he began to tense up. Robert Billings had a unique, if not annoying way of sneaking up on people, and Henry was in no mood for any of the ex-Marine's charades.

* * *

Sam Robertson ducked into the woods about a hundred yards before the gated driveway leading to the lighthouse, stepping gingerly over the crisp, frozen underbrush. He felt like a teenager sneaking past his parents' bedroom door on the way to a late night rendezvous, but knew the repercussions for getting caught would be far more drastic. Yet when he saw Henry McKay turn his truck into the old quarry lot and then dash across Cranberry Lane as though someone were chasing him, Sam's curiosity was piqued. He had passed the village commons a few minutes before beginning the long walk out to Kyle Foster's. He would surely have noticed if the blue light outside the gazebo was illuminated, signifying a meeting of the Lighthouse Society.

Membership in the Society was supposed to be secretive, yet having been the sheriff of Carroll Island for twenty years, Sam had become privy to island secrets, which were little more than gossip at the lunch counter in the Village Dock Store. And while he might have retired from that position a few years ago, there was something about that pesky Henry McKay sneaking around the island that drew Sam into those woods.

* * *

"Henry," a voice whispered softly, followed by a light chuckle.

Henry jumped backwards from the railing of the porch, almost falling over Robert Billings, who had crawled silently across the porch before startling his friend. His short, muscular frame was decked out in black from head to toe. He pulled the black watch cap from his head, and Henry could see steam rise from his military-style crew cut.

"For crying out loud, Robert," Henry said.

"Oh come on, McKay. I was just playing a little prank on you," Billings replied with a wide smile. "Besides, you're the one that asked me to come all the way out here tonight. What could be so secret that you couldn't have just asked Arlington to call a meeting? I don't like sneaking around—"

"Yes you do," Henry interrupted, cupping his left hand as he lit a cigar with the other. "If you were younger, you'd still be running through the woods with your Marine buddies."

"True, but you haven't answered my question, McKay. What's so important and why aren't the other members here?"

"As you know, there are some matters that can't be discussed in front of the other members. This happens to be one of them." Henry walked back to the railing where he had waited earlier and looked out over the rocks below. The sound of the waves crashing calmed him.

Billings walked over and leaned against the railing. "Okay. So you don't want Foster to know what's on your mind. What is it with the two of you anyway?"

"This has little to do with my relationship with Kyle Foster," Henry replied sternly. "But you're right. What I'm about to tell you needs to stay between us. Not that everyone else on the island won't find out, but given our island's history, I feel it's best that the two of us get a jump on the situation."

"What situation, McKay?" Billings had a sense of urgency in his tone.

"Tell me what you see out there on Chandler Point."

"Lights on in the old Chandler house," Billings said, seemingly dumbfounded at first. "That…that could be a problem."

Henry reached into his pants pocket and pulled out some folded paper. "I had phone monitor duty this afternoon and recorded this conversation" He handed the paper to Billings, hoping that the documentation would ease the skepticism. "I know that the rest of you seem to think I've been paranoid in the past—"

"This is a joke, right?" Billings interrupted. "Jack Chandler called Sally today and told her he's coming back to the island. You're damned right we've got to get a jump on the situation. When Foster hears about this, he'll probably organize a parade. Where's the rest of it? It's cut off in mid-sentence."

"We're lucky we got that much. The tape ran out. He told Sally that he and his fiancée are planning on moving out here next month… to live," Henry explained. "Asked her if she could help get the house ready for them. She's been looking after it for years. Ever since her mother died."

Billings let out a deep sigh. "What makes you think he'll cause trouble?"

"Told Sally he's going to work on his novel," Henry replied. "A novel he began around the time he wrote those damned editorials. He said that he wanted to write out here because the story is set on a small Maine island. Now what do you suppose that book could be about? And don't tell me I'm being paranoid. I know that the thought of him poking his nose around here scares the hell out of you, too."

"Yeah, it does, but we'd have a hard time selling it to the rest of the Society, never mind Foster," Billings explained. "As odd as it is for him to come back here after so many years, they'll think it's just a coincidence. Besides, it's been ten years since he wrote those editorials. Why now? And who'd believe him if he did start poking his nose around? He's not going to find the bodies. No bodies means no case, as far as I'm concerned."

"Be that as it may be," McKay said angrily. He hadn't thought Robert Billings would be such a tough sell. He imagined that the very thought of Jack coming back to Carroll would illicit the hard-line stance he was accustomed to from Billings. Not only was Billings his best resource, he was also a barometer for how the rest of the Society would react. If Henry couldn't get Billings on his side, he wouldn't have a chance with the others. "Jack wouldn't have written those editorials if he hadn't had some sort of proof."

"And what kind of proof would he have? Damned kid nearly drowned that night."

"That's what I want you to go find out," McKay said, insidiously.

"You're the man with all the connections. When are you going to your office in Portland next?"

"A couple days. Sooner if need be."

"Well then, why don't we just leave it up to your imagination, my friend." Henry had a grin from ear to ear. He knew that Billings couldn't refuse the challenge Henry had just thrown at him. "And remember, this conversation never took place," he said, turning to get some sort of acknowledgment, but Billings was gone. He had slipped away as quietly as he had approached.

* * *

As Sam peeked around the corner of the keeper's house and looked up at the porch, he saw a shadow move swiftly down the stairs to the side lawn while McKay stood alone. He was too late. In the time it took Sam to quietly make his way through the woods leading to the property, McKay had seemingly concluded his secret meeting.

Sam was angry that he hadn't been able to overhear McKay's secret conversation, but he was far more disturbed at what it could be. He knew that McKay wouldn't risk being exposed as a member of the Society unless his meeting was of the utmost importance. *Why not just wait till the next meeting?* Sam wondered. Yet he knew the answer. A little over two hours ago, Sam had heard mention of Jack Chandler's name while picking up a six-pack of beer at the Village Dock Store. The owner of the store, Sally Reynolds, had been telling a story to her lone employee, Sandra Carter, not realizing he had been listening to their conversation. At the time it had meant little. The Chandler family had founded Carroll Island, and Sam had assumed the conversation between the two women was merely some story about Sally and Jack as kids, but this meeting had changed that assumption. He knew that the one thing that scared the Society more than having its members' names and faces known to the island residents was the idea of someone connecting them to the deaths of Timothy and Laura Chandler. It was a fear that had changed the Society from being an overly protective governing organization to an oppressive, totalitarian-style government. They ruled the island by keeping the residents quiet and afraid. The only difference was that instead of one tyrant yielding his power over the masses, there were five men who hid behind the mask of the secret Society. A society that had been founded for the purposes of charity and brotherhood had become an underground organization driven by power, money, and the collective need to keep Carroll Island's darkest secret. If Sam was right, Jack Chandler was coming for that secret.

Chapter Five

S pecial Agent Nathan Richardson hesitated as he stepped out of the elevator and approached a tinted-glass door, just across the hallway from the elevator. To his left, the dim, sterile hallway extended about fifty feet to the office of the director of the Federal Bureau of Investigation. To the right was a door that was slightly ajar. Nate was able to see through the crack, but saw nothing more than a long conference room table.

It was his first time in the penthouse of the Bureau headquarters in the J. Edgar Hoover building. His former supervisor—now deputy director—Benjamin Chambers, received the promotion after his predecessor was forced to retire by the new Homeland Security Chief, Tyler Cochran. Nate wasn't privy to the details. He was, for all intents and purposes, just a financial analyst.

Nevertheless, Nate had news that he knew would light a fire in his mentor and former boss. He glanced down briefly at the newly attached nameplate, adjusted his tie, and knocked on the door.

"Come," a stern voice commanded.

Nate took a deep breath and ran his hands through his soft red hair. *Just be confident*, he thought as he straightened his back to make the most of his five-foot-eight frame. Nate couldn't help but think of the last time he requested to go into the field. A situation that almost got the Bureau sued.

Nate opened the door and walked speedily into the center of the office. A huge oak desk and three floor-to-ceiling windows behind him dwarfed Chambers. The walls on either side were covered with certificates and diplomas of various shapes and sizes. Nate was awestruck.

"Deputy Director, thank you for agreeing to see me on such short notice," Nate said. "And may I compliment your new office. It's, well... big." Confidence had always been a problem for Nate.

"Agent Richardson, will you do away with all the cloak and dagger crap. You said you had something important to tell me."

Nate walked over to a wooden coffee table and set down his briefcase. He snapped two small gold-colored buttons on the side and lifted the top. The inside was nearly empty except for one file. Nate took the file in hand and approached the desk, eyeing one of the two chairs, which were perfectly situated in front of the desk. He knew better than to make the assumption that he could make himself at home.

Chambers stiffened up in his chair. His square face was clean-shaven with fair skin. Despite his grayish-white hair, cut high and tight, he exhibited almost boyish features.

"Sir, I got a call from Jack Chandler today. Now I know what you're thinking. I didn't exactly accomplish much the last time I was assigned to him, but—"

Chambers interrupted. "You went to Colorado and became ski buddies with the guy. If I recall, we sent you there to find an inroad to that damned island. As you might imagine, I don't have a lot of patience for this topic. You made me look like a fool."

"With all due respect, sir," Nate replied, "you sent me out there to see if Jack had any intention of returning to Carroll Island. I couldn't exactly force the subject. I would have blown my cover. Now as it turns out, he's engaged to a woman who has been trying to talk him into moving back to the island."

"Who is this woman?"

"A lawyer by profession, but she apparently fancies herself as an artist," Nate explained. "Artists flock to islands in Maine. Seems there's some attraction to seagulls and pine trees. Regardless, they're both moving to the island. Soon."

"These two are just moving out to an island on a whim?"

"Not exactly," Nate replied. "Jack said he's sick of the insurance business and wants to get back to doing something he enjoys. Said he's going to go work on an unfinished novel."

"Let me guess, Richardson. He's writing a book about a family torn apart by a tragic accident. That's slippery territory for us to get involved in," Chambers replied. "Besides, the statute of limitations ran out years ago on that case."

"Well, sure. We're not going to find out what happened to all the money lost on that ferry, but if Jack's theory is correct—"

"Whoa, whoa, hold on a minute, Richardson. We'd been following a money trail for years. Nailing Robert Billings and that town government for money laundering would have gotten me up the ladder a lot faster, but the fact of the matter is that the case ended in the middle of that bay when we lost our one credible witness. Besides, I never bought into that whole conspiracy theory about the ferry being intentionally run aground."

"Sir, Jack thinks there was a cover-up. Now you may be right. It might all be nothing more than emotional overreaction, but if I go in undercover, we've got nothing to lose. If something does turn up through Jack's research…" Nate sighed. "There's no statute of limitations on murder."

Chambers twisted anxiously in his chair. "And how do you propose we get involved in this? You going to offer to be his literary agent?"

"Jack asked me to help him move his boat up the coast from Portland and spend a few days with him on the island," Nate explained. "He'd have no suspicions that I'm with the FBI. If nothing comes of it, no harm done. If he does uncover something, we'd be able to control him."

Chambers stood up and glared at the young agent. He tapped his fingers methodically on the shiny desk. "I've barely been in this post for a month, and you want me to not only break protocol, you want me to authorize a mission that may well be out of our jurisdiction?"

Nate stood tall, his arms grasped behind his back. His stomach was full of butterflies, but he felt a renewed sense of confidence. "Sir, I just want a shot at this. Please."

Chambers sat back down in his leather armchair and sighed deeply. He punched a few keys on his computer keyboard and stared at the monitor. Gently rubbing his chin, he turned back toward Nate. "Okay, Agent Richardson. You *will* work closely with the Coast Guard and you *will* take orders from Agent O'Neil, who has been working with the NCUA in Portland. If this goes sour, it could mean your career."

Chapter Six

The crash of shattering glass jolted Jack and Kendra out of a peaceful sleep. They both bolted upright, their hearts racing. They froze in fear when they heard the floorboards creak.

"That came from the kitchen," Jack whispered, his hands trembling.

"Why isn't the alarm going off?" Kendra asked, grabbing Jack's arm.

"Get under the bed, Kendra," whispered Jack, slowly pulling back the covers. "Stay there until I come back."

"Under the bed? What are you going to do?"

Holding his index finger to his lips to silence Kendra, Jack saw her still lying on the bed, too afraid to move. He crawled across the bed to her and said, "Kendra, please get under the bed. Stay quiet."

Jack rolled over to the edge of the bed and grabbed his grandfather's old .38 caliber Smith & Wesson revolver from the nightstand. He sat and listened, trying to figure out where the intruder was. He instinctively knew that their safety depended on his ability to make it to the rear staircase and stop the intruder before he or she found them.

Fear gripped him like a vise; his airways constricted. He grasped the gun in his right hand, cocked the hammer, and reached for the marble doorknob with his left. He was relieved when the hinges didn't screech and alert the intruder to his position. Crouching down to a crawl, Jack inched his way downstairs. Just before he reached the landing, he paused and listened carefully. The sound of rustling paper stopped him from moving forward. *Who would break in to look through papers?* he wondered. *No robber would be careless enough to make so much noise.* Then he heard the rustling again and realized it came from the old antique desk by the front foyer.

Blood rushed to Jack's head while he inched closer to the corner of the stairwell. The landing between the flights of stairs would be his cover. It was dark and high enough above the first floor for him to remain out of sight. Jack knew he had the upper hand. From his perch, he saw all the way through the dining room to the front of the house.

Jack crouched and waited with his eyes focused straight ahead. Where would the intruder go next? If he chose to climb the mahogany front staircase on the other side of the house, Jack would hear the steps and be able to get back to the bedroom in time to defend Kendra. Any other route through the house would cross his line of sight.

Jack waited, remaining still. Suddenly the sound of rustling paper stopped. He secured his grip on the gun and waited with the concentration of a sniper, while a stout man's shadow appeared on the living room wall. The shadow moved toward the open French doors separating the living room and dining room. Jack took a deep breath. The shadow turned and Jack saw a gun in the intruder's hand. He made out the outline of the hammer and the barrel extending from the man's fist. Jack put his finger on the .38's trigger and held it in his outstretched hands.

Suddenly the shadow was gone, and he had the stocky man in his sights. He pulled the trigger and the gunshot rang in his ears. The force of the blast made the gun jump right out of Jack's clammy hand. He peered around the corner to see where the intruder was; then he heard a click—the sound of a round being chambered into the intruder's gun.

Jack shuffled out of the line of fire when he heard the gun blast, and was showered with glass shards when the gunman's bullet hit the window above him. The sound of glass breaking was matched only by Kendra's scream from the bedroom. Jack scrambled back up the stairs and slid down on the hardwood floor toward the bed. He breathed a sigh of relief when he heard the back door slam, and knew the man had left.

Crawling out from under the bed, Kendra lunged at Jack and hugged him. "Are you okay?"

"It's okay. I'm fine—he's gone." Jack's torso was still trembling from his encounter.

Kendra's skin was pale, ghost-like in the half-light of the bedroom. "Who was it—why was he in our house?"

"Don't have a clue," Jack replied, out of breath. Something in his gut told him the break-in wasn't connected to the string of burglaries the neighborhood had experienced since Christmas. *What in God's name were you looking for?*

Looking over Kendra's shoulder through the window, Jack saw two beams of light through the fog, which had rolled in from Portland Harbor. On a clear day, he could look out the window and see most of the South Portland peninsula, the Fore River, and all the way out to Cape Elizabeth, but the pea-soup fog made it impossible to see past the lawn across the street.

Prying Kendra's hands away, he ran to the window and saw the thickset man looking back toward the house.

"He obviously didn't find what he was looking for," Jack said. His fearful tone had been replaced with anger. The .38 again grasped in his right hand, he ran toward the back staircase.

"Where are you going now?" cried Kendra, tears streaming down her face.

"Calm down and call the police."

While Kendra reached for the phone, Jack shuffled down the stairs and through the shattered glass; shards of fibers pierced his bare feet. Hobbling into the living room, he barely noticed the pain. He saw the door to the secretary desk left open, papers strewn everywhere.

"Jack, the police are on their way," Kendra yelled from the second floor. "My God, honey, did you run through this glass?"

"I'm fine. Don't worry about it," he replied.

Sifting through the paper on the desk, Jack realized exactly what the intruder had been looking for. All the papers were copies he had made of police reports and public statements made by Carroll Island residents. Jack had spent days in the Portland Library prior to writing his editorial about ferryboat captains drinking before getting into the pilothouse. The references were obscure. None bore the necessary proof Jack had been looking for—an admission of some sort. Even the most obscure link to Davidson being drunk, by one of the residents or survivors of the accident, would have solidified a case against the captain. Jack knew. He wasn't able to remember much from that night, especially after being knocked unconscious, but he had heard his father commenting on the beer bottle being thrown from the pilothouse window. And that had been the last thing he ever heard from his father.

It had been enough to drive Jack to write the editorial. He hadn't needed proof. It was an opinion piece, one that after years of coming up with nothing, the authorities frowned upon. The State Police and the FBI had censured Jack, but he liked to think of it as cooperating with their ongoing investigation.

Jack knew the investigation had ended years before, yet the mere fact that those four hundred words had gotten so much attention made him realize he might have been on to something.

Where the hell is it? Jack tossed loose sheets of paper and newspaper clippings onto the floor until he found what he was looking for. The quarter-page cutout from the Portland newspaper had a slight tint of yellow to it now. He held the ten-year-old article up to the light and read the title: "Are Ferry Captains Getting Away With Murder?"

As he set it back down on the desk, it became painfully obvious that the intruder had not been looking for the article. *Whoever that was thinks I actually have proof Davidson was drunk.*

More confused than ever, Jack closed the door to the desk and waited for Kendra to come down. *What more could they think I have?* he wondered, and then realized that probably wasn't the point. The idea that someone was afraid Jack could uncover the truth of his parents' deaths meant that there must have been some kind of cover-up. There must have been something the police and the FBI never found.

Jack had written in the editorial that he believed an organization called The Lighthouse Society had covered up the accident. He hadn't an iota of proof to back the assertion, yet while he may not have had evidence, The Lighthouse Society must have been afraid he could prove wrongdoing regarding his parents' deaths.

Jack didn't know much about the Society, but from the stories he'd been told, The Lighthouse Society had the connections to make things happen, or not happen, as it were.

"Find anything?"

Unfazed by Kendra's sudden appearance, Jack stood staring out the window.

"My God. Honey, I've got to get you to the hospital."

Finally overcome by the pain in his feet from the glass shards, Jack fell to his knees. In his left-hand pocket, he crumpled the newspaper article...

* * *

A streetlight from the adjacent parking lot shone in Jack's hospital room and projected his shadow on the opposite wall. The dark silhouette, which mirrored every move he made, bothered him; it was like the intruder in his house, a man without a recognizable face. It summed up how Jack felt about himself. Despite the beautiful girlfriend, the large home in Portland's historic district, and all the family money left over from the prosperity of Carroll Island's granite quarry, Jack was empty inside. It wasn't till he picked up the old manuscript and decided to write again that he actually felt normal. Yet his encounter hours before made it painfully obvious that in order to finish his novel, he'd have to come face-to-face with old, emotional wounds that were never properly healed.

The wounds on his feet were minor in comparison to ones he suffered when the Carroll Island ferry ran aground in Penobscot Bay sixteen years ago, but the hospital room seemed all too familiar to the one he awoke in after his two-week-long coma. The darkness reminded him of the loneliness he felt after his grandparents came in and informed him that his parents wouldn't be coming home.

When Jack moved to Portland to live with his grandparents, he stood out from all the other kids at his school, not because of the way he looked or acted, but because of how he felt. He knew he was different from the others and he was jealous of them. He was jealous of how their parents picked them up from school in their minivans and cheered them on during youth soccer games.

Now and again, a friend would ask, "Why do your parents look so old?"

"Those aren't my parents," Jack would respond with a heavy heart.

Jack might have slipped off into adolescent obscurity altogether if it hadn't been for the loving grandparents who took him in. Their constant supervision forced him into a life of normalcy. He excelled at everything he did, not because he felt he had been given another chance at life, but because he wanted to please them. He was afraid that they, too, would be gone, and he would be left with nothing.

When the light in the parking lot next door finally went out, Jack looked into the same window and saw the reflection of a man, but felt helpless like a boy. *Had the intruder been sent to just look for what The Lighthouse Society believed to be evidence in my home, or did he have orders to kill me in my sleep?* Jack wondered, knowing he couldn't wait around for their next visit. The decision to go back to Carroll Island had new meaning for him—to finally learn the truth about his parents' deaths, which had been buried for nearly two decades.

"Knock, knock," Kendra said as she pushed the heavy metal door and walked into the room. She wore blue soccer shorts and a gray University of Maine sweatshirt. Her strawberry blonde hair was pulled back into a ponytail, and her sapphire eyes matched her shorts. "You awake, honey?"

"Unfortunately," Jack replied, tiredly. "What are you still doing here? Thought you were going home to get some sleep?"

"Like I could sleep in that house right now. Besides, I wasn't going to leave you here alone," she said, collapsing one of the bed's side rails and sitting down next to Jack.

"Have the police left the house yet?"

"Yeah, about ten minutes ago," she replied. "Said they could wait till tomorrow to get your statement."

Jack turned and looked out over the empty parking lot as a glimpse of sunlight began to peek over the distant horizon. "Did they mention any leads?"

"Not that they shared with me."

"God, it's going to be so nice to get out of here," he said, turning back to the window. It was barely dawn, but he made out the outline of the *Island Holiday* making its morning run to Peaks Island. The yellow and black bow of the ferry crashed through the windblown whitecaps, and a chill ran down Jack's spine.

Chapter Seven

Adam Cyr pedaled his 22-gear mountain bike away from Carroll Island's town center while the afternoon sun burned down on him. He passed two-story Cape Cod homes with neatly manicured lawns and blooming flowers set amid majestic balsam firs. He turned and glanced toward the harbor as his bike rolled over gentle hills surrounded by moss-covered boulders and patches of purple lilacs. He could see his boat bobbing amidst the incoming tide, the white hull forced upwards with each swell, only to come crashing down in the dark green water. At the mouth of the harbor, he saw Carl Swanson navigating his way around scores of lobster buoys, each with a different color scheme, but all staking claim to similar traps resting on the muddy ocean floor below. Adam didn't have as many traps as most of the other lobstermen on the island, but he took pride in maintaining the ones he had by adding fresh coats of paint to his buoys each winter when the island's inner harbor was iced in.

Carroll, like dozens of other islands that dot the whitecap-frosted waters of Penobscot Bay, is a giant mass of granite. And similar to its inhabited neighbors, the island was founded on the value of a plentiful commodity—an igneous rock that was quarried along the coast of Maine for centuries. Adam sped by the entrance to the old quarry about a quarter mile outside of town. His father, Vincent, had worked there for years, and Adam remembered when Timothy Chandler closed it down. Before the shutdown, sounds of screeching steel cables and crashing slabs of granite echoed all over the island. Such sounds were like ghosts now.

Like most people on the island, Adam didn't own a car and didn't have need for one. He lived and worked on his lobster boat most of the year, except in the winter, when he squatted a room on the second floor of Sam Robertson's carriage house.

The quadriceps muscles in his legs pumped up and down like pistons. His rear end stayed off the seat of the bike. His elbows rested on the horizontal padded handlebar, and his hands extended forward to the mounted racing grips. With a simple flick of his right hand, the bike switched into a higher gear, and his chiseled face grimaced. Streams of sweat poured down as if he was training for a triathlon.

Adam leaned into the bend in the road, striving to maintain his momentum. As he rounded the turn, he saw Jenny Cooper standing in the middle of the road, kicking and cursing at her blue ten-speed as it lay on the ground.

Adam's jaw dropped as he came to a stop just short of Jenny, who acted as though she hadn't even seen him coming. He forgot all about his ride or her bike when he saw her toned midriff below her white cotton cutoff t-shirt.

"Hey, lobster boy," she said, "you going to help me with my bike or just sit there and stare."

Adam peered down at her shredded tire. He didn't want to look up at Jenny and have her see him blushing, but she had caught him staring and he was embarrassed. He jumped off his bike and crouched down toward her bike's front tire. "Jesus, Jenny, what the hell did you do?" he asked, glaring at the mangled rubber. "This tire's spent."

"How the hell do I know?" she said. "I was riding along and all of a sudden I heard a popping sound. Damn near killed myself when I fell. See?"

Adam looked down at the scrape on her kneecap. "Might want to have someone take a look at that knee."

"If you can't fix my tire, I might as well start walking into town," she said, seemingly ungrateful he had even stopped to help her. "Besides, I should tell the sheriff about that fence being broken before Mr. Tucker's cow gets out."

Adam had been so taken by Jenny's beauty, he hadn't even noticed the wafting stench of cow dung until she pointed to the large animal pacing back and forth along the fence. He looked over her shoulder and saw a strand of barbed wire missing from the top of the fence bordering the field. Towards the bottom he could see the barbed wire in a pile. "Was that wire by the fence when you got here?" he asked.

"No. It was in the friggin' road and—"

"You ran over it with your bike," he interrupted. "That's why your tire's so ripped up. Why would someone drag that wire into the road?"

"How do you know someone put it there?"

"Just a hunch. Don't worry about the sheriff. I'll call him when I get home," he said. "Leave your bike here and I'll pick it up later. I might have an old tire that'll fit it."

Adam mounted his bike and began pedaling hard. After about a hundred yards, he'd gained the momentum he would need to climb the hill up to Kyle's.

Adam suspected the barbed wire was put there for him to run over. He figured that whoever it was wouldn't be far behind.

In the distance, on Carroll Island's highest point, Adam saw his destination. Kyle Foster's house was perched on a hill on the other side of the island from town. He continued on his fast pace for the final leg of the trek. Such fast-paced rides were an everyday activity for the thirty-four-year-old.

Adam's loner status had been solidified sixteen years earlier. After claiming responsibility for the ferryboat accident that killed Timothy and Laura Chandler, he'd been shunned, cast aside from Carroll Island's close-knit community. There were some who doubted Adam's role that night, and some who even figured the Society had coaxed him into the confession, but no one talked about it. The guilty stigma followed Adam everywhere he went on the island. Some residents believed the concocted story, while others felt the official judgment of the Society had been force-fed to them. For the most part, though, people were just afraid to voice any other opinion for fear of their personal well-being.

Sam Robertson was one of the skeptics. As a younger, career-driven man, the former island sheriff agreed to cooperate with the Society when the FBI investigated the island in 1994. He feared that as the island's sheriff, anything uncovered by the Feds would weigh negatively on his job, if not indirectly make him partially responsible for the cover-up. Adam often wondered if Sam's regret for the past had led to the free rent Adam enjoyed at his home.

Despite the years of social isolation, Adam wasn't a bitter man. He realized he could have moved away and started over, but like most other folks who were born and raised on Carroll, he chose to stay.

He believed in the circular effects of karma, which is to say that he knew, someday, the Society and Captain Davidson would get what they deserved.

About halfway up Kyle's driveway, Adam came to a stop. He jumped off his bike to walk the rest of the way.

If Adam hadn't been used to the adrenaline rush, he might not have felt the anxiety of the moment. He knew that Kyle was a member of The Lighthouse Society, as most people on the island did. Being a member was supposed to be a secret, but Kyle had revealed his membership in the Society to Adam some time ago. Adam figured it was out of guilt, and surmised that giving away such information could have had dire consequences for Kyle. It was that conversation, and Kyle's candor in particular, that gave Adam the confidence to approach Kyle.

* * *

Looking up from the blackish-gray soil in his garden where he knelt, Kyle said, "That you, Jimmy?" The glare from the sun forced him to look away as he squinted.

"No sir," Adam replied, his throat constricting while anxiety washed over him.

Adam realized that Kyle must have been expecting Sheriff Reynolds. "It's Adam—Adam Cyr, Mr. Foster."

"Mr. Foster—who the hell is Mr. Foster?" Kyle chuckled. "Come out of the sun. I can barely see you with the damned glare. Didn't I tell you last time you were here, not to call me Mr. Foster?"

"Force of habit, I guess," Adam said as he approached Kyle.

Kyle placed his hand on top of a wood stake and pulled himself up. His thin, frail body leaned over onto the stake like he was using it as a cane. The knees of his faded khaki pants were black from the ground-in dirt, and it was well known that Kyle spent more time in his garden than anywhere else.

Kyle shook the loose soil from his pants, laughed, and said, "Not bad for an eighty-two-year-old, huh? I got a phone call last month from some place in Rockland. Said I should think about moving into an assisted living apartment. I'd be better off dead."

"Looks like you're doing okay to me," Adam said, eyeing the old man.

"Would you tell me if you thought otherwise?" Kyle asked. "Don't answer that, son."

Adam smiled.

Kyle leaned over toward Adam and removed his straw hat. His head was almost totally bald except for small white patches above his ears. "Top of my head burned?" he asked.

"It's a little pink," Adam replied, "but I wouldn't say burned."

"Good thing," Kyle said. "Wouldn't want to get some skin disease and die in my youth. I was out here a good two hours before I realized I'd left my hat inside."

Kyle's humor made Adam feel comfortable, yet the thought of bringing up Jack hung heavy on him while he made small talk with his elder.

"What are you picking in there, sir? I mean, Kyle."

"Jeez, I'll tell you—goddamned heat this summer is killing everything in my garden, but I managed to get a few strawberries today. Not enough to make a pie, but if I didn't pick 'em now, they'd be ruined before long." Kyle again took his straw hat from his head and tossed it into a wicker chair nearby. "You like ice tea?"

"Sure do," Adam replied. The idea of a cold drink was more enticing than the warm water Adam had in the plastic bottle attached to his bike. He was parched after the ride over.

"Good to hear," Kyle said, directing Adam to the shade of the back porch. "I assume you didn't ride all the way out here to talk about my garden."

"I don't know if you recall, but you said that if the time was ever right—"

"I'd help you confront Jack Chandler," Kyle interrupted. "Oh, I remember."

"Jack needs to know the truth about his folks," Adam said. "I guess I'm here to find out the truth for Jack and for myself, as well."

Cringing, Adam waited for Kyle's response.

"The truth," Kyle repeated, his friendly demeanor changing. "Son, weren't you in that wheelhouse with Davidson? I've told you I feel guilty about the cover-up, but what else is it you think I know?"

Adam made a fist, his nails biting the skin on his palms. "Why'd Davidson kill Jack's dad?" he asked. "And before you give me the same damned 'oh he was just drunk' crap everyone drilled into me back then, let me just say that you're right. I was there, and was fully aware Davidson was drunk, but when those two began to fight, it was like there had been tension building for a long time."

"What if I was to tell you I don't know anything you don't know about that night?"

"With all due respect, sir, I don't think I'd believe you. You knew that family better than anyone. Besides Davidson himself, if there is anyone that would know why he and Mr. Chandler would have reason to fight, I assume it would be you."

Kyle glared at Adam. "Money and sex. You know—the usual things men fight over," he explained. "Don't get me wrong—you wanting to help Jack is admirable, but there are things neither you, nor anyone else on this island, needs to know about those times."

"I'm not following you. What are you trying to tell me?"

"You look like you've seen a ghost or something," Kyle said. "I'm not trying to scare you, but if you'd help Jack find the truth without exposing yourself, you'd be better off."

"You do a damn good job of scaring people when you're not trying to," Adam said. "I just feel that Jack deserves to know that his parents' death wasn't an accident."

"I agree. But listen, Adam. There are people who would kill us if they knew we were having this discussion. That said, the answers you seek and what Jack wants to know are two different things."

"How do you mean?"

"All you need to know is that you were used to help cover up Jack's parents' murders. Now Jack—Jack probably needs to know why." Kyle let out a deep sigh. "I dread telling him, but until the day I do, I shouldn't go into any more detail than I already have. Do you understand?"

"Yeah, I guess so." Looking over to Kyle, Adam saw his eyes tearing and wanted to switch topics. He felt uncomfortable around people who got nostalgic about dead family and friends, but he couldn't think of anything else to talk about. "Does anyone know when Jack's coming to the island?"

"Sally Reynolds says he's coming this weekend," Kyle said. "She's the only one who's talked to him."

"So soon?"

"Guess he called a couple days ago and asked if she'd get the old house ready," Kyle explained. "Don't know if the short notice was intentional, but it's taken the Society off guard, to say the least."

"Why not just wait and see what Jack's intentions are?" Adam asked. "Maybe he has no intention of trying to uncover the Society's plot. Maybe he doesn't know enough about it to even matter."

"I don't want to take that chance, Adam. The others only care about covering their tracks. Maybe if it was only about the accident, but it's so much more. When Timothy found out what was going on and threatened to go to the FBI, the Society fractured."

"So this really isn't about Jack?" Adam's curiosity was piqued. He knew that Kyle was drifting into the subject he'd just sworn not to discuss. "What were the others trying to cover up, besides the accident, Kyle?"

"No, I've already said too much," Kyle replied. "Either you want to help Jack or you don't. You don't need to know the rest right now. We haven't the time."

Exasperated, Adam got up from his chair and began to pace. For the first time in years, he felt rage drifting through his veins. "So what if I just walk?" he asked. "Let you and the rest of the Society duke it out over this."

"Like I said, if they knew we were talking about this—"

"Yeah. Yeah, I know," Adam said, his tone almost flippant. "We'd be floating with the fish. It's old, Kyle. I think you want this to be more than it is, just as much as the others."

"The others," Kyle said angrily, "have already begun!"

Now we're getting somewhere. Adam stopped and hovered over Kyle. Sweat was dripping from the old man's brow, and Adam could sense the fear. "Begun what?"

"Sam Robertson overheard Henry McKay instructing someone to break into Jack's house in Portland," Kyle replied.

"Who?"

"He got there too late. Just caught the tail end of the conversation," Kyle explained. "My guess would be Robert Billings."

Adam's heart was pounding uncontrollably and he began to feel faint. He slipped back down into the wicker chair and gulped some of the iced tea.

"It doesn't matter though. They aren't in control of the situation. These men are at the distinct disadvantage of not knowing Jack's intentions. Did they succeed in breaking into Jack's house? I don't know. What I do know is that young Jack is a resourceful man. The sooner he knows the truth about his parents, the better off we'll all be." Kyle stared intently at Adam. "That's where you could be of most help, Adam."

"Are you suggesting that I should go find him and let the cat out of the bag?"

"Not really. Think about it. If you were in his shoes, would you listen to some guy who everyone said was responsible for your parents' deaths, or would you think that person had ulterior motives? Now, if you were to spark Jack's curiosity anonymously, I'm sure he'd come to his own conclusions."

Adam looked at Kyle and was intrigued by the intensity in his eyes. Yet he knew that behind the gaunt expression, Kyle was hiding something. He knew Kyle had also been hurt by the ordeal. He lost a person he considered a son and, because of it, another he considered a grandson. Peering into Kyle's eyes, Adam saw something bordering on revenge.

"Okay then, what should I do? We're pressed for time."

"I have an idea that'll kill two birds with one stone—bring your innocence to light, and prove that The Lighthouse Society covered up the murders," Kyle replied.

"And then you'd end up in jail too."

"I did what I did and I'm willing to face up to it. The others want to take the cover-up to their graves. I don't want that to happen."

"Okay, so what should I do?" Adam asked.

"Help Jack find some answers—that's all."

"How do you mean?"

Kyle took a handkerchief from a small coffee table between the two wicker chairs and wiped the sweat from his eyebrows. "Do you recall the summer I was sent to Seguin Island?"

"Not really," Adam replied. "Should I?"

"It was my turn in the rotation to go to one of the lighthouses the Society helps maintain," Kyle said, straightening up in his chair with excitement. "So I went off for four months and lived on Seguin."

"Why on *earth* would you want to live out there?"

"I didn't," Kyle replied, "but things were heating up out here. We'd just pulled off the biggest scam this island's ever seen. The Feds couldn't find any evidence, but we sure had it. The others had the idea that one of us should go away and take all the minutes from the Society meetings, along with anything else that could implicate us."

Adam's lower lip twitched as he tried to force a smile. "Why didn't you guys just destroy them?"

"We'd all sworn an oath to uphold the bylaws, which entailed making sure they survived. The minutes included every financial detail of our organization, who owed the Society money, and more importantly, why they owed money. If we got rid of the documents, we'd lose much of our leverage over some of the island's landowners."

"So that's what this is about?" Adam said. "Blackmail?"

"It was so much more than that, Adam. We're talking about detailed logs of money laundering, racketeering, blackmail—"

"Why did you need to blackmail people?"

"Let's just say some lobsterman happened upon a meeting that was supposed to be secretive and involved people who didn't want their identity known," Kyle explained. "Then said lobsterman starts asking questions about what he saw, and, well, you can either ask him to be quiet or you can make sure he's quiet."

"And how did you make sure?"

"That's what's in those minutes, son."

"Kyle, I have the right to know," Adam demanded.

"It's simple on an island. A man has but one thing to protect—his family."

"So you threatened people's families?"

"Not in the way you're thinking, Adam. You see, the Society controls the credit union and the tax assessor. The tax assessor decides how much someone's land is worth, which decides the amount of taxes someone owes to the town. Then you have the mortgage rates being decided by the credit union, and—"

"And you basically had whoever you wanted by the balls?" Adam scoffed. "So what did Davidson have to do with this?"

"Nothing," Kyle said, "except that he wanted Timothy Chandler dead, and so did certain members of the Society."

"Why would anyone besides Davidson want him dead?"

"Timothy wanted to close the quarry, and the Society didn't. They threatened to disclose all these financial records to the authorities, after they'd been doctored a little, so to speak."

"You mean even Timothy was involved in this?" Adam shook his head in disbelief. "I don't buy it."

"Maybe not as much as others, but he at least knew what was going on, and his signatures were prevalent."

"So why have him killed? Why not just go through with the plan?"

"Chandler called the Society's bluff. He claimed to have his own proof. Apparently some of the others felt they had been pushed into a corner."

"And there was nothing you could do?"

"Those were tense times. I knew what we did was wrong, but I was in the minority. It was a tough summer on Seguin, but being out there gave me lots of time to think about how stupid the whole thing was," Kyle replied. "Even if we hadn't killed anyone, we might as well have. Covering it up's the same thing."

"That makes perfect sense," Adam said, his hazel eyes narrowed with suspicion. "If you're going to send someone away with incriminating evidence, it might as well be a place in the middle of nowhere. Hell, being alone like that, anyone would be strained by his conscience."

"I thought about going to the police. Just might have if I hadn't been all the way out there."

"So you want me to go to Seguin and find those minutes?"

"They're not there. I may not have had the balls to go to the police then, but I figured I might someday. So I took the documents and hid them about halfway between Rockport and Camden. Out near the water."

"So why not just tell Jack where the minutes are hidden?"

"To be honest, I'm not exactly sure where the place is. It was all pastures and fields back then. Who knows what could be there now?"

Adam laughed. "How could you just forget where it is?"

"Because a lot of the land's private. Things change, Adam. People build houses, swimming pools, and God knows what else," Kyle said. "When I hid the documents, there was a construction site in the middle of an arboretum. Not sure what it was, though. Sort of looked like a log cabin."

"Why would you go hide something important without leaving yourself any way of finding it again?" Adam asked.

"I recorded the coordinates to the location."

"Okay, where are they?"

Kyle cringed. "They're etched on the base of the lighthouse lamp…on Seguin."

"Fine, I'll just get on my boat and head down there right now." Adam knew the evidence in that trunk would exonerate him.

"Don't be foolish! The Society would be after you in no time," Kyle said. "Let Jack worry about getting out there."

"I think they're already suspicious of me," Adam said. "Someone sprawled out some barbed wire across the road by Tucker's farm."

"Sounds like something they'd do," Kyle said. "It get wrapped up in your tires?"

"No, but Jenny Cooper ran over it. Shredded her tires." Adam paused. "You mean to tell me you didn't know about the wire?"

"They think I'm soft, Adam. They don't tell me about the nasty stuff like cutting traps or screwing around with people's credit. They know I don't like it. Wait till they find out I've helped Jack."

"How will we clue him in on this idea and get him to go to Seguin?"

"Head over to Vinalhaven and call him. The Society can't trace the call from there," Kyle explained. "You make an anonymous call. I'll see that you get an alibi."

"What sort of alibi?"

"I'll make sure the Society thinks you're heading out on a scallop trip with some friends over on Vinalhaven. Stop by your mailbox in the morning. There'll be instructions waiting for you."

Chapter Eight

Kyle paced back and forth on the front porch of the old Chandler house. On one side of him, gray clapboard shingles surrounded a set of bay windows. On the other, the Atlantic Ocean crashed into the granite ledges below. From the perch on Chandler Point, Kyle could see clear across Penobscot Bay. The granite-topped Camden Hills rose majestically above the small villages, dotted with whitewashed houses and towering church steeples.

The Chandler house was more than just an empty 19th century mansion; it was a historical landmark on the eastern shore of Carroll Island. For more than a century, it had been home to the most prominent family on the island. In 1994, that history came to an abrupt end with the deaths of Timothy and Laura Chandler.

While a strong northwesterly wind blustered around him, Kyle looked down at his watch and continued to pace impatiently. From below the deck he heard a familiar, yet somewhat concerned voice. "Kyle, where are you?"

Kyle leaned over the edge and looked down to the strip of grass between the stone foundation and the edge of the cliff. Staring up at him with probing eyes was Adam. "Jesus. What are you doing down there?" Kyle said. "You're liable to fall off the cliff."

"Probably make some folks around here happy," Adam said, walking around to the porch stairs. "Besides, what are you doing out in the open?"

"Who's going to see me out here—the damned squirrels?"

"Yeah, well, I saw Davidson sitting in his truck across from Sam's place last night. Must've found out the barbed wire didn't get me." Adam stroked the neatly trimmed beard that covered his boyish face and smiled at Kyle. "You sure the Society doesn't have any plans for me?"

"Not unless you provoke 'em," Kyle said. "They'd be worried if they had any idea about our conversation yesterday, but they think you are going on that scallop trip."

"What if they have Davidson follow me tonight?"

"Sam and I made up this special bottle of whiskey and delivered it to Davidson. Ou-wee, that stuff's probably knocking him silly right now." Kyle's laugh carried in the wind. "And don't you worry about the Society knowing anything's amiss. Sam will have you over to Vinalhaven later this evening. You can take off from there and head south. He'll take your place on the boat. By the time the Society finds out you're not on the fishing boat, the plan should be in effect."

"If that's the case, why did your note say to meet you out here? Why didn't you just leave instructions like you said? Just seems like an extra risk."

"I think you will find the 'extra risk' will be worth it," Kyle explained. "Plus, the fact that Davidson's been following you has helped us."

"How so?" Adam asked.

"First, it isn't the Society as a whole that has had him following you. There are certain members that operate that way. They have their own agendas, but they don't influence the lot of us. Davidson found out you're going on the scallop trip with Sam and told the others. Drunk bastard helped us create your alibi."

"I suppose that makes me feel a little better," Adam said disbelievingly. "But you still haven't said why you had me come all the way out here?"

Kyle knew he couldn't fend off the subject any longer. He had been up all night trying to convince himself he had told Adam everything he needed to know, but the reality was that he was keeping the whole truth from him because he was ashamed. "You have the right to know the whole truth."

"So there *is* more?"

"Yes. Davidson was paid to kill Jack's father." Kyle felt tension lifting from his shoulders. "The reason I thought it was Billings out there with McKay the other night was because Billings paid Davidson to cover up his own mess."

"I thought you said that people were upset Jack's dad closed the quarry?"

"They were," Kyle said, his voice soft and defenseless. "Quarries were closing down all up and down the coast. The one here was one of the last. Timothy kept that place afloat as long as he could—"

"But the Billings family didn't have any ties to the quarry," Adam interrupted. "Why would he care either way?"

"He didn't." Kyle's voice resounded. "He couldn't have cared less about the Chandlers, but about a month before the accident he got a call from the FBI. It seems that the export business he'd been running out of Portland had caught some federal attention. I don't know all the details of it, but apparently millions of dollars were getting from U.S. banks to rebel fighters in Northern Ireland."

Adam had a perplexed look on his face. "Robert Billings was funding the IRA?"

"No. He was laundering money from wealthy contributors," Kyle explained. "He'd take their money and wash it through Carroll Island's credit union—"

"Which has always been run by the Society and therefore everything was documented in those minutes!"

"Exactly," Kyle exclaimed. "Made it easy for any traceable numbers to disappear, but once the money left Carroll, Billings couldn't control what happened. Seems the Coast Guard did a random inspection of a fishing boat off Georges Bank and found five million dollars."

"I thought you said the money wasn't traceable?"

"It wasn't, but the fishing boat was. It was a boat that had been leased from Jack's father. Of course the FBI first went to Timothy, but he had all his papers in order. Didn't have a clue what was going on. Then he called the yard in Rockland he'd leased it through, and Billings' name came up."

"Was it Billings who leased the boat?" Adam asked.

"No, but whenever Billings needed a boat, he'd pay someone under the table and take her out for a one-time deal. Like I said though, this was information that the Society knew nothing about, and McKay wasn't even a member. It was Timothy who brought the information in front of the Society and basically told Billings he could deal with the FBI, or Timothy would give them the information they needed." Kyle was beginning to hang his head. "We couldn't have known what would happen next."

Adam's eyes grew large and his breathing became heavy. Kyle could tell that he was filling with the sort of rage that many others had felt over the years.

"The reason I wanted to tell you this is because I needed you to know how dangerous Billings and anyone around him can be."

"And who else might that be?" Adam asked, staring at Kyle intently. "Davidson?"

"Not quite," Kyle replied, hinting at a smile. "But his daughter could be a problem. Have you ever met Julie?"

"No. Did she grow up out here?"

"Off and on," Kyle said, "like her father."

"So why should I be worried about her? Is she into smuggling money to terrorists as well?"

"Julie recently replaced one of the keepers out on Seguin this summer and, like her father, she's an ex-Marine."

"Okay, what does that have to do with me?"

"There's a good chance Jack's going to need your help." Kyle saw Adam's eyes widen and he thought about how much he was asking of Adam. "Julie will be looking out for Jack. Especially with Billings and the others thinking the minutes are still on Seguin."

"Her being out there is no coincidence, is it?" Adam asked.

Kyle nodded.

"I'm supposed to go out there and cover him if he gets in trouble?" Adam almost sounded eager for the challenge.

"Sort of," Kyle said. "You know how to get to Five Islands?"

"Yeah."

"I have a friend there who's willing to give you a ride out to Seguin on his boat. He owes me a favor and I called it in. He's gotta go out there to pull traps anyway. He'll drop you off on the other side of the island," Kyle said. "Besides, I don't want you to wait for trouble. I think you should be on that island as a precaution."

Adam nodded in silent acknowledgment.

"The best-case scenario is that Jack goes to the island, Julie doesn't have a clue who he is, and your work is over." Reaching into his backpack, Kyle handed Adam a gun and said, "Take this. It's a Magnum I've had for years. I just had it cleaned last month and I'd rather you be prepared if need be. You're going to be just fine, my friend."

* * *

Jack lay sprawled out on his psychiatrist's Italian leather couch. For years it had been one of his comfort zones. Once a week, Jack went to that tiny office to pour out his soul, talk about his nightmares, and try to sort through the demons that still haunted him from his childhood. Regarding his parents' deaths, his psychiatrist was his only confidant.

Doctor Daniel Turner had been Jack's shrink going on ten years. Jack was nervous about telling him of his plans to go back to Carroll Island. The moment Jack realized the intruder had searched through his research notes, he knew he had to face his past and effectively lay it to rest.

The office door suddenly swung open, and Jack was startled to see the six-foot-tall, balding man before him. "Sorry, Doc," he said. "Your receptionist said you were running late and didn't think you'd mind if she let me in."

Doctor Turner looked surprised to see Jack. "No. It's fine," he replied. "I didn't see you in the waiting room and thought you might have forgotten the appointment. Besides, the staff has left." He settled into a large armchair opposite Jack. He crossed his legs, put on his reading glasses, and picked up Jack's file from his desk. "Let's see. It's been about two months or so. I got your email, and it sounds like a lot's happened since our last meeting."

"You could say that."

"According to my schedule, we weren't supposed to meet till next week. What's so important?" The doctor smiled.

Jack cringed. "Well…I'm going on a long trip."

"Oh. Where are you going?"

Jack looked away. He couldn't bear to see the reaction. "Carroll Island."

"I see. Are you sure you're ready for this?"

Jack sat up. "I've quit my job and decided to give writing another shot, but I assure you, I have nothing but the best intentions. Kendra brought up the idea years ago and I just wasn't ready, but I truly feel that I am now."

"What exactly have you decided you're ready to do, Jack? Why not go somewhere else to write?"

"'Cause I own a house there," Jack replied. "And…the storyline of the novel is somewhat similar to my past."

Turner stood briefly and inched the armchair closer to his patent. Jack could see the intensity in his eyes and could tell he was being studied.

Doctor Turner sighed. "You told me yourself, you had absolutely no conclusive evidence that anyone did anything malicious the night your parents died—other than a slight recollection of your father and the captain having an argument. The FBI couldn't even come up with anything. What makes you think you can go out there and find some hidden truth after all these years?"

"Because they think I have evidence," Jack replied. "They sent someone into my house to try to find it. If someone broke in to steal something of value, they sure as hell wouldn't go rummaging through an old desk."

The doctor began gently rubbing his chin as if he was deep in thought. "Does Kendra know that the break-in wasn't random?"

"I didn't want her to be scared, so I didn't tell her. What good would it have done?"

"It would have let her know she was going back to the island under false pretenses," the doctor replied.

"Listen, Doc, I didn't go to school for six years to sit behind a desk and pore over other peoples' misfortunes."

"Be that as it may, but I think you're really going out there to solve what you perceive to be an act of malice. How much writing do you think you'll actually do?"

Jack rolled his eyes. *This is what I get for being honest.*

"Listen, I think I've made my position on this fairly clear," the doctor explained. "But I know that you've already made up your mind about this, and all I can ask is that you be careful."

Jack stood by the door and reached for the knob. He genuinely felt bad, but he knew that if he got into a long, drawn-out discussion about the pros and cons of his decision, it would just make it all the more difficult for him. He had to stand by his decision. He took a deep breath, extended his hand to Dr. Turner. "Thanks, Doc…for everything."

As Jack walked out of the building, the bright, late summer sun made him squint. He patted his pockets in search of his sunglasses and heaved a sigh of relief as he began walking down Exchange Street, navigating his way through the mass of seasonal vacationers. When he got to his car, his cell phone began to ring. He took it from inside his jacket and held it up to his ear. "Hello."

"Jack Chandler?" an unfamiliar voice asked.

"Yes?"

"Mr. Chandler, there isn't much time. When you leave for Carroll Island, you must stop at Seguin Island."

Jack looked dumbfounded, but curious nonetheless. "Seguin Island—why would I go to Seguin?"

"Mr. Chandler, if you really want evidence of the Society's plot, go to the lighthouse on the island and look for a set of coordinates that are etched on the base of the lantern. Find those coordinates, and you'll find your answers."

"Who the hell is this?" Jack yelled as tourists frowned at him.

"Beware of the island keeper."

The line went dead and Jack stood there in the center of Portland, his heart racing. Was the person really trying to help him, or get him killed?

Chapter Nine

J ack gave another good tug before tying the anchor line on the cleat. Shading his eyes from the sun with his hand, he looked up to the sparse, but fast moving cumulous clouds. The simple fact that the current and the wind were both flowing in the same direction gave Jack an extra sense of security. He wasn't sure what was on the ocean floor below, but he was confident the anchor would hold.

"Honey, what are you doing?" Kendra asked. She was lying flat on a beach towel just behind Jack. She had brought a boat cushion from the cockpit and was using it for a pillow as she bathed in the afternoon sun. "You're blocking my rays, Jack."

"God forbid," Jack said, coiling the excess line from the anchor. "You sure you remember what to do if the anchor comes free?"

"I've set the anchor before," she said.

"Not in water like this," Jack explained. "It's not like anchoring her in a secluded cove."

"If you're so worried," she said, "don't go ashore."

Jack crouched down, leaned over, and kissed her on the forehead. He could taste coconut oil from her tanning lotion. "We have to. Besides, you'll be fine out here. Sure you don't want to go with us?"

he asked, looking over his shoulder as he walked back to where his two friends were getting into the dingy.

"All set, thanks," she said.

Rob Ackerley knelt gingerly on the bow of the ten-foot inflatable dinghy. He steadied himself with one hand on the pontoon and the other grasping the boat's bow line. He turned and smiled as his golden-blond hair swirled in the southwesterly wind. "I really hope I don't cut my feet," he said before jumping into the shallow water below.

"Should have worn shoes, moron." Nate laughed as he crawled toward the bow. He watched his longtime ski buddy, as if waiting for him to begin to shriek in pain.

Rob looked up with a dumbfounded look on his ruggedly handsome face. "Not to worry, the rocks are smooth," he said. "Be careful though. They're pretty slippery. "

Jack leaped over the side of the dinghy from his seat in the stern and waded through the thigh-deep water. All three got a good grip on the dinghy and hauled it in several feet from the shoreline, just above a row of sun-dried seaweed that extended the length of the shore.

"This is far enough," Jack said as he let the bow down and wiped a bead of sweat from his eyebrow. He glanced briefly at *Vigilance*, which was anchored about forty feet from shore. He saw Kendra look up toward the sun and reposition herself on the bow. Paperback in hand, she rolled over so the sun could reach her back. She looked so innocent lying out in her turquoise one-piece bathing suit, and Jack felt a hint of guilt.

Just a few feet away, the earth rose sharply from the narrow beach. Seguin Island was nothing more than a huge hill peeking out of the

Atlantic. It was like a volcano that had been weathered for millions of years. Down the beach from where they landed was an old boathouse. Next to the frail-looking red-painted shack, a set of rusty tracks ran from the shore all the way to the top, near the lighthouse.

"Hey, that's pretty cool," Rob said, his eyes widening. "What is it, a train?"

"An old tram, actually," Jack replied. "It's only used to haul supplies these days."

Rob shot a glance to Jack, sneered, and said, "Are you saying that instead of riding in the tram…"

"We're taking the stairs." Nate patted his friend on the back and began to walk toward the first section of stairs, which climbed the grass and dirt-covered granite slope of the island.

Jack had almost forgotten how steep it was. He had forgotten how the island's ominous look from afar was magnified up close.

"You gotta be kidding me," Rob said as he lagged behind the other two, who had swiftly begun climbing the steps.

After noticing that Rob was out of earshot from them, Nate slowed, grabbed Jack's arm, and said, "It's a good thing Kendra stayed on board."

"My God, we'd never hear the end of this," Jack replied. "It was hard enough just to get her to come on the boat with us. She wanted to drive to Rockland and take the ferry out to Carroll."

"Well, it makes sense. You could have had anyone take your boat up the coast."

"Yeah, I could have, but I wanted to take it myself," Jack explained. "Why do you care? Thought you and Rob wanted to get a couple of days out on the water?"

"Hey, I'm not complaining. I love being out here with you guys. Just think it would be better if you were honest about why we came here—to Seguin."

Jack stopped and faced Nate. "What the hell are you implying, Nate?"

"I want to know why we're here today. I want to know why we went out of our way to anchor in such a dangerous place."

Jack scoffed at him and brushed by. "You wouldn't understand."

"Try me, Jack. I'm not dumb. I know more about what's going on than you think."

Jack continued up the stairs as if he hadn't heard what Nate had said.

"Where should I begin? I know about the articles you wrote to the papers when you were eighteen. I know the FBI demanded you stop pushing the issue of your parents' accident—whether or not it was a result of the captain being drunk. What more do you want me to say, Jack?"

"Speaking of which," Jack said, "why do you think the FBI was so concerned with my articles?"

"Perhaps the Bureau was trying to mount its own covert investigation, and your interference wasn't helping."

"Yeah, well, those articles are all public knowledge," Jack replied, quickening his pace. "Anyone could know about those."

"Maybe, but how many people know about the phone call you got yesterday?" Nate asked, his eyes focused on Jack's.

Jack turned and shrugged. "I don't know what you're talking about."

"Sure you do, Jack. You expect me to believe that you just decided to move back to Carroll Island to research a novel? No, of course not. Don't get me wrong. I'd want answers as well," Nate continued as he kept pace with Jack. Their distance from Rob continued to grow.

Jack turned abruptly and raised his fist in anger. He wanted to give Nate a good smack in the mouth—rough up that pretty surfer-dude face, which seemed to have a permanent grin. He had so much built-up rage inside, he could barely keep it in. With a drawn-out grimace on his face, he said, "What the hell do you want? And, how the hell do you know about the phone call?"

"Because I lied too, Jack. We didn't meet by chance. I mean, sure, Rob was a buddy of mine from way back, and he even thought he was just on some ski trip with me, but the truth of the matter is that, four years ago, I was sent to Colorado to meet you. I was supposed to get to know you. It was my job to find out if you still had ties to Carroll Island," Nate explained, looking Jack straight in the eyes.

"Sent by whom?"

Nate heaved a sigh, rolled his eyes, and said, "The FBI, Jack. I work for the FBI."

Jack didn't know what to say. He glared briefly at Nate as he turned back up the hill. He pretended the admission either wasn't heard or that he didn't care. He did.

"I never meant to hurt you, Jack. We needed a way onto that island, and quite frankly, you were—and are—our best shot," Nate said. "Hell, the Bureau dropped the case about your parents after I told them you weren't connected with the island. Then out of nowhere you call me up and ask me on this trip. I mean, seriously, why go back now? It's been what, sixteen years? Couldn't you find another place to write your book?"

Jack's eyes sharpened. "They broke into my home!"

"Who broke into your home—The Lighthouse Society?"

"I doubt it was one of them," Jack said. "You think the FBI got a kick out of those editorials I wrote? Well, believe me, ever since I wrote 'em, those bastards have had their eyes on me. They obviously think I've got something on them. Then a couple of days ago, some guy broke into my house in the middle of the night. He rummaged through some stuff in an old desk before the two of us exchanged shots."

"Exchanged shots?" Nate said. "Report said that the perp fired once, then fled the scene."

"I actually fired first, and missed. They didn't even call in forensics."

"Why lie about shooting at someone breaking into your house?"

"I don't know. I mean, I was afraid I might get into trouble. I didn't have a permit for the gun."

"So what really happened? You two exchanged shots—then what?"

"He ran. If the Society was worried about me having incriminating evidence against them or Captain Davidson, I assume someone must," Jack explained. "I knew I needed to find it."

"I guess it's a good thing I caught up with you before you got out there."

Jack shot another glare at Nate. He wasn't sure what to say. He turned and began walking again.

When the two reached the top of the stairs, they turned and looked out over the water below. Jack acted as though he was alone—barely looking at his friend. He pulled a water bottle from his backpack and took a swig without offering any to Nate.

Nate said, "Do you want my help or not?"

Jack scoffed at him and said, "Do I want your help or the FBI's help? There's a difference, right?"

"Let me put it this way. You want to bring down The Lighthouse Society, and so does the Bureau. What if I could guarantee you the two of us would have total freedom from any bureaucrats or bosses? We could work together—do it our way."

"Before we get into any of that, explain to me how the FBI even had the right to be involved in the accident in the first place," Jack said. "What jurisdiction would a federal agency have in a Maine case?"

"It's simple. The ferry was the mail carrier for the US Postal Service and the Carroll Island Credit Union. The NCUA would've been on our tails if we hadn't at least checked it out."

"So the FBI had no indication of foul play..."

"Not until you started questioning the cause of the accident."

Jack thought about everything Nate said and realized he couldn't exactly fault him for lying about how they became friends. He, too, had lied about his intentions, but Jack knew there was something more. He sensed the FBI had more of an interest in Carroll Island than finding out the real cause of an old ferry accident. *What aren't you telling me, Nate?*

"So, do we have a deal?" Nate asked.

"Let's worry about that later. Right now we have to make sure Rob stays away from that tower and out of harm's way. Then we need to get to the top of the tower. Think you can handle that?"

"Why would any of us be in harm's way out here?"

"The keepers out here are working for the Lighthouse Society," Jack said, looking at the twenty-foot white and black beacon. His plan had been simple. Perhaps too simple, as Nate hadn't been fooled, but both Rob and Kendra really believed Jack had been asked by someone in Portland to deliver mail to the keepers. Jack had stuffed a large manila envelope with junk mail and disguised it as a package to be brought to Seguin. He only hoped that if they did meet the keepers, he could persuade them they were visitors stopping by to see the historic landmark.

"For the love of all that's holy. Think you guys could have taken a break earlier?" Rob asked, gasping for air—his brawny frame bent over.

Nate grinned at him. "Tell you what, Rob. You just wait here. I'll go in with Jack. We'll be back in a few, okay?"

Rob looked up at Nate with heavy eyes and said, "If I'm asleep when you get back, just roll me down the hill."

* * *

Jack was surprised to find the house was empty. Maybe he had been overly paranoid, but the caller had a sense of urgency that made Jack suspect there would be danger awaiting them on Seguin. He was careful to keep his eyes and ears open.

Breathing heavily, Jack and Nate reached the top of the spiral staircase inside the lighthouse tower. Sunlight streamed through the black, iron hatch-door, which had been propped open a few inches to light the inner shell of the tower. Mystery, imminent danger, and spotty cumulous clouds overshadowed the day that began so many hours earlier under a canvas of sun. Searching the lantern house atop the tower, Jack was a little more at ease than earlier. He looked over at Nate, who was busy looking around the small room. He would never discount his love for Kendra or her unwavering support, but she didn't know what was really going on. For that simple fact, Jack felt guilty.

He told himself that he was merely protecting her, but protecting her had always meant isolating his fears and bottling them up inside. For sixteen years, Jack had no one to turn to, no one to vent to without some kind of recourse, but that had changed with Nate's interest in the situation—an interest spurred on by the desire to help a friend.

The mysterious phone call allowed him to believe there were others who were looking after his interests, but they weren't tangible yet. Their clues—whatever they might be—could be leads to other clues. Other truths. The mere thought that Jack's alliances could actually grow was uplifting.

Inside the lantern house, the crystal-glass-encapsulated Fresnal lamp, which was one of the last in the United States, astonished Jack. Its lasting presence had been assured by a group of Maine lighthouse historians.

"You really know about all this technical lighthouse stuff?" Nate asked.

"Not really. I looked up the island history up on my phone on the way here." Jack grinned as he searched the circular, transparent room overlooking everything from the far-off White Mountains to the Monhegan and Mount Desert islands.

"Okay then, wise guy, what are we looking for?"

"The guy on the phone said there are coordinates on the bottom of the lamp." *Bottom of the lamp?* Jack looked for a plaque or something with writing, but there was nothing visible to the naked eye. Kneeling on the grated-metal floor, Jack got as close as possible to the shiny fixture. Looking up, he smiled. "They're engraved in the copper."

Nate knelt down beside him.

"How 'bout these?" Jack pointed to a set of numbers. "It may be a little faded, but here they are. 'North forty-four degrees, twelve minutes and fifty-two seconds by west sixty-nine degrees, three minutes and two seconds' —stands for latitude and longitude," he pointed out.

"Okay, so where is this location?" Nate inquired.

"Don't have a clue, but we can find out when we get back on the boat and pull out a chart," Jack explained.

Jack was startled by the sound of a gunshot followed by a sheering sound. It sounded like cable fibers coming apart and a line snapping.

"I am an expert on some stuff, and that sounded like a .38," Nate said.

"And it sounds like it hit a cable," Jack said as they both ran around the circumference of the tower looking for where it could have come from. "Oh my God! Rob!"

They looked in amazement as the tramcar began racing down the track. The speed increased before it was out of their line of sight. The sound of clanging iron echoed from the tower as the two ran down the stairs to help their friend.

Someone had shot the century-old cable, splintering it until the weight of the tramcar was too much.

Jack and Nate raced down the spiral staircase. Reaching the bottom, they stopped just short of two doors. Nate reached his arm back to keep Jack from rushing past. Field agent or not, Nate's training would dictate their next move.

"Hold up, Jack," Nate whispered, "we don't know where the shooter is."

Jack was breathing heavily. "Nor do we know where Rob is. We can't just wait here—we have to help him."

Nate surveyed the area. One of the doors entered the keeper's quarters and the other led to the outside. "Turn around," he said as he reached for Jack's backpack, quickly unzipped it, and rummaged through the contents.

"What are you looking for?"

Nate pulled out a small flashlight and held it in his right hand. He peered briefly through the window and looked back at Jack. "I'm going to throw this in the opposite direction from the museum. When it hits the ground, we're going to sprint to the trailhead by the museum. If the shooter's waiting for us, he'll hopefully be caught off guard. With any luck we should be able to get cover before making a break for the stairs." Nate drew a small pistol from a holster under his vest. "We don't even know where they are," he said. "They could be hiding anywhere and ready to take us out. By the sound of it, they severed that tram cable with one shot. I hope Rob wasn't in there when it went.

"Okay, one, two, three, go!" Nate ordered as he tossed the flashlight. Almost on all fours, they ran across the front yard and ducked behind the museum—just as they planned. Another shot rang out and a small cloud of dust rose from the area where Nate had thrown the flashlight.

"Perfect," Nate said, shooting a glance toward the dust.

From the dirt-covered trailhead they could see the tramcar at the bottom of the track, shattered into hundreds of pieces, yet no sign of Rob.

"Jesus, where the hell is he?" Jack pulled a small pair of binoculars from his backpack and surveyed the expansive landscape from his position on the ground behind the corner of the whitewashed museum building. Despite a growing sense of guilt at the predicament he had put his friends in, he knew he needed to focus on getting out of there. Nate was now in charge, and they needed to help Rob before it was too late.

Nate said, "Look, about halfway down. See that patch of grass? I bet if he was on the tram, he would have tried to jump out there for a softer landing."

"Maybe, but at that speed, he could've been thrown all the way down to the water."

"There! You see him? The orange spot," Nate said, pointing to a small patch of orange. From the distance, it looked like a lifejacket amidst a sea of dirt and knee-high brush.

"Damn. That's about fifty feet from the grass," Jack said. "I don't have a good feeling about this."

"Hold up, Jack. Not so fast." Nate grabbed hold of Jack's collar, keeping him in place. "Here's my idea. When you make a break for Rob and duck down the trail, stick as close as you can to the track. That little bit of elevation could make a world of difference. I'll wait a second and see if you draw someone out. Don't worry. You'll be covered!" Nate sounded confident in his plan. Seasoned pro or not, he spoke with a candor suggesting he was accustomed to the danger. "Hold a sec; is that a handheld in your pack?" he asked. "We can try and call Kendra to get the engine going." Nate took the small handheld VHF unit out of Jack's backpack. "Okay. You ready? Go get 'em, kid."

The distance from the museum to the maintenance path was only about fifteen feet, but Jack had gotten no farther than a couple of strides before hearing the first shot.

"Holy crap!" About halfway to his intended distance, he dove to the ground to avoid the shot, which whistled over his back—barely missing him. After rolling over twice, he jumped back to his feet and stayed in a crouching position. Without further hesitation, he dove toward the edge of the trail as a second shot was fired. Again, it barely missed him; the slug lodged into a birch tree stump a couple of feet away.

Nate, who had disappeared behind the museum, reappeared on the other side and fired two shots toward the northwest corner of the keeper's house. The first hit the brick facade and took a sizable chunk out of the wall. The second shot may have found its intended target, but a plume of chalky smoke clouded the area. "You okay, Jack? I think I hit her," he said as he crouched down and scurried toward Jack.

"Her? I almost got shot by a chick?" Jack peered over the edge of the banking as Nate ran toward him. His clothes were covered with patches of green and brown from the dirt and grass he'd rolled through.

"Looked like a woman to me. Hell, I just saw the gun smoke from over by the house, and shot when I saw a figure. Looked like a woman, though." Nate dropped to the ground and rolled next to Jack. He was nearly out of breath, but not as roughed-up as his friend. "You okay, buddy?"

"Yeah, I'm all right. She missed me," Jack said as he pulled up his t-shirt and wiped the sweat from his brow. He quickly jumped to his feet and ran down the path. "Let's go, Rob needs us."

Nate jumped back to his feet and followed suit.

Jack began to slow down when he was about fifteen feet from Rob, whose body lay motionless and twisted over root-covered dirt. He had landed close to a rock outcropping, which dropped several yards. Fresh divots in the grass and dirt showed that he had tried to jump to the grass, but tumbled about fifty feet before coming to a rest near the ledge.

"Rob, can you hear me? Rob?" Jack yelled, dropping to his knees and letting his backpack fall from his shoulders.

"Careful, Jack. Don't move him." Nate slid down on the other side of Rob, whose clothes were severely torn. A small stream of blood drizzled from a wound on his side. They looked at the wound and then each other.

"What do you think—superficial?" Jack had seen more than his fair share of injuries from falls in the mountains, but none so gruesome. The pictures that occasionally accompanied insurance claims didn't compare to this.

Rob made a dull grunting noise as his head rolled to the other side. "That could be a good sign. He couldn't move his neck if it was broken." Nate took hold of Rob's wrist and checked his pulse. "Seems a little slow. Rob, you need to wake up, man. Come on, Rob."

"We don't have much of a choice here. We gotta move him now," Jack said, gasping for air.

"His back may be broken," Nate insisted.

"Yeah, and his spleen may be ruptured, but no one's coming out here to help. If he has internal bleeding, getting him out of here is his only chance. Let's pick him up on three. You get the legs and I'll support his head." Jack wasn't afraid to take charge of the situation, and Nate complied. "One, two, up." The two of them picked Rob up with ease and began to move slowly back toward the maintenance path, veering away from the railway, which extended down over giant boulders.

When they reached the cove, they set Rob down on some coarse gray sand. Jack tried to look out to the boat to see if Kendra had gotten it started, but the gusting wind blew sand in his face and obstructed his line of sight. A steady rain began to fall, and grew more intense with the force of the wind.

"Listen, Rob, if you can hear me, we'll be right back." Jack jumped to his feet and ran toward the boathouse.

"Jack, we need to get him on the dinghy. Where the hell are you going?"

"Nate, come with me…" Jack reached the side door of the boathouse, which was locked with a steel chain. Through a small window, Jack could see a boat with an outboard engine.

Nate caught up and said, "What are you doing?"

"Shoot the chain."

Nate pulled out his gun and took aim at the padlock. His one shot severed the lock, and Jack kicked in the door.

"It's much faster than mine," Jack said as he pointed to a nineteen-foot Boston Whaler, which was perched on a short railway of its own, leading through two wooden doors and into the water.

"Do you think it runs?" Nate asked.

"Hope so," Jack replied. He had already climbed aboard and stood on the bow, where he quickly untied the cleat. "If nothing else, we can keep anyone from coming after us. Quick. Get on. When I pull this lever, it's going to slide down through those doors."

"Should I try to start the engine?"

"No. Not yet. Wait till we're in the water," Jack answered.

"What about Rob?"

"We're going to get him, and then stop to get Kendra. We can get to the mainland about five times faster in this than we can on my boat.

Besides, there's ample room to lay Rob down on the boat's deck. I just hope that it's fast enough to save him. Ready? Hold on." Jack pulled the lever and the boat slid down the rusty track, slamming through the garage-like doors.

The engine started with ease and they sped over to the beach to get Rob. The two jumped off and ran to their friend, who was quietly moaning again. Nate and Jack agreed that it was probably a good sign. They picked him up and quickly brought him over to the boat, which was already starting to drift in the crashing whitecaps.

Kendra was on the side of the *Vigilance* and appeared to be waiting for them to arrive. Jack kept one eye on his course and his other on.

Kendra was standing on the rail of the boat on the outside of the lifelines, holding on with both hands.

"I thought you couldn't get hold of her?" Jack said.

"I couldn't talk to her long enough to tell her to start the boat's engine, but I told her we were on our way and that Rob was hurt. She doesn't know what's going on. Probably couldn't hear the gunshots with this wind." Nate's attention shifted quickly back to the island "Look." He pointed to someone hobbling down the stairs toward the shore. "That's the woman I shot. Guess I hit her. She's definitely limping."

"Give me your gun." Jack extended his hand.

"Jack, she's too far away. You'll never hit her from here."

"Perhaps." Jack took the gun and fired one shot at the dinghy, which was up on the high-water line. Upon impact there was a loud popping sound, and one of the pontoons burst. "Now she can't come after us at all. Get ready to help Kendra aboard." The Whaler pulled alongside of *Vigilance*. The choppy seas made it difficult for Jack to maneuver.

"What the hell is going…? Oh my God! Rob!" Kendra yelled as they approached the yacht.

"Honey, we'll explain. Please get ready to jump on the Whaler."

"We're just going to leave your boat all the way out here? Didn't you say a boat couldn't stay moored out here in bad weather?" Kendra had taken her attention off of Rob and looked back at the well-equipped vessel they were leaving behind. She had an intense look on her face, which was red from the driving rain.

Jack steered clear of the bow of *Vigilance* and headed toward the mouth of the Kennebec River. "Weather's bad and Rob has blood flowing out of his side. Which one do you think we should worry about here?" Looking like a scolded child, she turned away from Jack and knelt down to help Nate with Rob.

"Don't worry about it. He's upset. He's blaming Rob's accident on himself. I'm sure he didn't mean to yell at you," Nate said to her, placing his hand on her shoulder.

"Accident? Was it an accident that after pointing to some handicapped person on that island, Jack took a gun shot at his own dinghy?" Kendra asked, confused.

"Kendra, there's a lot more to it than what you just saw," Nate said.

"Didn't you guys go up there to deliver some mail?"

"We can get into that later. I think we have some more important things to worry about. Rob is obviously hurt, and we don't know how bad it is. We haven't been able to get through to anyone on the radio with the interference, but I'll keep trying," Nate explained. "Here; sit and hold the towel against the wound."

"Sure, but shouldn't we slow down? These waves are going to hurt him more," she pleaded.

"No. Jack can't slow down. Rob could die if we do." Nate grabbed the handrail and got to his feet, making his way to the bow.

"Anything yet, Nate?" Jack asked.

"Hold on. I'm trying the Coast Guard again now." Nate held the VHF to his head with one hand while holding the bow railing with the other. "Coast Guard Group, Boothbay Harbor, Coast Guard Group, Boothbay Harbor, come in. This is the crew from the pleasure boat *Vigilance*. Over."

"Vessel calling Coast Guard Group, Boothbay, come in. Over," a voice finally responded on the radio.

"This is Special Agent Nathan Richardson of the Federal Bureau of Investigation in need of emergency assistance. Over." Nate looked over toward Kendra, whose eyes had widened in amazement.

"Agent Richardson, what is the nature of your emergency and your location? Over."

"We are a party of four en route from Seguin Island, just northwest of The Sisters Ledges. We're currently heading toward the Sheepscot River. One aboard is seriously wounded and requires immediate attention—possible internal bleeding. Over." Nate clearly knew a lot more about the ocean than he had let on before they had arrived on Seguin.

"Okay, Agent Richardson, keep on your current heading; we'll be there before you get to the mouth of the Sheepscot River. We're dispatching a chopper to assist with the wounded. ETA, seven minutes. Over."

"Understood, Richardson out and returning to sixteen."

"Coast Guard Group, Boothbay Harbor will continue to monitor channel sixteen, out."

Nate turned to Jack, who looked just as confused as he was. "Well, at least they're sending a chopper to get Rob." Nate looked back toward Kendra, who was tending to Rob and hadn't heard the end of the radio transaction.

"I think we've done all we can do for now," Jack said. "Are we going tell her everything now or…"

"I don't know, Jack. That may be up to you."

"You still plan to go to the island, don't you? Nate, aren't you at all concerned for Rob?"

"You know damned well that I'm concerned for Rob, but you also know that there is going to be nothing more we can do for him. I think he'd want us to find out who tried to kill him, along with your parents."

"I agree," Jack said, turning to his friend. Although he was upset he hadn't known Nate's true identity, he understood it was for the good of the cause he was trying to achieve. As he looked into Nate's eyes and saw the raw determination, Jack knew he had found a true partner.

Chapter Ten

Since its incorporation as a town, Carroll Island had been governed by a secret organization known as The Lighthouse Society. Jack's great-great-grandfather, William Chandler, and four fellow Freemasons he recruited, moved to the island in 1851. William purchased the island with the intention of establishing a year-round community that would be economically based on the island's rock quarry. The United States government agreed to sell the island for the sum of one dollar. In return, Chandler agreed to maintain the island's lighthouse, which had been built at the turn of the century.

In the early months, all five men occupied the lightkeeper's house until their own homes were built around the island's sheltered harbor. Each night they huddled around a woodstove, smoked cigars, and debated the numerous details regarding the development and government of the island. All were previously members of a Masonic lodge on the mainland and figured that creating a new lodge on the island would serve two purposes: they could practice their fraternal traditions, and create a structure of government based on their Masonic ideals. With this in mind, the men wrote the charter and constitution for the island. Two years later, in 1853, the island was incorporated as a new town in the State of Maine. Soon after, their lodge had a new charter under the umbrella of the Grand Lodge of Maine.

When other men and their families moved to the island, laws and regulations were already established. Membership within the Society was private, yet people had a good idea who some of the members were. Like Jack's great-great-grandfather's selection of the other four members, The Lighthouse Society, as it came to be known, chose its own members. There were no public elections for any position on the island, but the voice of the people was still heard. At each town meeting, the town secretary would take minutes and drop them off in the keeper's mailbox. Likewise, decisions made by the Society were read aloud at the town meeting. Regardless of the residents' opinions, however, all final decisions were made by the Society. For all intents and purposes, proper democracy didn't exist. The majority of residents were most concerned with putting food on their family tables, and the wages men received on Carroll were better than on the mainland or other islands. The secrecy was publicly sold to them as being tradition. Tradition, they were told, which came right from their founder. People from Carroll Island loved and embraced tradition.

* * *

After the accident in 1994, the Maine State Troopers and the Federal Bureau of Investigation came to the island looking for answers. The fierce mid-winter storm made it nearly impossible to investigate the wreckage until time and saltwater had cleansed the rusting remnants on "The Graves."

The arrival of the authorities would have been a perfect time for someone to come forth about the Society, yet no did. There was never a mention of the secret institute, and the island knew that the reprimand the Society would face from the government would be deflected onto them as a community. Everyone did their share in disguising the truth about their home. Late at night, letters mysteriously arrived at the residents' mailboxes with instructions on what to say to police. Without question, the residents complied. The two most popular questions that investigators asked were: "Who was behind the helm of that ferry?" and "Was it Captain Brian Davidson?" No matter who was asked, the answer was either "I don't know, I wasn't there," or "That's between him, his first mate, and God."

When the investigation ended, the FBI and state officials were furious over the lack of information they were able to gather. They were suspicious that the Carroll Island residents were intentionally being obstructive, but they couldn't prove it. With nothing more to go on, the case was closed. It wasn't that people wanted the Chandlers dead or that there was any ill will toward them, but they knew they couldn't bring them back. The Society decided that turning on Davidson, an island resident, would be counterproductive to island morale.

* * *

News of Jack's return was scattered over the island. Those who spoke about it had mixed feelings about his homecoming. Some looked forward to seeing the person they knew only as a young child, yet others feared the possibility of a conflict with the Society. Most of the gossip, however, surrounded his plans to bring a mainlander to live on the island with him. Unbeknownst to Jack, the topic was actually discussed at a town meeting. The islanders had always been skeptical of mainlanders.

When news spread that Jack was leaving Portland, the blue light on a seemingly useless lamppost, near the center of town, lit up and people knew that The Lighthouse Society was to meet. Jack actually hadn't left his port at the time, but someone obviously thought that his departure and subsequent arrival were important enough to call a meeting to order.

The night before Jack, Kendra, Nate, and Rob left Casco Bay, a blue light, similar to the one near the town center, shined outside the keeper's house. People talked as though some big to-do was happening, but they were all just curious as to what could be going on up in the old stone house they weren't allowed anywhere near.

Of the five Society members, Kyle Foster arrived last that night. He always arrived last. Being the oldest member of the Society, he was becoming frail, but he still insisted on walking everywhere. This worried the other members. They were afraid someone might follow him, thus giving away their secret location. Little did they know, he had already done far more than give away their secret location.

The rules of membership in the Society were simple. Once chosen, or "tapped," as it was called, there was no refusing membership or even quitting until near death.

"Why are we here? We met last week and conducted regular business." Kyle Foster's craggy six-foot frame appeared in the candlelit room located in the basement of the keeper's house. If anyone arrived at the keeper's house during a meeting, they would never find the Society. Other than the narrow, zigzagging staircase that led to the bottom floor, the only other way out of, or into, the room was a tunnel-like bulkhead, which came up to a water tower near the building. It was the perfect hiding place.

"There's nothing regular about this business," Henry McKay said.

"Shut up, Henry!" Foster shouted back. "You got what you

wanted." It had become apparent that Old Man Foster knew exactly why they were meeting and was perhaps trying to rouse McKay just a little. It was working.

"I did, Kyle. We all did, and it is our duty to uphold the decisions we made all those years ago," Henry replied.

The two had been arguing about the cover-up for more than a decade and a half. Henry and Kyle had been at odds over what to do when agents came to the island back in 1994 and 1995. Foster believed that the captain should have been investigated and held responsible for his actions, but Foster's voice had been quieted by the likes of members who felt that Kyle made decisions based on personal feelings toward the Chandlers and not for the overall good of the island or, of course, themselves. They knew that any investigation would have, in all likelihood, sent the whole group to jail for their parts in the cover-up.

It was the simple fact that the Society was unaware of Jack's intentions that got them so riled up. Jack had given them no reason to worry about anything, but just like before, the members were more worried about themselves than they were for anyone else. Because they were that the ones who made the decision to obstruct the investigation, they were responsible if someone like Jack came looking for answers.

"Why would he make a fuss now? What could he prove?" Peter Jacobs, the island minister, spoke from the corner as he tapped the cherry of his cigar.

"I doubt the validation of proof ever kept a man from vengeance," McKay replied. "We've tried to ascertain whether or not he actually has any proof or if the editorials he wrote were just hot air. We came up empty."

Jacobs said, "What are you talking about?"

McKay glared at Jacobs. "For the love of Christ, Peter. Not everything that happens needs to be approved by the rest of you. Let's just say that Robert and I arranged for a little investigative work. We found nothing."

"Maybe we should arrange for Captain Davidson to go into hiding so we can assess what young Jack has on his mind," Robert Billings said. He didn't often say much and spent most of his time off-island on business trips, but nonetheless, Kyle didn't like him and thought he was a greedy man always looking out for himself.

"That would be too obvious," Jacobs said.

"Too obvious? You're all paranoid. I say, if he asks, we tell him the truth. Doesn't this island owe him that?" Kyle insisted. He hoped that the whole conversation would be irrelevant if Adam was successful in reaching Jack in the morning.

"Nonsense," uttered McKay.

"Nonsense is right, Henry. The way Adam Cyr has been treated, that is nonsense. Which one of you has arranged to have him followed around everywhere he goes? What are you afraid the man will do? Hell, who should we be more afraid of, a guy who hasn't been here in sixteen years, or a guy down the street whose life was ruined by this group? Besides, you can be at ease if you're worried about him. He took off today with Sam Robertson and some folks from Vinalhaven to go scallop fishing."

"Gentlemen, settle down," Arlington Cooper said. Cooper was the group's leader, a position in the Society referred to as the Cleric. It was his job to interpret the Society's decisions and preside over any internal disputes. The leader of a normal Masonic lodge is known as the Master, but when it was decided that the lodge would be the island's governing body, some of the rules and procedures were changed. When a member became the Cleric, like membership itself, it was meant to last till his dying days. "Have any of you really given this whole matter any genuine, rational thought since they closed the investigation? I hadn't so much as thought about it at all until, like you, I got the news that he was coming back to the island. Honestly, I never thought a Chandler would come back here, but he is, and he has every right to. It is not our job to sit around here and scrutinize what some young man may or may not do based on our own beliefs or past actions. It is our job to take whatever situation is presented to us and make a decision accordingly. Quite frankly, Kyle's right. You are all a little too paranoid for your own good. We can't just go on up to Captain Davidson's house and tell him to take a trip or hide him in an attic somewhere. Even if we could, that would solve nothing. If Jack does cause some sort of trouble, and I'm not so sure I'd blame him, then we can deal with whatever it is. Until such an event arises, I suggest you all relax. However, we all took part in an elaborate cover-up of the accident, and we need to make sure that our stories are straight. I suggest we all go home and give this situation some more thought and perhaps cool down a little. We'll plan to meet again in closed lodge in two nights' time. Until then, there will be no petty arguments between any of you." His sermon silenced the rest, but the silence was deafening. Everyone could tell that neither Kyle nor McKay were done with their argument.

"Before we go, I feel it pertinent to mention something that could become of serious consequence to us all." Kyle looked straight into the eyes of McKay. "Have any of you given thought to the fact that young Master Chandler has the right—by our very own charter—to become a member of this Society?" Kyle had no malicious intent in providing this information.

"What the hell are you talking about?" McKay asked.

It was true. If Jack put a letter of personal petition into the mailbox at the keeper's house, the Society would be forced to give him a seat. It had been written, and practiced, that if a current Society member were to die, his firstborn male would assume his spot at a time of maturity. Timothy Chandler was a member of the Society at the time of his death. He was hardly active, or even on good terms with the other members, but he was a member and the rules were strict. If Jack had stayed on the island, he would have been recruited to be a member when he reached the age of eighteen. That was the custom. After nearly a year of being a four-member body, the remaining members of the Society voted to suspend their bylaws for the purpose of voting in a new member. They had gone too long without full representation and were weary of the lack of family lineage available, but the ruling was necessary. The new member was Henry McKay.

"Henry, when the Society made its exception and voted you in, it was noted that a Chandler male heir held a seat in waiting." Foster was proud that he had even remembered such a clause. He may have been old, but he was as sharp as a tack.

"Brother Foster is right, yet let it be known, no one's seat is at stake here, nor does this body need to offer a position to young Jack. If he truly wants a seat, he must come forward himself. The likelihood that he even knows we exist is slim. The idea of him becoming a member is not a concern," Cooper explained.

"And I wasn't suggesting otherwise. Just providing the body with some insight which may have been overlooked," Kyle noted.

"Gentlemen. Brethren, don't say a word of this to anyone and it won't be an issue."

The five all nodded in agreement, but Foster had made his point. He would abide by his oath, but he wouldn't let a chance pass to rub something in Henry McKay's face. In truth, he didn't really care either way about Jack Chandler's membership, but he wanted to be fair. He knew full well that he was the most fair of them all. If not for his bout with cancer and resulting weakened health, he would have been named Cleric years ago, but when the time came, he was too ill and passed the position to Arlington Cooper, his nephew and neighbor. Cooper and Foster were longtime friends and allies. If Foster was doing nothing else, he was merely making sure that all his cards were accounted for.

Kyle remembered the year the Society consisted of only four members, and official business had been suspended until the appointment of McKay. The death of Timothy Chandler notwithstanding, it had been a horrible year for the island—a year that they would all rather forget. If not for the honesty and conscience of Foster, perhaps they would have. The disparity of the Society and its paranoia were evident by the fact that all meeting minutes from 1994 through 1995 had either been destroyed or hidden.

After the other three left the lighthouse, Cooper offered to give Foster a ride home. Normally, Kyle would have turned the offer down, but he agreed to get out of the rain, which had begun falling while the group met. The two got into Cooper's Jeep Wagoneer and drove off in the opposite direction from the others.

* * *

With one hand on the wheel and the other collecting the light rain outside the rolled-down window, Cooper turned to his friend and said, "What were you doing in there, Kyle?"

"Just feeling out the situation," Kyle replied.

"No. What you were doing was trying to piss people off," Cooper said with a smirk on his narrow and aged face.

"Perhaps a little." Kyle laughed. "Seriously, Arlington, do any of them really have a reason to be so damned paranoid?"

"Doubtful, but I get the feeling if it weren't for Henry, you would have just kept to yourself."

"Not true. I distrust them all equally. Except for you, of course," Kyle said.

"What is it about Henry that upsets you so? I can see why he may still resent the past, but why the resentment on your part?"

Cooper was right, Henry McKay did have a good reason to hold a grudge against Kyle. When Kyle was sick and decided to pass on the position of Cleric, he didn't follow tradition. He should have named McKay the new Cleric, as McKay was the second-ranking member, yet Kyle passed him over in favor of Arlington Cooper.

"You weren't there, Arlington. That son of a bitch manipulated everyone. If not for him, there may have never been a cover-up."

"It would have destroyed the island to do anything else. What would the authorities have thought of our local government?" Cooper pleaded.

"And what about the Chandler family? Had it not been for that family, none of us would even be here. You know that as well as I do. When Timothy shut down the quarry, people like McKay were furious. They probably thought it was some sort of sick justice."

Cooper cleared his throat and said, "Wait a minute. You really think the cover-up was some sort of punishment for the Chandler family?"

"Makes sense, doesn't it? McKay was town secretary when the quarry closed, and lots of his constituents lost their jobs. Perhaps he told them he was in a position to provide them with payback."

Despite the role of town secretary being a superficial post, such information was not public. While the position was dictated by the Society, the mere fact that the islanders didn't know allowed some influence.

"Are you suggesting that the accident was a setup? Come on, Kyle. Davidson was drunk and he hit a damned ledge in the fog. The Chandlers weren't even supposed to be on that ferry. Talk about being paranoid."

"As I said, Arlington, you weren't there. Adam Cyr said that he heard Tim and Davidson arguing." Kyle's scratchy Maine accent thickened.

"Perhaps you're right, Foster. Who the hell knows? Those records are long gone. Probably buried off on some island. Frankly, if I knew that all this was going to come up, I would have pulled you aside long ago. I just don't have the energy for it anymore."

"Just forget about the whole damned thing," Kyle said as he got out of the car. He stood for a moment at the end of his gravel driveway and watched as Cooper drove off.

The taillights faded quickly in the thick mist, which had replaced the gentle rain from before. Standing there in the half-light of the moon, Foster pondered his part in the whole mess. What was he to do?

If it were up to Kyle, Jack would be informed of the Society's indiscretions. He would tell him Davidson was drunk, and that Adam was used as a scapegoat. He didn't know if he could tell Jack about his mother's improprieties. That would be much more difficult.

Although the existence and makeup of the Society were secretive, there weren't supposed to be secrets among its members with regard to its business affairs, governmental actions, or judicial proceedings. Prudence suggested that silence was his best and only option.

* * *

Kyle Foster's house was at the end of Cranberry Lane, on the northeastern point of the island. His modest three-bedroom Cape was built in the early 1900s, when the island and the federal government had thought about building a second lighthouse. The house in which he lived was to be the lightkeeper's house, but due to budget cutbacks, the beacon was never built. Pine trees and firs surrounded and camouflaged the property. It was the highest point of land on the island, and part of about twenty acres Kyle owned.

Until the late 1980s, his land, although fairly far from town, was the most popular wintertime place for islanders, including young Jack. A field near his house was once home to the island ski slope. Along one side there was a 400-foot rope tow, which was powered by a 1926 Dodge pickup truck engine. Foster provided the land for use, while the island paid for maintenance and other costs. Every islander was welcomed. At the bottom of the hill, there was a small pond where island kids would skate and play ice hockey. The lingering nostalgia invoked a feeling of sadness and loss. As he walked up the driveway, Kyle looked toward the remnants of the old slope. Those were good times for Carroll Island, but like the old rope tow, the island was a broken-down, rusted version of what it used to be.

"Not friggin worth it," Kyle uttered out loud, approaching the front door of the house. A single light next to the back door was lit for him to find his way. Sometimes the fog off the ocean got so thick, not even the light was visible from the driveway. Foster liked the mystique of his home, with the surrounding trees on three sides forming a natural canopy and cliffs plummeting to the sea. He knew that no one would ever hear him if he got into trouble out here. He often joked that if he were to die it would be days before anyone even knew. For the most part, this was true. It was no secret Kyle was getting up there in age, so the sheriff would stop by from time to time to check in on him.

In 1995, when The Lighthouse Society decided to conceal the island's secrets, they sealed the meeting minutes and hid them. Included were a new set of laws and rules the islanders were to follow. The Society tightened their financial grasp on the islanders who dared to question the way things were run. Many islanders became paranoid. The investigation of the island and realization that their lives were so different from other people's made them realize how much freedom they didn't have.

One of the downsides was that residents knew they had lost their sense of identity. The new island laws made people fearful. The worst part was the secret identities of the decision makers. Not knowing if one's neighbor was a member of the Society. Not knowing if your next-door neighbor was also Big Brother.

The island's sense of community was lost for years. People stopped going out to Kyle's land to sled, ski, skate, or even walk their dogs. He missed the company, but remained hopeful that the island could someday regain its illustrious and bright past.

The thought of Jack's return brought a smile to Kyle's face. He hadn't seen Jack in sixteen years. He heard Jack had gone through some tough times since leaving Carroll, but Kyle's memories still conjured up the red-cheeked, runny-nosed boy who showed up on his hill without a care in the world.

At eighty-two years old, time was running out for Kyle. Jack may be his last hope. Leaning over to the end table, he picked up the phone.

"Hello, Sheriff Reynolds?"

"Kyle? Jesus, it's eleven o'clock." Jimmy Reynolds was off duty, a rarity that his wife, Sally, looked forward to.

"Listen, Jimmy, I've got to see you. Are you busy tomorrow around ten a.m.?"

"No, why? What's up?"

"Just thought we could have a little chat," Kyle said as a loud whistling sound came from outside. He heard his shutters bang against the clapboard siding. "Jimmy, you there?"

There was no dial tone. Nothing.

Kyle put the phone back on the receiver as another gust of wind howled under the eave of the roof. Looking out the window, he could see the trees swaying back and forth. *Damned wind must have knocked out the phone again.* He settled into his sofa and turned the light off. If the phone line had gone down, he knew the power would soon follow.

Kyle wasn't afraid of a little darkness. As he sat and reflected, he realized it was the Society he was afraid of. He hoped Jimmy would come to see him like he asked. He hoped Jimmy would be the only one to come to see him.

Chapter Eleven

The arrival of a massive white and orange chopper in the ominous gray sky gave mild comfort to Jack, Nate, and Kendra. Rob had slipped in and out of consciousness, but hadn't opened his eyes since Nate's call for help. He lay on the deck, motionless and silent. His breathing was steady, but weak, and his eyelids fluttered as if he were dreaming.

Kendra kept pressure on his wound but had yet to receive an explanation of what had happened. The wind from the expansive rotors overhead was making it difficult for her to stay in her crouching position, and she dropped to her knees to keep from falling on top of Rob.

Neither Jack nor Nate had figured a good way to tell her all that had happened and knew that such an explanation needed a lengthy and possibly painful preface. She was better off not knowing for the time being. Her naivety would ensure her loyalty to Rob. He had nothing to do with Jack's deception or Nate's lies and deserved the care of a gentle woman.

The ten-foot seas were nearly flattened by the sheer power of the helicopter's rotors forcing air down below it. Jack and Nate stood, staring skyward at the giant machine that floated around the sky like a fly caught in the path of a fan. A giant sliding door on the side of the aircraft opened, and a man in a helmet peered out over them. The pilot had tried to radio down to the Whaler, but there was too much interference for the signal to get through. It was obvious that the chopper was trying to get into position, yet every time it inched closer and closer, a gust of wind would push it away.

After much anticipation, a longline dropped out the door, splashing in the water a few feet from their boat. A husky man in an orange survival suit with a built-in harness clamped onto the line and began to rappel down. Jack grasped the line with a boat hook, but had not tied it down for fear that a giant gust of wind could push away the helicopter, having drastic consequences for everyone aboard. The man, with a helmet twice the size of his head, made his way quickly down the Kevlar rope before stopping about halfway down and looking upward toward his colleagues onboard. A single hand sprouted out of the cockpit window, giving him the thumbs-up sign. The would-be rescuer then slid the rest of the way down, falling to the deck of the Whaler too fast to be caught by either Jack or Nate. Seemingly unfazed, he got back to his feet and removed his helmet.

"I'm Squad Commander Scott Morelli, United States Coast Guard, Boothbay Harbor. How bad is he?" The commander, a man about six feet tall and stocky, appeared to have the energy of a monkey. He had a five o'clock shadow that barely hid the small wrinkles that appeared when he forced a smile. He looked up to the fleeing helicopter and back to the other three, who appeared a little taken aback. "Don't worry. They'll be back. They're just giving us some time to assess the situation without all the noise." He looked up and said, "They're rigging the rescue basket right now."

"How bad? We don't really know," Jack said. "He's been unconscious for the better part of the past hour. He came to a couple of times, but was totally incoherent."

"Okay, we only have a minute or two before that chopper comes back and we get our one shot at getting him aboard," the commander explained. "Radio had a lot of interference, but I heard something about internal bleeding?"

"Just an assumption," Nate replied.

"And you are?" Morelli asked.

"Special Agent Nathan Richardson. FBI."

"Can you tell me what happened?" Morelli said, looking down at Rob's limp body. "Did you assess the danger of a broken neck or back?"

"When we first got to him, he moved his head a couple of times. So we ruled out a broken neck. He also wiggled his legs a little, which convinced us his spinal column was most likely undamaged. We didn't have much choice but to get him off the island."

"Your assessment was probably correct, but why didn't you stay on the island? It would have made this rescue a lot easier."

"Commander, we'd be more than happy to discuss that later, but I'm more concerned with the well-being of our friend," Nate said. "Besides, staying on the island was not an option."

Jack kept silent. He knew that this was where Nate's experience would be important. He trusted Nate's discretion about how much information to provide about the ordeal on Seguin.

"Fine by me, sir, but I have to know how he got like this."

"He was on the tram car on the island and the cable snapped," Nate replied, leaving out the part about the gun being what snapped it. "From what we could tell, he tried to jump off and landed hard. He slid about fifty feet from the original point of impact."

Morelli said, "Fifty feet? Jesus, the man's lucky to be alive. Have you had pressure on that wound since?"

"Except to wash it out, yes." Kendra added.

"Okay, well, I can't do any kind of internal diagnosis out here, but it seems safe enough to move him. This is how it's going to go down. When I give them the thumbs-up, they'll reposition above us and lower the basket. We'll get your friend in and then they'll be off to Maine General in Portland. We have to treat it like a worst-case scenario, and that's the closest trauma unit. I'm going to stay on board and bring you guys into the Boothbay Harbor station for debriefing," Morelli explained.

"Wasn't there supposed to be another boat out here to meet us?" Nate inquired.

"Yes sir, originally, but once I saw your boat was in good shape, I ordered it back to base for safety reasons. We've got an ever-changing weather forecast and line squalls coming out of nowhere."

"Fair enough," Nate said, "let's just get him to safety."

Morelli looked back toward the helicopter. "Okay, y'all ready?"

The helicopter was in position. With the signal from the commander, the basket was lowered to the Whaler's deck. Nate, Jack, and Commander Morelli put Rob's pale, wet body inside and it was hoisted to the safety of the chopper. In seconds, the aircraft had veered off and was on its way south.

Jack shifted the engine into gear while the others scrambled for seats. He headed the boat toward Boothbay Harbor and opened up the throttle. Following the contour of the shoreline, Jack piloted the boat with confidence as they headed to the Coast Guard Base.

The commander stayed silent and didn't try and get any more information out of them. Either he knew that he would have plenty of time once at the Base, or there was something about Nate's governmental status that made him cautious.

Jack made sure to hug the shoreline when possible as he knew that the land mass would give enough cover from the rough weather. Bobbing lobster pots made him feel he was speeding through a slalom course.

As the Whaler approached the entrance to Boothbay Harbor, Commander Morelli insisted on taking the helm from Jack. Without question, Jack throttled down into idle and got out of the chair, making room for the commander. He turned and walked back toward the stern, where Kendra sat, exhausted.

Commander Morelli navigated the boat with ease while hugging the coastline and cruising through a narrow passage, keeping Burnt and Moose islands to his port side. Cutting through the thickening fog, he banked a sharp turn to port and rounded McKown Point.

Like a typical Maine harbor, lobster boats dotted the anchorage. On the shore there was a large hangar-like building that opened onto the harbor. The front of the massive sky-blue building was secured with several garage-like doors, which were closed and had no windows. On the one side of the building that was visible, the acronym USCG was painted in large orange lettering.

Commander Morelli slowed the boat and looked around under the steering column. As they got closer to the building, one of the doors began to open and the commander steered toward the entrance. "Welcome to Coast Guard Group, Boothbay," he proclaimed as the boat floated into the hangar, which was like an enclosed port.

Directly in front of them were six docking slips. Four of them were occupied with standard Coast Guard vessels, the others, vacant. The commander steered toward an open slip as a lone man walked down a set of stairs that led down to the docks. Morelli said, "That your man, Agent Richardson?"

"It is, Commander. He must have arrived after you left." Nate pulled a navy blue windbreaker from his backpack with bright yellow letters—FBI—on the chest and back.

"They said that some Fed had showed up. Said it was routine, but everyone's been real hush-hush about him."

"You know how it is with clearance issues and all. I'm surprised you weren't told, though," Nate said. "It is your base."

"Well sir, I just got back from leave a couple hours before your call. The guys that normally would have gone out after you today went on leave when I got back. It's been a little mixed up around here." The commander threw a line to another man, who appeared from beneath the deck of one of the other boats.

Jack looked around in amazement.

"So, you guys want to tell me what's going on?" Morelli asked, looking a little impatient.

Jack shrugged his shoulders. "Good question. I can tell you we got shot at."

"That much I gathered. But by whom?"

"You don't mind if we wait till the briefing, do you?" Nate said as he walked down the wooden planks toward his boss, who was a short man, around five and a half feet tall, but in pretty good shape. His dark suit hid most of his physical features.

"No, not at all. I'll be right in. You're welcome," the commander said sarcastically.

"Don't feel bad, bro. This is all new to us too." Jack patted the commander on the back He and Kendra brushed past and followed Nate. Jack paused briefly, turned to Morelli, and said, "Thank you, Commander."

Morelli motioned as if tipping a nonexistent hat and smiled slightly.

Kendra tugged on Jack's sleeve and said, "Hold up a minute." She continued to hold onto his sleeve until he had stopped and faced her. "Jack, what the hell is all this?"

"Honestly? I'm as much in the dark as you are," Jack replied. "To most of it, that is. I had no idea that Nate was in the FBI, or that Rob was going to get hurt, but I did go to Seguin with the hope of finding some information about my parents' deaths."

"That much I figured," she said with a disgruntled-looking frown, "but people with guns?"

"Hopefully we'll have some answers in a few minutes." Jack turned and looked toward the stairs.

"So you have nothing to do with this?" Kendra asked.

"That depends on what you mean. As I said, I didn't know Nate was an FBI agent and obviously didn't know his people would have the foresight to be here, in Boothbay Harbor, of all the places in the world," he replied. "As for our predicament today, I suppose I have a lot to do with it." Jack was caught between a rock and a hard place. He wanted to divulge a lot more to her, but in the back of his head, he also thought that Nate would come through for him and they would indeed be partners as they had discussed. He knew that it was Nate, and not Kendra, who could provide the most assistance to him on the island. Having them both would be invaluable, but he was out of his element now. Nate hadn't talked about his boss being at the base, but he obviously knew about it and would know the best course of action.

* * *

Jack and Kendra regrouped with Nate by the stairs, and they all looked up toward the strange man in a black suit. He looked like a Secret Service agent without an earpiece.

Nate tugged at his lower lip with his teeth, and Jack could tell he was waiting for a cue from his boss. A cue to release more information that was bound to him by orders rather than a sense of duty.

Kendra turned to Jack and said, "I'm going back to Portland to be with Rob. This whole cloak-and-dagger thing just isn't for me—"

"Rob's not going to Portland. He was brought somewhere else to keep this little incident from going public," Nate interrupted. "Don't get me wrong, you can go back to the city if you want to, but Jack and I are going to the island. We'll get a car and try and make the last ferry to Carroll." He turned from the others and began up the stairs where his boss was waiting.

"Jack? Are you seriously going to take off with Rob in this condition?"

Jack nodded, his emotion drained by fatigue.

"He's your friend, Jack!" she pleaded.

"And you heard what Nate said. He's not in Portland."

"Which is your fault, Jack. You brought him out here today. The least you could do is try to be at his side."

Jack knew Kendra was right, and she didn't even know the whole truth. She didn't even know that Rob had no idea he'd be in danger. Like a showdown at a poker table, his eyes were caught in a dead stare with hers. He didn't have to flinch though. Kendra was too good at reading people.

"He didn't even know, did he?" she asked.

"Sorry?"

Kendra's look intensified. She glanced around at the surroundings, then back to Jack. "All this. You, Nate, and the excursion to Seguin; he didn't know?"

Jack sighed. He ran his fingers through his short, damp hair. "No, he didn't know he'd be in danger. In fact, Kendra, this was all my idea. Nate was sent by the FBI to tag along and see that I stayed out of trouble."

"So you lied about all of it? Your novel? Your reason for going back to Carroll? All of it's been a—"

"No, Kendra," Jack interrupted. "I made the choice to go back to Carroll for all the reasons I told you. It was the break-in that made me realize that it wasn't just me who wouldn't let the accident go. That break-in wasn't random. I suspected it wasn't and then I got confirmation. I don't have a choice. Unless I go to Carroll and find out what really happened to my parents, there will be people following me—following us. The people who broke in think I have all the answers already, but I don't have anything more than the same suspicions I've had for years. I have to do this, and I need you. I need to put this to rest once and for all."

"So I'm just supposed to come along for the ride?"

"No. We need to go back together; they think you're coming, too."

"They're obviously onto you. Do you think there will be some welcoming party when we get to the island?"

"Only a fraction of the residents are a part of this, Kendra," he pleaded. "And if we get there and make contact with the right people, their hands will be tied. That's why we have to go tonight."

Staring down at Jack's feet, Kendra exhaled deeply through her nose. A curious look on her face, she lifted her eyes to meet with Jack's. "You actually think we can get the last ferry?"

"I have no intention of even trying to catch that ferry," Jack said. "I have a feeling that Nate's boss will be more comfortable with us going out to the island if we tell him where we are going to be. We just won't be there. Know what I mean?"

Kendra said, "But you plan on going into some meeting upstairs? You're not the type to even listen to authority, but yet you plan on sitting in on a debriefing? You're going to lie to them too?"

"You're right about the authority part, but we have to sit in on the debriefing. I'm sure there are people with big guns who will see to that," Jack replied.

"Fine," she said begrudgingly, "but you still haven't told me how Nate got involved in this. I know you didn't call the FBI and tell them your plans."

"Nate and I will fill you in on the ride up to Rockland. I promise."

Jack was into the cloak-and-dagger mission. Unfortunately the safety of his friends, and worry for Rob, had been thrown out the window. He wanted to be there when Rob came to, but he also knew he only had one chance at this.

* * *

"Jack, Kendra, this is my boss—Special Agent In Charge Richard O'Neil," Nate said, flanking his superior.

"Ms. Davids, Mr. Chandler, how do you do? I feel like I know you, Jack. Although I must say, it's been a long time since your name has come up," O'Neil said.

"Not to be rude, but can we get on with this debriefing? We need to get on the road soon," Jack snapped back.

"We'll do the best we can. I have lots of questions for you all, though."

The four walked up the stairs, turned left through a door, and entered a normal, office-style room complete with cubicles. It was a separate building attached to the hangar, but the aluminum wall that separated the offices from the boat depot had been covered with a layering of sheetrock to improve the aesthetics of the room and perhaps hide the contents of what was behind it. The hallway they followed hugged the hangar wall on one side, with the office on the other. The room was empty.

At the end of the hallway they came to an intersection. In front of them was a door that read "Private — Military Personnel Only." Jack thought it was odd as the Coast Guard, although a branch of the armed services, wasn't considered military. Then again, the FBI agents looked as though they felt right at home there. He didn't know of any public relationship between the FBI and the Coast Guard.

They entered a simple conference room with a large twenty-seat table in the middle. Two men in suits stood immediately as the group came through the door. One of them was Commander Morelli. His jacket was snug. Jack could tell it wasn't his.

"At ease, gentlemen. Nathan, Jack, Kendra, please take a seat and make yourselves comfortable," O'Neil instructed as he took a seat at the head of the table, his demeanor serious. "Okay then, Agent Richardson, could you give us a breakdown of today's events so we can get them on record and decide how to proceed?" He took out a pad of paper and a pen.

There were cameras and recording devices in the corners of the room. As the four sat down, Commander Morelli stood up and proceeded to pull down a projector screen.

"Oh great. We're going to watch a movie?" Jack was uncomfortable with the tension in the room and thought it was the perfect time to act a little playful. It helped calm his nerves.

"Mr. Chandler, this is a very serious matter. I think we would all appreciate it if you would address it as such," O'Neil said. "A friend of yours is currently lying in a hospital bed in a coma."

Jack shrugged, turned to O'Neil, and said, "Yeah, you know, I heard you talking about that with my buddy here. I also heard you say that he was taken to Brunswick. That wouldn't by chance be Brunswick Naval Air Station, would it?"

"Yes it would. They have an excellent medical facility there," O'Neil replied.

"If I may interrupt, sir, I told them originally that their friend would be taken to Portland, but that was before we knew all the details," Morelli said.

"Thank you, Commander. As the commander pointed out, you had not informed him of the shooting when you called in; thus he wasn't aware of the containment issues."

"Containment issues?" Kendra sounded interested in what legal grounds they would have to contain Rob at a military base. "Are you holding him as some sort of prisoner?"

O'Neil replied, "No, I think you all have a distorted perception of what's going on here. Perhaps we are all suffering from a lack of communication. To be honest, we didn't want him to go to the hospital in Portland for fear of media attention. It is our understanding—from

Agent Richardson—you want to go on with the operation. Your cover would be completely blown if this leaked."

"Excuse me, folks, what operation? Would it be okay if someone filled me in a little?" Kendra asked.

"Ms. Davids, I don't—"

"Jesus. My name is Kendra," she said.

"As I was going to say, Kendra, I'm unaware of the extent of your knowledge. I don't want to assume anything, so I figured it best if Agent Richardson would just do a briefing about everything. I'm sure he will add any information that may be helpful to all of us."

"Okay. By Agent Richardson, you mean Nate, right? Sure, gotcha, I'm listening." Kendra rolled her eyes.

Jack shot a glance over at Kendra. He couldn't tell if she was really as frustrated as she sounded or if she was going to bat for him.

The lights in the room dimmed and the projector came on, showing what appeared to be a slide of the Cape Small, Seguin Island, and Kennebec River area. It looked like a chart, but not one that Jack had ever seen published before. Nate turned away from the chart and spoke about the background of Jack's parents' untimely death and how he had gotten involved in the case soon after his rookie year in the Bureau. His description of the relationship he'd formed with Jack and Rob shocked Kendra, who remained silent. It was the same story that he had told Jack out on Seguin earlier in the day. He proceeded to go through the day's events and explained how he revealed himself to Jack before they entered the tower of the lighthouse. He then turned to the projection, which had a detailed insert of Seguin in the lower left-hand corner. He used a pointer to show where Rob's incident had taken place, where he thought the shooter was, and how they escaped down the maintenance path to the shoreline. After a recap of the events that transpired on Seguin, Nate informed them that with Rob in stable condition, he and Jack had still planned to go out to the island.

"What about me?" Kendra asked.

"The only thing that changes for you is that you are going to the island a different way now. We realize that we may find out nothing, and that this could be an isolated incident. It's not likely, but it is possible. Regardless, there is no reason that it should interfere with you moving out there. I'm the one that's going in undercover, and Jack's going to help me. We all know that the islanders are skeptical of anyone going out there," Nate explained.

"What are you really trying to accomplish by going to the island?" Kendra asked. "Are you trying to expose this secret organization? I guess I don't see what there is to gain for the FBI."

"We really don't know what we are looking for, but we hope we'll find something at the coordinates we found engraved at the lighthouse." Nate looked to the other side of the table. "Commander, have your people figured out where this is?" Nate stepped back from the screen and a new slide came up.

Jack couldn't look at Kendra. He'd just got done explaining that going to Seguin was his idea, and now Nate was telling her differently.

"The first slide is of the greater Rockland area," the commander said. "If we look closer to the minutes from longitude and latitude, we are brought to a small area in Rockport called The Children's Chapel. To the best of our knowledge, it is a park of some sort. Is anyone familiar with it?"

"I went there often as a kid," Jack said. "My parents were married there." The thought of his parents' wedding brought memories, and his eyes began to well up. "The Society must have known that. Why would they hide something so important there?"

"Jack, we may have found some coordinates, but we haven't found anything nefarious. I think the three of us just need to get up there and search the place," Nate said as though he had been formulating a plan.

A hard knock sounded on the door, and the group turned their attention. "Come in," O'Neil commanded. A man in normal Coast Guard attire came through the doors and walked over to O'Neil, whispering something in his ear. O'Neil nodded to him and he left, never once laying eyes on the rest of them. "Okay, folks, we just got confirmation from our boys who went out to Seguin. They found a woman, believed to be in her late thirties—dead on the shoreline."

"Dead? I only shot her in the leg. I think. Did she die from loss of blood?" Nate asked.

"No, Agent Richardson, she died from a close-range gunshot wound to the head, with a .45 caliber gun," O'Neil exclaimed.

"So she killed herself?" Kendra asked.

"It doesn't appear that way. It wasn't her gun and the shot wasn't close enough to be considered self-inflicted. If someone wanted to make it look like a suicide, they were awfully sloppy," Morelli said.

"Sir, there's no way someone else could have made it out to that island. Not that fast. And we didn't see anyone else there with her." Jack paused for a second. "Wait a minute. You don't think one of us..."

"Not at all. We have a team going out to investigate the scene and hopefully get Jack's boat. As for what happened, there's nothing we can conclude for right now. We assume that she wasn't alone out there, but she isn't one of the original keepers on record for this summer."

"What do you mean, sir?" Nate looked up from his legal pad, which was filled with cryptic notes. "Was there someone else who can't be accounted for?"

"This year, the organization that funds it chose a couple to live out there for the summer. That couple was David and Norma Peterson from Rangeley. Our men just got off the phone with Norma. She's at home with some virus. Extreme flu-like symptoms."

Jack said, "Who replaced her?"

"She said the lady's name was Julie Billings. We've confirmed the name. Julie Billings is a resident of—"

"Carroll Island," Jack interrupted. "I grew up with her, but I don't think she was in her late thirties, maybe early thirties. What about Norma's husband— David is it?"

"That's what we don't know. Hell, for all we know, he's on your boat en route to God knows where, but he could have gone home with his wife. We didn't have time to ask. Mrs. Peterson said she was about to be sick and dropped the phone. We have planes out looking, but as you know, the fog is thick out there." O'Neil got up from his chair and began to pace around the room. "So, what do you guys want to do?"

Nate and Jack looked at each other, smiled, and then looked toward Kendra.

"What do you think, Kendra?" Nate asked.

"I say we do it, but right now, I'm exhausted," she said.

O'Neil said, "Why don't you go outside and take a break before you guys leave. I would like to have a word alone with Agent Richardson."

Commander Morelli and the other man, who never said so much

as a word, both got up and left the room. Kendra and Jack followed them outside. Nate stayed behind to talk to O'Neil.

* * *

Kendra and Jack followed Commander Morelli through a double doglegged hallway, up a set of stairs, and through a door that left them in a small lobby. Flipping through a glossy-covered fashion magazine, a receptionist sat behind a raised desk. Opposite the desk, two leather armchairs flanked a coffee table with magazines neatly arranged. Jack couldn't tell if the woman at the desk was military or not, but she was part of the cover. Chewing gum loudly, she looked up from her magazine and informed the two that they had to sign a departure log before going outside.

Jack took off after the commander as Kendra signed her name. "Hey, Commander, you have a smoke?"

The two exited through the front door together.

"Nope. I don't smoke, nor should you," he replied with a smile.

"Yeah, thanks. I'm well aware. Just a little stressed out."

"You'll be fine, sir. I've been on missions like this before."

"What do you mean by that? You haven't been ordered to go with us, have you?"

"Yes, sir," Morelli said. "Captain Arnold and I will escort you to the island and spend a few days there."

"What the hell is going on…?" Jack ran back to the front door, brushed by Kendra, and back down the stairs.

"Hey, you have to sign…" the receptionist shouted, but Jack hadn't so much as glanced at her.

When he got to the conference room, Nate and O'Neil were in some sort of argument. Jack pushed open the heavy door, and the inside knob slammed against the wall. The bang echoed in the hall.

"Guess how quickly this operation will fail if we have to bring those two," Jack said, almost out of breath. They looked up, startled.

"This is for your protection, Mr. Chandler," O'Neil said.

"No sir, it is absolutely insane for you to think that anyone on that island is going to let those two clowns just walk on there with us. How much luck have you had getting people on there in the past?"

"These are supposedly your people, Mr. Chandler. I'd think they'd believe any story you came up with," O'Neil responded.

"I doubt that. They'll hardly let Kendra on the island. They had a damned town vote about it."

"Yet you think they'll let you bring Agent Richardson?"

Jack sighed. "Again, they know he is coming and that he is supposed to stay for a couple of days, helping us with the move."

"Wouldn't you think that things have sort of changed in the past twelve or so hours? Aren't they going to be waiting for you? They probably think you killed that woman." Special Agent In Charge O'Neil made sense. Jack had no way of knowing what the reaction would be. Had she radioed someone before being killed?

"Jack. Sir. Hold on a minute. Remember when I gave my briefing? I said that there were—or are—seemingly two groups of people? Well, what if this Julie woman was working for the Society and she was shot before being able to relay any news back to the island? Maybe the person who shot her is on our side." Nate grinned.

"You think I have some sort of guardian angel?"

"That call had to come from someone who wanted to help—"

"Or set us up. Julie Billings knew we were coming."

"Maybe whoever it was that called you was made."

"Then how would they be able to get out to Seguin and shoot Julie?" Jack was becoming even more frustrated. *What if they are waiting for me?* "You're disproving your own argument, Nate. If the caller was made, the Society would never let them off the island."

"You mean to tell me you think there's only one person out there wanting to help you? You're jumping to conclusions, Jack."

"Regardless, your boss's goons aren't coming along for the ride." Jack stood his ground.

"Jack, think about it. Who would have shot her? If she were one of your allies, she wouldn't have shot at us. She knew that we found those damned coordinates and tried to get to us before we got off the island."

"I would love to believe it, but what if she did get word out before she was shot?" Jack thought for a second and then turned back to O'Neil. "Did you guys intercept any radio transmissions from Seguin after ours? You must have been monitoring."

"Yes, we were. There wasn't one VHF or even cell call from the island," O'Neil confirmed.

Nate said, "So I could be right?"

"You could be right, but even if you are, we couldn't get on that island with two more guys," Jack explained. "You have to trust me on this one. Please." His tone was laced with desperation. "We'd be watched every second we were out there—followed everywhere."

"Okay. Okay," O'Neil conceded. "You guys can go without them, but at the first sign of trouble, I'm sending them out there. We already have enough to get a warrant."

"Good. We'll need to go to Rockport first and look for whatever it is they've been protecting," Nate said.

"Yes, you do. Then I want you—Agent Richardson—to report back to me before you get on that ferry."

"It's too late to get a ferry tonight. We can get the morning one, but I think we should probably try and get to the chapel tonight in case someone else is on to us and Nate's theory is wrong."

"A theory of mine—wrong? How rude." Nate smiled. "Let's get your girlfriend and get out of here. Sir, call us as soon as you locate Jack's boat."

"Good luck, gentlemen." O'Neil tipped his hat, turned, and left the room, leaving the two friends alone. Jack whispered into Nate's ear, and the two made their way to the exit. Jack was afraid to say anything out loud that he didn't want heard. He assumed the room was being monitored.

* * *

When they got outside, Kendra waited for them with a set of keys to a car.

"Where'd you get those?" Nate asked.

"Your boss just made a call up to that overly friendly girl at the desk in there. She brought them out to me. She said he wants us to be careful taking the car on the ferry." She snickered. "Of course, we're not taking the ferry. So, little does he know, he has nothing to worry about."

"Why aren't we taking the ferry? I thought I was in charge of this mission," Nate said, frustrated.

"You know damned well that O'Neil will have those two on one of those ferries. If we don't take one, they won't dare get off on Carroll. So we aren't going to take the ferry. I've got some friends in Camden who will lend us a good boat." Jack smiled. He thought he was pretty tricky. "Let's get the hell out of here."

They got into a brand-new Mercedes S-Class, belonging to Nate's boss. The car wound its way over narrow back roads and onto the mainland. Although it was evening, the light from the sun had returned to the sky over the western horizon, which had been filled with thunderous black clouds for the latter half of the day. Jack looked out the rear window and stared at the blurry headlights tailing far behind them. Despite the lack of snow, just traveling on that road again made him recall the day his parents died. He was clouded by an overwhelming sense of déjà vu that he just couldn't get out of his head.

Unaware of the significance of Jack's memories, Nate and Kendra were in the two front seats talking away. They chatted about things that didn't matter. They had that luxury. Their past wasn't being reinvented right in front of them, but it was different for Jack.

Chapter Twelve

J ack sat in the backseat of the Mercedes, his mind elsewhere. His thoughts drifted in and out of the past. It had been sixteen years since he'd seen this stretch of Route 1. The very thought of it made him feel cowardly, yet perhaps his psychiatrist was right. Maybe he truly wasn't ready to take this step. What had been a life-altering move to begin with had become so much more complex. Would they find out some truth that was so horrible they would return to Portland— return to the boring life they left behind?

Traveling the northbound lane, the towns whisked by like pages of a matchbook cartoon; Damariscotta, Nobleboro, and Waldoboro all passed like blinks of the eye. The charming little tourist towns that dotted Route 1 had no meaning to Jack. Even if he'd had an interest in any one of the massive flea markets or taffy shops, he wanted to be alone, to be lost among the lush trees that lined the highway. The emotions he had kept in the back of his consciousness for so long had caught up with him, and he fought back tears.

If they hadn't checked in the rearview mirror, Kendra and Nate might not have noticed. Jack was in the kind of pain that medicine couldn't heal, only time. Maybe he hadn't given himself enough time.

Worse, maybe he'd never really felt the pain before. Twelve years old was a young age to comprehend loss.

"Honey, are you okay?" Kendra asked.

"Fine, thanks," Jack replied. The short response was all he could afford.

"Is there anything we can do, Jack?" Nate asked. "Wanna stop anywhere? You hungry?"

"I'll be fine. Thanks."

It was around 8:30 in the evening and the sun was all but gone from the sky. The purplish-dusk sky turned to night, but the three-quarter-full moon provided an eerie light. In the distance, the commanding presence of the Camden Hills grabbed their attention—the rocky, rounded peaks rose above the mist with a majestic presence. Cruising down the secluded highway, theirs was the only car on the twisting and turning road.

A half-hour later they arrived at the base of Mt. Battie, perhaps the most recognizable of the hills. The Camden Hills brought a mystique all their own to the towns of Camden, Rockport, and Lincolnville. On brochures throughout the state, the area—placid nine months out of the year—was dubbed "Where the Mountains Meet the Sea." Thousands of tourists flocked to this quaint corner of Maine each year, fighting the crowds of cars that scurry up Route 1.

* * *

The black Mercedes pulled into downtown Camden, with its bustle of summer guests. They passed the post office and the bank, just off Main Street, and Nate pointed out that he had seen such buildings in Stephen King movies. Jack was quick to tell him which ones and when they were made. The man who had seemingly regressed to a boy in the backseat was now alert and eager to share his knowledge of the famous mid-coast town.

The three were anxious to check into an inn and find some food before the local eateries turned their attention to the late night drinking crowds, which were most popular along the inner harbor.

Jack asked, "Anyone think to book a room for tonight?" The thought hadn't crossed his mind until that moment. "'Cause, if not, we might as well head back to Rockland. There won't be any vacancies here."

"Not to worry, my good man, O'Neil called ahead and booked us a couple rooms at a place called the Mt. Battie Inn," Nate said.

"Great, let's check in. I'm starving."

* * *

After settling into their room and changing into some fresh clothes, Jack and Kendra met Nate in the lobby before heading into town. The inn was only about a mile from the center of town, but none of them were up to the walk after such a long and exhausting day.

"Did Dick say anything about my boat?" Jack asked, deciding he just couldn't deal with the mouthful that was Special Agent In Charge O'Neil.

"I almost forgot to tell you," Nate replied. "O'Neil said that up till nightfall, the fog was still too thick to send up any helicopters. They weren't sending anything up except for distress calls."

"Hey, hey, *Vigilance* is a four-hundred-thousand-dollar boat. If a loss like that isn't distressful, what is?" Jack was only kidding, but he had worked for many years on that boat, and it was his pride and joy.

"Vanity isn't exactly the main focus of the Coast Guard or the FBI." Nate laughed.

"Oh no, of course not. That's why Dick's company car is a Mercedes," Kendra said.

As they drove down Main Street in Camden, there were a surprising number of people still out, given that it was 9:30 p.m. Tourists peeked in the lighted windows of closed art galleries and fashion boutiques, and the line at the ice cream shop extended out to the road.

Having passed the main strip of shops and restaurants, Jack pulled the car into the parking lot of the Camden Yacht Club. There was a large sign stating, "Parking Is for Members and Guests Only." He parked adjacent to the red clapboard clubhouse and reached for a piece of paper. He wrote his last name, followed by a three-digit number, and placed it under the windshield of the car.

"Won't the car get towed if we park here?" Nate asked.

"Not with my membership number," Jack replied.

"Honey, I didn't know you were still a member here," Kendra said. "We haven't been here in years."

"Neither have half the other people who are members, but like them, I pay dues every year."

"Like I said, it's all about vanity," Nate said.

"Shut up, cop," Jack said. "Jealousy doesn't become you." He and Kendra shared in the laugh as they walked a couple of blocks to The Salty Gull, a favorite restaurant of locals and tourists alike.

Although hungry from almost a full day without food, they were either too tired or too excited to enjoy their meals. When the waiter brought the entrees, the table was silent. There was none of the normal joking from Jack or even complaints from Kendra over the quality—or lack thereof, in her opinion—of the freshly brewed coffee she requested. Many patrons enjoyed coffee after dinner, but few asked for a breakfast blend. It was as though she was immune to the effects of caffeine. Ordering extra cream and extra sugar, perhaps her unrest had nothing to do with the coffee.

"Okay, guys, it's time to ante up," Kendra insisted. "I haven't put up too much of a fuss over the lack of information, but you want me to go out there to Carroll Island tomorrow and what, go bird-watching? What are we going to do out there? May I remind the both of you that I left Portland yesterday to go live on an island. You know, to get away from it all. I'm tired, I'm frustrated, and I'm damned sick of being treated as though I am not worthy of any info. Quite frankly, I feel like a pawn."

Nate felt she was ready to hear everything. "Kendra, we don't really know what we are going to do when we get out there. I'd love to say that we will know more tomorrow. We hope to find something at the chapel, which would put us on some sort of path, but honestly, it's just a hunch. Personally, I think someone's just trying to slow us down."

"All right, fine. What if we find nothing? No evidence, no smoking gun, just a bunch of flowers. Are you guys going to drop this high and mighty crusade and let it go?"

"We can't just drop it. Perhaps if we had skipped the visit to Seguin today, but not now," Nate said.

The shooting and the death of Julie Billings would mean a full-scale investigation of the island, which they couldn't prevent. The only thing pushing that back was the tip Jack had received.

"Let's look at it in a more practical way. If we don't find anything tomorrow—which is entirely possible—how would we proceed without having to bring in Dick's guys?" Kendra asked.

"We should think about every possibility seriously. Then we can plan some strategy," Nate said. "Let's see. Jack, one of your roles will be to hook up with your buddy Jimmy and his friends. I have little doubt that these people will put some kind of show on for us, so we need to get inside. You also need to get close to that Sally friend of yours. From what you've said about her, she'll talk."

Kendra laughed and said, "Oh, that's nice. You want my boyfriend to go hit on his ex-girlfriend?"

"Jesus, Kendra. Would you relax? We were ten years old, for Christ's sake. Nate's right. She loves gossip. She'll talk. The real question is whether or not Jimmy will. Hell, if we can get Jimmy and Old Man Foster with us, we'll be in good shape. No doubt one of them must be part of the Society."

"If they're a part of the Society, how can we trust them?" Nate said.

"'Cause I have a strong feeling whoever sent that note to me has contact with the Society. I think one or more of them may want out. Might just be looking for a way," Jack said. He knew the only way to find out would be to get out there and test the theory.

"Could I offer anyone some dessert?" the waiter asked, having crept up from behind the bar.

Perhaps he had been listening in? It wouldn't matter—anyone who heard this conversation would think they were all nuts.

"Oh, no thank you." Startled, they all answered in unison.

"Any coffee or tea instead?"

Kendra smiled and said, "Gee, no thanks, but could you tell us if there is a ..."

Jack interrupted, "No, we're fine. Thank you. Just the bill, please."

He wanted to cut off Kendra before she could ask the gentleman if there was a Dunkin Donuts around.

It neared 11:30 p.m. as they strolled down the dew-soaked road back toward the yacht club. They walked slowly down Bayview Street, looking in some of the lighted windows like the other tourists, but there would be no ice cream for them. The shop had closed its doors over an hour before. Jack complained that he should have ordered some ice cream for dessert.

"So back to those plans. Are we all set with what we're going to do when we get to the island?" Nate asked.

"Oh sure," Kendra replied. "I'm going to hang out at a house I've never been to—but pretend to like it there. Jack's going to flirt—something he does quite well. Kidding, honey," she said with a subtle wink. "And you—you're going to do whatever the hell it is you do. Sorry, I guess I wasn't paying attention when you said what that was."

"Weren't you the one who was all uptight about this?" Nate asked.

"Yep, but once you told me, I became indifferent." Kendra appeared most content when being a bitch. "From what you said earlier, it doesn't really matter until the two of you go on your egg hunt at the chapel."

"She's right, Nate. I think we should just worry about getting some sleep before we worry about riding in on the Trojan horse. Besides, it'll take us a while to get out there tomorrow. Plenty of time to plan," Jack said as he patted his pockets for the keys to the Mercedes.

As Jack continued to search, Kendra poked at him and tickled his side. She only had a couple of beers with dinner, but it was enough to make her a little silly. Nate had jogged ahead a little and turned into the yacht club.

"Go get 'em, cop," Jack yelled to his friend, laughing.

Nate slowed and turned around with a puzzled look on his face. He said, "Jack, I think you might want to see this."

Jack and Kendra quickened their stride. "What'd you do? Bust somebody?" Jack said.

"Seriously, man, this is just weird. I think your boat's here," Nate replied. He turned back toward the water and started to walk to the dock. Jack and Kendra released each other's hands and ran after him.

Jack's heart pounded as he ran up the small hill. Having turned down the driveway, he slowed with the dock in sight. "Damn," he said, nearly out of breath. "That's not my boat. Looks a lot like it in the dark, but not mine."

"You're kidding, right?" Nate replied.

"Don't get me wrong, I wish it were, but this is a Hinckley '42. *Vigilance* is a Sabre," Jack said, smiling. "You got the color right, though."

Glancing back toward the yacht club parking lot and pointing, Nate's jaw dropped as the three peered at a rustling shrub.

"Gentlemen and lady, good evening," Richard O'Neil said, wearing Bermuda shorts and a polo shirt. His exposed limbs were pasty white.

"Jesus, you scared the living hell out of me," Jack said, barely recognizing the man. "You look much different during the day. Personally, I liked the hat you had on, but the crew cut is working for ya."

"Very funny, Mr. Chandler. So, who's going to tell me what's going on here?" O'Neil pointed toward Jack's boat on the dock.

"It's not what you think, sir," Nate replied. "It's not *Vigilance*."

"Right, 'cause we really would have had the means to get my boat all the way up here in a manner of hours," Jack said, rolling his eyes. "I think it's you that should be explaining what's going on. You didn't say anything about being in Camden."

"I've been following you guys around. You didn't think you'd get far off the leash, did you?"

"Jack, can you and Kendra go for a walk or something, please?" Nate asked.

"No. My chain's been yanked a few too many times. As if weird phone calls and people shooting at us weren't enough, we got an FBI dude who orders around machine-gun-carrying Coast Guard guys? I think we'll stay right here," Jack replied.

"A little paranoid, are we, Jack?" O'Neil's grin was sinister-looking.

"I'm paranoid about anything having to do with the government, and/or bureaucrats. So let's get one thing straight. This is our battle. We agreed that we'd call you if needed, but, oh no, you had to appear out of the shadows like some *X-Files* character," Jack said, rolling his eyes. "The way I see it, we can stay here and argue about whether or not the three of us can handle this situation, but frankly, I think that would be a waste of time, so I'm going to bed. And don't even think about sending that pansy, Commander Morelli, or that other meathead with us." He turned and walked toward the car. Kendra quickly followed suit as O'Neil and Nate stood in shock at the display Jack had put on. Nate wanted to leave with them, but it was time for him to pay the piper for Jack's outburst.

Nate heaved a sigh and said, "Sir, I don't..."

"Shut up, Agent Richardson! That boy's good. Hell, he's better than you. No offense," O'Neil replied.

"None taken. I guess. So what do you want me to do? Us to do, I mean?"

"You heard him. Go get some rest. You'll need it."

"You're not pissed?"

"No. Why? He called my bluff. He's a wise guy and a loose cannon, but I think we can trust him. If I get any new info, I'll call your hotel. Otherwise, you guys can have it your way. We'll back off, but we won't be too far off if you need some help. Good night, Nathan."

The two shook hands.

"Night, sir. Thanks," Nate said.

They left in opposite directions, and Nate hurried back to the car before Jack drove off. SAIC O'Neil vanished much like he had arrived—somewhere into the shadows.

The mood in the car was tense. The three had been so gleeful, but reality had sunk in. Jack had set the stakes high for them, and although they might have been a little nervous, there was still an air of excitement among them.

"Rob would have liked this, huh?" Jack said.

"I doubt Rob will have any regrets about missing this part of the trip," Kendra said. "I just hope he pulls through."

The car's taillights faded in the dark fog of Route 1, winding its way out of the center of town and toward their hotel.

Chapter Thirteen

Carroll Island welcomed morning the same way every day. As the morning sun begged to dry the cobblestone of Main Street, front doors opened and sprinklers popped up.

Each stone on Main Street was cut by hand and placed together on the road stretching some 200 yards. Lined with neatly maintained brick sidewalks and granite curbs, Main Street was the only road on the island with sidewalks. In fact it was the only road on the island that wasn't dirt or gravel.

Like most small towns in Maine, the street was the focal point of all activity on the island. On one side a number of stores' front doors opened onto the faded red walk. Across the street, a small park with a finely manicured lawn and neatly trimmed hedges surrounded a post-and-beam gazebo.

Carroll Island rarely saw visitors, and the residents liked it that way. People were comfortable knowing every person going in and out of Hamilton's Hardware or the Village Dock Store. As it was, there was plenty of gossip going around without adding a stranger to the mix. Nate, however, would be an anomaly to such a rule. Conveniently, the residents had it in their minds that he was contracted by Jack to do some house renovation appraisals.

Although Carroll Island's characteristics were unique in many ways, the island residents woke up and worked a hard day, like any other town. In other parts of America, one may hear a rooster as they go out to get their morning paper, others hear the roar of the day's first 767 flying overhead. On Carroll Island, the residents woke to the same sound each day: the distant sound of the island ferry's foghorn as it entered the inner harbor to pick up the 6:15 passengers. Even on the brightest of mornings, the ferry would sound its horn; it was a tradition that people had come to admire. As the rusty white ferry floated slowly through the inner harbor, island lobstermen waited anxiously for the sound of its horn so they could start their own engines and begin their day. There was no rule or law that said they couldn't rev up their loud diesel engines at an earlier time, but each day—like clockwork—they waited. They waited out of respect for the people living near the harbor, and indeed they waited because it was part of their ritual. Carroll Island was big on rituals.

* * *

At 6:00 a.m. sharp, the screened clapboard doors of the Village Dock Store swung open, and its proprietor—Sally Reynolds—welcomed the day, and of course anyone waiting for the ferry. Each day, the smile on her face may have been ubiquitous, but the gossip she looked forward to was always different.

The Village Dock Store had a lunch counter where Sally and her closest and most vocal friends sat and discussed the latest news.

Colleen Thomas, Jenny Cooper, and Nancy Harding sat on the oak stools, crafted by none other than Kyle Foster. Sally poured their first morning cup of coffee before grabbing her own and pulling up a stool on the opposite side of the counter.

Sally's mother, Carla Stevenson, had opened the store in the early 1960s. Sick of sitting at home and worrying about her husband out on the ocean lobstering, she thought that it would be a good way to pass the time. It was the first store, and still the only general store, on the island. Despite its small space, it carried almost everything an islander could need.

Carla passed away in 2002, after a long battle with cancer that had left her confined to her home. Sally, who at only nineteen years of age had been running the store in her absence, took command for good. She had intended to leave the island and attend Bowdoin College in Brunswick, but her mother's death was like an omen that she must stay on the island. Her father, Earnest—a lobsterman still—wanted no part in running the store. His place was at sea, thus Sally felt a sense of purpose in staying. To this day, she said she had no regrets about staying. She had wanted to go on to medical school after Bowdoin, but despite her goals, there weren't many youngsters who left the island for academia. Most just accepted their places on the sterns of the expansive lobster fleet, which had replaced the island's former trade of quarrying.

In 2006, Sally took on the name Reynolds when Jimmy returned from the state police academy to work in the sheriff's department. Jimmy, too, could have gone anywhere; being a state trooper was even in his sights, but he always had eyes for Sally and knew that they could have a nice life together on Carroll.

Sally bent her sleek, five-foot, eight-inch frame and picked up a freshly delivered copy of the *Bangor Republican* from the corner of her store before returning to her stool. She tied her long blond hair in a loose knot and stuck a knitting needle through to hold it in place.

"Well, girls, what's happening in the real world today?" she asked the morning coffee crew as she opened the paper.

"To hell with the paper," Nancy said, grinning. "I hear you've been keeping a secret from us."

Sally shrugged and said, "What do you mean?" She had a fake look of innocence, displaying her coy and attractive smile, which she had inherited from her mother.

"Word is, you've been getting the old Chandler house ready," Nancy said. "I hear Jack's coming back this week."

"I didn't want to make a big deal out of it," Sally replied. "He's been through a lot. Jack and I were in school together—neighbors for twelve years. I lost a great friend when he moved away. He needs to know that he has true friends here, not just curious onlookers." Sally was sincere; the two had even been a pre-teen couple for a brief period. She used to tell the story of when they went to see the fireworks on the fourth of July, and her dad yelled at them for kissing. She couldn't help but still have feelings for him, but kept that to herself.

Like many women her age, Sally was a dreamer. She had been all her life, but that never stopped her from being practical. It was practical for her to stay on Carroll and run her mother's store, and it was practical to marry Jimmy Reynolds. Yet the loss of other options left her with an empty feeling inside. It was from within that empty place she conjured up her dreams. Sally knew that her occasional thoughts of an extramarital relationship with someone like Jack were both unfounded and unrealistic, and that's all she wanted them to be.

There was little doubt she wanted a more exciting life, but she knew that one should never take a good life, such as hers, for granted.

Sally snapped out of her daydream. She rubbed her eyes and brought her attention back to the lunch counter. She said, "I'm sorry. What were we talking about?"

"Told you guys she was spacing out," Nancy said, chuckling. "We were talking about your favorite subject—Jack."

Sally sighed and said, "That's not my favorite subject. Jeez, Nancy, you're liable to get me in trouble with my husband. Besides, what would Jack want with an island girl who runs a lunch counter?"

"Jack was always a good guy in my book. Real cute, too," Jenny said. "I never really knew him that well, but my dad and his were pretty good friends I guess. That is till, well, you know..." She returned to her copy of the new *People* magazine, realizing she had stumbled upon a sore topic. "Imagine if Brad Pitt dumped Angelina and moved out here. Now that would be something to talk about."

Sally laughed at Jenny's imagination and got up to get more coffee for her friends. The phone started ringing in the kitchen. "I should probably get that," she said, shuffling away from the counter. It wasn't often she got phone calls at the store. Anyone coming in by boat, wanting to rent one of her moorings in the harbor, would call the store on their VHF radio.

"Good morning, Dock Store, this is Sally," she said.

"Hey, Sally. It's Jack."

Sally looked out to the counter to see if the girls could see her. She could barely contain her smile, but she didn't want them to know it. "Oh, hi, Jack. How are you?" She could have smacked herself for saying something so stupid, so normal. She gathered her composure. "When are you going to grace us with your presence?" She intentionally tried to sound sarcastic so he wouldn't know how excited she was to see him.

"We should be out later on today. We'll see how the weather is."

"You sound tense, Jack. Is everything okay?"

"I hope so," he replied, "but in case anyone has any misgivings about me coming home, I'd like to think I had someone reliable to call."

"And Jimmy's not reliable?" she asked. "He's the sheriff, for heaven's sake."

"Precisely, Sally."

Although the conversation had only been going on for a short time, Sally's friends appeared curious as to what she was up to, and were trying to listen in. Pretending not to notice them, she turned her back to the pantry and spoke softly.

"Okay, Jack, good to talk to you, too. We'll see you soon." She hung up the phone and wiped the smile off her face before returning to her friends.

"Welcome back, Ms. Busybody. Who was that, Jimmy?" Colleen said as she took out a cigarette and struck a match on the table surface, which was incidentally made of polished granite.

"No, actually, it was Jack," Sally responded, like it was no big deal.

"Speak of the devil and he shall appear," Jenny said. "What was he calling for?"

"He's on his way and wanted to know if his house was ready," Sally replied. "Before you get that look in your eye, Jenny Cooper, you should know, he's bringing a friend. I mentioned it at the council meeting."

"Hey, I'm not the one schmoozing on the phone with him in the kitchen, Mrs. Reynolds."

Colleen's eyes widened and she said, "So, who is this chick?"

"I don't know much about her, except that she's a lawyer."

"Another lawyer on this island?" Jenny said. "Do we need more lawyers out here?"

Sally knew that Jenny only said that because her father happened to be a lawyer. The sad thing was, he hadn't had a client for as long as anyone could remember. Most disputes were brought to the council and then to the Society.

"She's not coming here to practice. Apparently she fancies herself a painter," Sally said. "She's also originally from Rockland."

Nancy laughed. "From Rockland? She must be a brazen hussy."

Nancy, not unlike Jenny or Colleen, was in what some may call an arranged marriage. Not in the tradition of 18th century English nobility, but in the Carroll Island tradition, which meant that families were friends with certain families, and when their daughters and sons were old enough, they got hitched. There were few options for one to choose if deciding to stay on the island. If you were a single woman, you were required to work. If you were married, most likely to a lobsterman those days, you could stay at home and live under the umbrella of your tax-paying husband.

Sally was an anomaly in her own right. She was both married and working. Her marriage wasn't unlike the other women's, but she was far less vocal about its ineptitudes. She claimed happiness where others might find blandness. She was a woman of simple needs. She loved Jimmy, but she also knew that she had little choice not to.

After being married two years, Sally and Jimmy decided they wanted children. It had been a few years and they hadn't been successful in their quest for offspring, but they maintained hope that it would happen for them. In a community the size of Carroll Island, there wasn't a soul who didn't know of their troubles, but it was nothing more than gossip.

* * *

As the time neared 10:00 a.m., Sally left the budding conversation with her friends and went about her daily cleaning routine. She had only made a couple of breakfasts that morning; it had been a slow but typical day. Once the lobstermen were gone for the day, the island was more or less a ghost town.

Outside on the dock she had three round tables with navy blue umbrellas covering them. Those who chose to come down to the docks for lunch could do so with a wonderful view of the harbor. The menu consisted only of simple items like grilled cheese sandwiches and a variety of burgers. If one truly wanted to have a dining experience, they would have to take the ferry to the mainland.

Each day, Sally left the store at 3:00 and took the rest of her day off. On the weekends, the store would close when she left, but during the week, eighteen-year-old Sandra Carter would take over till 7:00 p.m. Sandra, or Sandy as she was called, was much like Sally, a promising young woman who went to school with the other kids in Rockland and then returned afterward to work a few hours. She had played sports every season from grade six through last spring, but had decided to sit out her senior year and save up some money for college. Sally always smiled when she came into the store. She daydreamed of all that young Sandy could look forward to in her future: college, the chance to get away, to have a career, everything she herself had given up to stay on Carroll. Sandy's parents couldn't afford for her to go away to college, but her grades were good and she received a scholarship to attend McGill University as long as she kept an A average through her senior year. Sandy was fluent in French and hoped to major in foreign languages at the Canadian University before going on to live and work abroad.

Sally hadn't said anything to the others or Jack when he called, but after thinking for a while, she remembered a girl named Kendra who had gone to school with her in Rockland. "Kendra Davids," she said to herself as she dried off the stovetop with a red and white checkered cloth. "Guess it's not the same girl, but damn it sounds familiar. It isn't like there could have been many Kendras at our school. Maybe she moved from Rockland when she was younger and never went to school there."

Jenny cleared her throat and said, "Okay, honey, we're off. Gonna go down to the beach and see about getting a tan on my flabby backside." She wasn't flabby in the least, but had always said so, ever since she was a teen.

"Have fun for me, okay?" Sally replied in a tired voice. She wasn't jealous. She could go if she really wanted. It wasn't as if there would be any business, but if someone on the town council wanted anything and the store was closed, The Lighthouse Society would surely be told. The whole notion angered her, especially with her husband being the sheriff, but like most other residents who claimed to be unafraid of the Society, she was. "Hey, Jenny, watch out for the crabs. You wouldn't want to get those again," Sally said, laughing.

"Very funny, girl. I'll get you for that later, you little hussy." Jenny was good for a joke or two. "Heads up, Sally, here comes your boyfriend," she said as she pointed to the navy blue Jeep coming down Main Street.

"Jeez, I forgot to make him his sandwich," Sally said out loud, but not within earshot of the others, who were already up past the Town Hall. Perhaps the excitement of her conversation with Jack had made it slip her mind.

Jimmy Reynolds parked the Jeep across the street from the store. His Jeep was one of only a handful of cars on the island, and the only one the department owned. On both doors of the vehicle was the department insignia; not surprisingly, a lighthouse surrounded by the words Carroll Island Public Safety, in gold. He closed the door and reached for his baseball cap, which was the same color and had the same insignia on the front.

Jimmy was a tall and well-built man. His brown mustache mirrored his hair, which was cut short, almost military style. His baby-blue eyes stood out from his hair and sun-bronzed skin. He was an attractive man, and he knew it, but nonetheless, he was good people. He walked with a certain swagger that made it seem like he was the big man on campus, and indeed he was, short the members of the Society.

"Good morning, sunshine," Jimmy said as he crossed the street. Sally stood in the doorway using her hand as a visor from the sun, which was right behind him. When she left for work that morning, he was still fast asleep. Public safety wasn't usually a pressing issue on Carroll Island, and Jimmy didn't go into his office until he felt the need. Yet Kyle's phone call took him by surprise the night before, and he had had trouble falling back asleep afterward.

"Hey there!" Sally said. "Just coming in?" The two lived out toward the lighthouse and the point, which was one of the first places to lose power in a storm.

"Yeah, damned storm turned my alarm off again. I was supposed to meet Kyle right about now, but I figured I would stop in to say hi," he replied.

"Oh, I'm sorry, Jimmy. If I knew you had to be up, I would have reset it for you, but to be honest, I just kind of got up and got moving at my normal time." Sally didn't even use an alarm clock. Each and every day she woke up at around 5:00 to be at the store for opening. It was a good habit to have except in the fall and winter when it was still dark that early. "Everything okay with Kyle?"

"Oh, I think so," Jimmy replied. "He seemed a bit frazzled on the phone last night, but if he didn't need me then, I doubt it could be too important." He took his hat off as he crossed the threshold of the store. He was always a gentleman; the same could not be said of all the island's men. "Probably hit a raccoon with his truck and is afraid to pick it up off his driveway. You know him, always believing what everyone else tells him."

Kyle had seen a newscast a few years back about raccoons having rabies in southern Maine. Two days later he hit one driving down Cranberry Lane and insisted that his car was covered with rabies.

Sally said, "Well, paranoid or not, you put your rubber gloves on if that's the case. You hear?"

"Yes, ma'am. What's for lunch today?"

She had hoped he had forgotten about his sandwich and would just ask for it later on. It wasn't as though he would be upset, but Sally always tried to get everything right all the time. Jimmy, on the other hand, wasn't as uptight. "Well, that would depend on what you want. I thought maybe you'd be in the mood for something different." Sally twisted the truth a little, hoping he would bite.

"Sure, that's cool. What is it?" His mustache curled up with his smile.

"Well, Sheriff, I'll tell ya what, you come on back here when you're done with raccoon duty and we can eat together, or do you have more pressing business this afternoon?" It was a good save by Sally.

"Well, my lady, sounds good. You keep an eye out for me." He winked at her before turning around and leaving the store—same swagger in his step. "Tell the girls I said hi."

"Oh, they've all gone to the beach. They left right when you were coming down the street," she said.

"Lucky you," he replied. "Call me if you need anything." He jumped into the Jeep and sped off down the bumpy road before turning off the cobblestone street and on to a gravel road right past town hall.

Cranberry Lane went all the way out to Kyle's place on the northeastern end of the island—nearly two miles away. As the Jeep's wheels left the stone surface and made contact with the fine gravel, they spun, leaving a cloud of dust behind.

A drop of sweat fell from Sally's eyebrow. She had an extreme sense of guilt. She knew that she should have told Jimmy about the phone call, but just for once, she wanted something that was hers alone. She knew that she would have to tell him at lunch; she had told the girls, and they couldn't keep their mouths shut.

Sally sat on a stool on the customer side of the counter and stared into the kitchen aimlessly; there was surely nothing to see, but she was daydreaming. She couldn't help but think of how odd Jack acted on the phone. Maybe there was something bothering him that he needed to talk to her about. He wouldn't have mentioned the cell phone if that wasn't the case. But the risk... If someone were to walk in and find her on the phone that Jimmy gave her for emergencies, both of them would be punished.

"Stupid damned rule," Sally said out loud, wanting to yell it at the top of her lungs, but restraining herself. Maybe it would be good that she had to tell Jimmy. If there was something wrong with Jack, he would help. They had all grown up together, but then again, if Jack wanted Jimmy's help, he would have called Jimmy. It never occurred to her that Jack called her because he didn't know if he could trust her husband. For all Jack knew, Jimmy was a member of The Lighthouse Society and would be looking for his head upon arrival.

It was barely 11:30 and Sally didn't think she would see her husband again for another hour. With no one else around and the girls down at the beach, it would be the optimal time to get out the phone. She would have to stay in the kitchen, but that would be okay, she could mix dough for the next morning's bread. If someone happened to come in, she would have an excuse. Her arms tingled at the thought, and she felt a sense of adventure. Little did she know of the real adventures that were happening.

Sally took out her cell phone, which was buried in her leather handbag and inside a glasses case. The last time she had used it, she was in Rockland and had met up with some friends for the movies. She called Jimmy on the island to let him know she would get the late ferry. She hated to have him worry, especially if there was something she could do about it. She rummaged through her apron pockets, looking for the slip of paper that she had written Jack's cell phone number down on. "Where the hell is that thing?" she said as she pulled out several gum wrappers and old receipts. *I should be more organized.*

Sally finally found the number and took a deep breath. She dialed and waited for an answer. One ring, two rings; she wondered if his phone was playing a song to him or if it was just ringing normally. Hers played "Ode to Joy," but it was on silent, for good reason. After four rings, the voice mail came on, and she figured he was either busy or in a spot with bad reception. The Camden Hills were notorious for blocking cell phone signals. She put the phone back in her purse and decided that she would either try again after lunch or wait and see him when he got there. As she returned to the counter to take a seat, she had an anxious feeling in the pit of her stomach, with a little dizziness. After sipping some cold water, she realized that she had a case of the butterflies; she felt shame, but she couldn't help it. It was Jack Chandler she was thinking of.

Chapter Fourteen

J ack drew back the shade of the center bay window, and a sharp stream of sunlight illuminated the suite. He was up early in anticipation of another long and possibly frustrating day. His plan was to go look for the evidence and then get over to Carroll before sunset, but he knew that everything would be contingent on the search. When he woke the day before, he recalled mixed feelings of anxiety and joy, as he was to set out on his life-altering journey, but when he looked out over the willow trees and pointed firs, onto the dark, rippled waters of Penobscot Bay, he couldn't help but feel uneasy.

Kendra awoke with similar moans and groans as the day before. She had managed to get a hangover after attending a going-away party back in Portland, and after two drinks the night before, dehydration had again gotten the best of her.

"Honey?" Kendra spoke with a soft, angelic tone. "Come here, sweetheart."

Jack crawled over to her side of the bed like a spider nearing its prey.

Lifting the pillow that had been covering her face, she eyed Jack with a cunning, playful look. "For the love of all that is holy, would you close that damned shade?" Her yell wasn't loud, but the angelic tone was replaced with an annoying yelp like a wounded dog.

Jack laughed, jumped on the bed, and said, "Oh, is someone not feeling well, again?" He jumped out of the way before she could smack him. "Can I get you some water? Perhaps some Advil for the pain?"

"I wanna go back to sleep," she replied and rolled back over, wrapping herself in the sheets.

"No can do, sister. We have to be downstairs in twenty minutes. Don't worry. Nate went down to the Rockland Dunkin Donuts. We figured the only way to get you moving would be to bribe you with caffeine and sugar," Jack said, laughing. "And look what I've got." He pulled a large plastic bag from next to the bed.

"What's in the bag?"

"I was talking to the night auditor early this morning, and she had a huge box of clothes left by previous guests—let me take whatever I wanted."

"Early this morning?" she said. "Jack, it's six-friggin-forty-five right now. Exactly what do you consider early morning? Besides, you really think I'm going to wear someone else's dirty clothes?"

Jack rolled his eyes. "The clothes have been cleaned, and it's not like we have many options."

"I know and I'm sorry, it's just frustrating," she said, her facial expression softening as she pawed through the bag. She began to laugh as she pulled a large bra from within. "Are you kidding me? These cups are bigger than my whole torso. You thought this would fit me?"

"I guess I haven't had all that much bra experience. Anyway, we've got a big day ahead of us." Jack spoke with the enthusiasm of a kid who had just gotten a new bike and couldn't wait to pedal around the neighborhood. "So rise and shine."

"Oh my God," she muttered. "Could you please leave and bring back my boyfriend?" Kendra rolled over again and covered herself in the comforter. "Honestly, Jack, you do realize this isn't a game, right? People have died, someone tried to kill you, and more of the same might be in store for all of us today."

"Kendra, I know damned well this isn't a game," Jack replied. "I know more about this than anyone. I might not be able to prove what happened on that ferry, but I know that there are people who can—and with a little effort on our part—people who will. All of us are aware of the danger. If you're having second thoughts about this, let me know right now and I'll call someone to come get you. Hell, I'll even call your mother if you want."

"Leave my family out of this, Jack," she said, sounding like the girl in *The Exorcist.*

"Why? You weren't ashamed of your mom till, what, last year? Then all of a sudden you decide you won't talk to her because she argued with you in front of your friends? What is it you're afraid of?"

"You wouldn't understand, Jack. Can we just drop it, please?"

"Fine by me," he replied. "Seriously, though, we have to get going. I've had my shower, so it's all yours. I'll meet you downstairs." He was annoyed by Kendra's unwillingness to open up to him. They had been together for years, and her family was still a topic that was off limits to anyone. He knew crossing that boundary was unnecessary, but he at least knew her mother. She never talked about her father, except to say that he walked out on them.

A navy blue fleece flung over his shoulder, Jack grabbed his duffle bag and stormed out of the room.

* * *

"Aren't you forgetting something, Jack?" Nate said, leaning against the black Mercedes. His khaki shorts were lighter than the skin on his thin legs. He wore L.L. Bean boat shoes, just like Jack's. He, too, had a blue fleece, but no FBI logo today.

"What am I forgetting, my baggage?" Jack asked, walking down the hotel's steps toward Nate.

"Ah, no. It seems you have that," Nate said with an all-too-familiar smirk. "I was referring to Kendra."

"I know, my baggage!"

"Jack, none of us have time to deal with the two of you fighting. We have serious stuff going on."

"Yeah, thanks, bro. I'm well aware of our stuff. So is she. We'll be fine. I have no intentions on letting anything, or anyone, interfere with our plans. Besides, we're not fighting; she's just a little slow this morning."

"That's what I like to hear, my man." Nate smiled as he flipped down the black sunglasses that were resting on his forehead. "Oh, I almost forgot, Special Agent O'Neil called again—"

"Jesus, would you just call him Dick, please?" Jack interrupted. "It's not like we call you Special Agent."

"Anyway, as I was saying, Dick called and said that the lab reports had come back from the print dusting out on Seguin."

"And?"

"Five sets. The three of us, which were confirmed, Julie's, and another set that wasn't in any database from the Camden Police Department to Interpol," explained Nate, flipping through some notes on fax paper.

Jack rubbed his chin. "That's weird. Don't you need to give prints everywhere, even at the bank these days?"

"Sure do. But if he hadn't opened an account or cashed a check at a bank other than his own, he wouldn't have had to give one. Seems to me we're dealing with a local." Nate seemed pleased with his investigative work, which was apparent by his coy grin.

"The local part is obvious, Nate, but how do you know it's a guy?"

"We don't, but one would assume it's a man," Nate said.

"I would assume the same, but I would have also assumed that the person who had shot at us yesterday would be a guy as well. Obviously, it wasn't." Jack turned around as Kendra came out the front door decked out in long pants, a sweater, hat, and sunglasses. She looked more suited for fall than a seventy-five-degree day.

"Okay, point taken, Detective Chandler," Nate said, catching a glimpse of her coming toward them.

"Hey, Kendra, Christmas in July is supposed to be just a sale, isn't it?" Jack laughed and gave Nate a high-five.

"Guys, give me a break. I was going to wear shorts, but I look fat in them today. Besides, the selection wasn't too extensive," she said in a whiny voice as she got into the backseat of the car. Jack passed back a large coffee that Nate had gotten for her. "Oh, thanks."

Eyes forward, Nate grinned. "What do you say we head to the Children's Chapel?" He switched subjects to the one that was more important. "Where am I going?"

"Left, and straight until we get into town. Then turn left at the bank. That's Chestnut Street. It'll take us all the way to Rockport," Jack said, pointing as he sipped his coffee.

* * *

The sleek Mercedes turned south on Chestnut and followed the rolling hills through the outlying neighborhoods of Camden, where the houses were few and far between. Mansions and estates rose from the rocky landscape that turned from a suburban setting to countryside.

"I'm going to call Sally. I want to know if the news about Julie Billings has hit the island yet," Jack said as they got closer to the Children's Chapel.

"You are nuts, aren't you?" Nate said. "That's a bit risky, isn't it? She could tell someone we are on our way."

"First of all, I told you if there is one person I know I can trust, it's Sally. Second, did you honestly think we were going to sneak onto the island or something? People are expecting me. They just haven't been told when I'm arriving. And I don't know about you, but if word did happen to get back to the island about Julie, I'd like to know." Jack reached down between the front seats to find his cell phone.

"If that's the case, explain the anonymous phone call you got the day before yesterday," Nate said.

"Dude, these people are all about gossip. I'm sure that Sally told them I was coming this week. I think you're worried we're going to get sabotaged when we sail into the harbor. You have to understand that if there are people out there that want to get to me and shut me up, it's only a few people out of a few hundred. Hell, I wouldn't be surprised if half the island invited us to dinner."

"A little arrogant, aren't you?" Kendra said.

"Arrogant or not, my family founded that island. Good or bad, my name means a lot out there. Most of them have no idea what goes on politically—most couldn't care less. Guys, these are good people," Jack explained.

"Hey. I was just playing devil's advocate," Nate said. "Call your friend for all I care. You might want to leave out the part about the FBI though."

Jack laughed and said, "Gee, you think?"

* * *

"So, how's your girlfriend?" Kendra asked, her voice laced with jealousy.

"Give it a rest, Kendra. We've been over this a few too many times, or don't you remember?"

Nate slowed the car and made a left turn onto a heavily wooded driveway that opened to a circular parking area. The birch and pine trees seemed to bend over like a natural canopy.   "Wow, it's beautiful," Nate said as he climbed out of the car. "The flowers are absolutely amazing. Must cost a fortune to do the upkeep."

"I'm sure it does," Jack replied. "It looks like there are hundreds of different kinds of flowers here."

He sniffed as he walked by rows of purple and white lilacs surrounded large rosebushes unlike any he had ever seen. The petals were tiny in comparison to the roses he bought for Kendra in the store.

Kendra shed her sweater and said, "Hey, guys, go have fun on your treasure hunt while I take a stroll through the gardens."

"Sounds good to me," Jack said. He knew that the two of them would be able to cover the grounds faster that way. "We'll head to the chapel. Nate, we're looking for these coordinates." He handed him a piece of paper with the coordinates on it. "Latitude: west sixty-nine degrees, three minutes, two seconds. Longitude: north forty-four degrees, twelve minutes, fifty-two seconds."

Jack and Nate walked around the perimeter of the grounds with

Jack holding a handheld Global Positioning System about an arm's length from his chest. A navigational expert at sea, Jack had never tried to use the device on land.

"We're at the forty-four by sixty-nine degree mark, but we're off a few seconds," Nate said, peering over Jack's shoulder. "I didn't really think this would work."

"Well, I'm sure there are a couple people out there that were hoping for the same thing," Jack said. "I doubt most of them even know about this location, though."

"Come again? That doesn't make any sense, Jack. If they didn't know about it, we wouldn't be here."

"I have a theory that the Society doesn't know that whatever we're looking for had been moved here." Jack looked at every stone and every tree; he had no idea what he was looking for, but was sure he would know when he found it. When they got to the Children's Chapel, they walked up the stairs and into the open-air room.

As Jack stood in the center of the chapel, the GPS in his hand began a sequence of beeps, which startled him. He looked around for any closets or cabinets, but everything was open. Could the device be malfunctioning? He started to recalibrate it by resetting some of the dials next to the antenna.

"Are we there?" Nate asked.

Looking confused, Jack said, "Well, I don't know. According to the GPS we are. I guess it means anywhere in this general vicinity. Just look around. Maybe there's a hidden door or something around here."

"I see. So we're going to break and enter? Perfect."

"If need be. You have a problem with that? You sure didn't when we stole the Whaler yesterday."

"True, but the situation was a little more dire, wouldn't you say?" Nate pulled out a travel package of tissues. "Man, these flowers are killing me."

Jack paced back and forth, checking and re-checking places where he had already looked. Every once in a while, he would stare at one of the engraved initials as if it had some clue for him, but there was none. With an impatient stride, he stomped out of the chapel and said, "God, this is so infuriating." He looked back at Nate to see if he would follow suit, hoping he wouldn't. He needed to clear his head a bit. The constant trivial conversation from his friend was getting to him. He needed to think, but his confusion brought anger, anger brought fear, and fear brought outrage.

Jack followed the gray gravel and clay path that wound its way around the chapel, descending the hill and passing in front of the chapel about a story below. The path was lined with a rusted chain-link fence to keep visitors from going over the precipice, which hovered over a private road between the chapel and the ocean.

Jack stood directly in front of the chapel on the path below. He found a spot where the foliage was thin enough for him to see out onto the ocean. He rested—both physically and mentally—with his arms on the rusted fence. The fence was like a crutch, and as long as he held on, he needn't worry about searching. He was a tourist now, a sightseer. His eyes focused far away on the horizon. Over a dozen miles out he could see the tip of the opening to the harbor of Carroll Island. He would have been anxious, but he was too tired. His mind raced too much to worry about a place so far away, yet his very mission that day had everything to do with the island.

After a few minutes of standing there in silence—picking petals off a flower he couldn't name if he'd been told a hundred times—he shook his head and winced. "Of course. Goddamn. If anywhere, it would be…" He turned back toward the chapel, which, although built into the fall line of the sloping terrain, had a small wooden frame underneath it. Mostly pine beams strung together by frayed two-by-six planks. On the side of the building, which formed a sideways triangle fitting in with the slope, there was a small door. The door was no more than three-feet-by-four and he didn't think it could be anything other than a utility closet—perfect for hiding something. *Who would think to look in there?* The door itself had a padlock, much like the one on the door of the boathouse on Seguin, but no chain. With a flathead screwdriver he could just take off the hinges. He took out his trusty Leatherman tool and went to work. Focused, he did his best to get the screws to budge, but each screw was stripped as though his task had been tried before. He used all his strength and put added pressure to make up for the lack of rigid surface. Slowly, the first screw came out. He set it down next to the wooden door.

About five minutes had passed and he had managed to free only two screws when he heard Nate come from behind him. Jack said, "Look what I found." Squinting from the sun, he turned his neck, which had become red from constant contact with the hot sun.

"Hmmm. Sure looks like a possibility," Nate said, seemingly unimpressed with Jack's find. "Pretty cool view." He pointed to where Jack had been staring before. Jack turned, not realizing that his friend had fooled him into looking away.

Nate drew back his leg and kicked the middle of the door, breaking at least two panels. He said, "Oops. Guess we'll need a new one of those. Too bad actually, you'd think they would have built it with some more expensive wood. Broke pretty easily."

"Jesus, Nate. Why'd you do that?"

"We'd be in jail before you got those off," Nate exclaimed. "Besides, why do you care so much? It's just a cheap door. We'll send 'em a check. Okay, that would be dumb. How about a money order?" He pushed Jack out of the way and tore the rest of the door off.

Jack nudged him. "You made your point. Now get the hell out of the way, please?" He grabbed Nate by the collar and yanked him back.

Nate rolled over backwards and out of the way. Jack crawled into the confined space. The only light came from the cracks in the thin walls. The room had no obvious purpose, no gardening tools or equipment, just a floor made of earth and lots of cobwebs. The inside of the room was like a wedge of cheese as it sloped upward toward its ceiling, the floor of the chapel.

"Over here. I found something," Jack said, his eyes lighting up like a firefly in the dead of night. The ground was damp; the sunlight—although streaking through the cracks—couldn't impact the dense clay ground. On his hands and knees, he edged forward slowly as the space decreased. In the corner was a box about half the size of an army footlocker. Someone had wedged it into the ground to fit the dimensions of the room. Erosion had created a natural cradle for it. It was black and slightly darker than the clay surrounding its bottom. Jack took out his Zippo and gently ignited the wick.

Nate looked in and squinted. "Can you see anything?"

"Yeah, there's some sort of box in here. Pretty big one too. Looks like it's been in here an awfully long time."

"Like what, sixteen years perhaps?"

"No, wouldn't be that long, but it's been here for at least a few years, I can tell by the erosion around it." Jack blew out the flame. The lighter was getting too hot to hold. He rubbed it against his sweat-moistened shirt to cool it off and struck the flint again. "Ah huh, just as I thought. Can you see up here past me to the box?" He tried to twist on his side.

"Yeah, wait a second," Nate said. "That's the Mason symbol, right?"

"Yep. The square and compass. And we know The Lighthouse Society was a Masonic lodge for many years. I can feel a handle on the end here, but I don't know if I can get it out." Jack's pulse had quickened and adrenaline was rushing to his head. He hadn't felt this alive in a long time.

Directly overhead, Jack heard footsteps. *Was it Kendra or another tourist? Perhaps it was O'Neil?* They knew he had been following close behind them, but Jack knew that he would keep his distance. He was more worried about a local calling the police. He turned back to Nate and whispered for him to be quiet.

"Seriously. Shut up," Jack said softly.

"Sorry," Nate said, motioning as if to zipper his lips.

Jack rolled his eyes and the two lay there, still, but restless. Ants and other tiny insects were crawling close to Jack's face, only about an inch from the ground.

The echo of steps faded. It seemed that whoever was in the chapel had seen what they had wanted, or had they? Regardless, Jack began to tug feverishly at the end of the box, hoping to jar it loose.

"You think you could hurry it up a little?" Nate coughed as he spat out a black fly. "I'm eating insects back here."

"I never asked you to crawl in here with me. Why don't you get the hell out and let me do my work." He yanked the handle back and forth, unearthing chunks of clay that rolled down past his face and settled against Nate.

Nate began to slither backward, blowing cobwebs out of his face that had come loose from the ceiling amidst Jack's violent jarring. He said, "Fine, just move a little faster than you did with the door."

"Whatever," Jack said. "It's not like you can just kick it open."

"Sure about that?"

"I've almost got it," Jack said, "but there's another lock. Jesus, can't any of this be easy?"

"Just relax and get the box out here."

"Okay, I've got it loose, but now I'm stuck. Listen. Once you're out the door, you're going to have to pull me out by my feet. Damned thing's heavy." The light of the Zippo gleamed on Jack's dirt-covered face. He looked like a chimneysweep from *Mary Poppins*.

"You look kind of sexy in earth tones," Nate said, inching his way out of what was basically a hole. He hobbled to his feet. "Oh man, my leg's asleep." He stumbled to the ground again, laughing as he landed on the rocky turf. He rolled over and rubbed the muscles in his legs that had fallen asleep. "All right, tell me when you're ready and I'll start pulling." Nate seemed excited at the opportunity to share some of his pain with Jack.

"I don't know if I should trust you," Jack replied, one arm outstretched, grasping the black box. He knew Nate wouldn't take it easy, and he prepared for a heavy jolt. He covered his face with his hand, but the space was too confined to reach an arm down to protect his family inheritance.

"Oh, don't you worry, buddy." Nate had a sinister look on his face as he grabbed both of Jack's feet, raised them up, and literally let himself fall backward. The force of the gravity along with his pulling flung Jack out like a snake out of a burrow. A cloud of dust swirled in the light breeze.

"You prick!" Jack yelled, "For the love of Christ." He was out of the structure and rolling around in agony on the ground, one hand still firmly attached to the end of the box, which had withstood the harrowing ride. "Hey, anytime you want to grow up is fine with me."

Jack was still on the ground, covered in dirt and clay from head to foot, his eyes resembling a raccoon's as their blue hue stood out against his dark, soiled skin.

"That's a big box. Should have told me, I probably wouldn't have yanked so hard," Nate said.

"Oh sure, don't worry," Jack replied. "I'll remember this one." He wasn't one for vendettas, but some friendly banter or tomfoolery was all in a good day's work.

"Let's get that bad boy open," Nate said, nearly salivating.

"No. We'll get Kendra, get it into the car, and open it on our way back. We've made enough of a ruckus here already. Someone's sure to notice." They had only been there for about forty-five minutes, and several cars had arrived in the parking lot. Most of the visitors set about admiring the flowers in the adjacent and surrounding gardens, except for the one person they heard in the chapel as Jack tried to get the box loose.

Nate grabbed Jack by the arm to slow him and said, "What if this isn't it?"

"If this isn't it, I doubt it exists, and we'll go ahead with another plan, but I know in my gut that what we are looking for is in here."

Jack wandered through the plush, forested grounds looking for Kendra so they could get out of there, while Nate went back to the car to guard the box.

Kendra sat quietly beneath an apple tree that might have seemed out of place in any other season among the wild colors of the other flowers, but the tree was in full blossom, with thousands of white petals attached.

"Kendra, let's go. We got it," Jack said.

Kendra shrugged her shoulders. "Well, where is it?" she asked. "What is it, for that matter?" She hopped to her feet, giving Jack the once-over. "What'd you do, go swimming in the mud?"

"Very funny. Let's just say it was in a very dirty place," Jack replied, glancing over at Nate. "It's over by the car with Nate. We haven't gotten it open yet, but it's some sort of trunk."

"By the looks of you, that place must be pretty clean by now," Kendra joked.

The Mercedes was covered in white petals from an overhanging tree that had been swaying from the offshore breeze, reluctantly freeing its hold on the budding flowers.

"Kendra, you drive, okay?" Jack took command as if he had the whole thing planned out. "Quickest way back will probably be back down Beauchamp. Stay away from Route 1. We don't want to get held up in traffic."

Nate and Jack placed the black box in the middle of the backseat, each taking a place on either side. Nate pulled out his gun and hit the lock with the butt end, breaking it with little difficulty. It had obviously been there for a long time. The edges of the cover were coated in a rubber-tape-like band that extended all the way around and was altered to be airtight. The makeshift job had done the trick, as the inside was dry. It was stuffed with crumpled-up newspaper, like it had been a package waiting to be sent somewhere. Jack sifted through the paper, taking each ball out without risking the integrity of whatever it may be protecting.

Nate took one of the balls of newspaper and unwrapped it. It was a comic section of the *Bangor Republican* featuring Charlie Brown. "Wow. Check out the date on this page," he said, handing it to Jack. The top of the paper read *July 25, 1995.*

He continued to take out small balls of newspaper until he came to a much smaller box, a letterbox. It was inside of what looked like a Ziploc bag, minus the Ziploc. Jack took the box out of the bag and opened it. Inside was a stack of paper, pages, some stapled together, like newsletters, but handwritten. He looked at the date on the top of the first page. Below, perfectly centered on the page were a few lines. It looked like the cover page to a term paper or a resume.

The Lighthouse Society Meeting Minutes
Carroll Island, Maine
Sealed Documents 01/01/1994 – 07/21/1995

"So this is it, huh?" Nate said. "All that fuss over a bunch of notes someone took at some meetings?"

"Nate, look at the time period. This is a year and a half of meeting minutes from secret meetings. No one's ever seen these. Hell, no one's been able to prove that this organization has ever existed," Jack explained, smiling nervously. "Whatever happened must be in here.

Why else would someone go to all the trouble to hide these?" Jack knew he was onto something, but wondered why the notes hadn't been destroyed. "This stuff is amazing. I wish I had penmanship like this guy. Weird though, there are no names in here."

"No names, Jack?" Nate inquired. "That doesn't make sense."

"No, I mean there are, but they are all blacked out under the roll call section. Added security I guess." Jack was fascinated by his findings. He scrolled through, page by page. "So they met once a week and basically discussed island business. They make a decision, and then give it to the town secretary to deliver to the town. That's odd."

"Very odd, and not very democratic," Nate said. "It would go against any town charter in the United States." He suddenly appeared interested in Jack's reading. "Wait a minute. This means that the town thinks they are deciding something and effectively they have no vote or anything? They're like pawns."

"That's what it looks like," Jack said, flipping through the stack of pages. "Obviously not what we're looking for, though."

"Well, it's all evidence," Nate replied. "It would be nice to have a table to go through all this."

Jack had the last page of the whole stack out and squinted to make out the small print at the bottom. "It says here that these minutes are to be sealed until further notice by order of The Lighthouse Society Cleric, John Oxford. I guess they forgot to black out that name."

"What's a Cleric? Is this religious?" Nate asked. "And who the hell is John Oxford?"

"Religious? No, don't think so. It refers to the leader as the Cleric. John Oxford was a friend of my dad's. He's dead now, passed away a few years after my parents. Heart attack or something. Apparently he was the leader, or Cleric, whatever." Jack looked perplexed. "This is weird. There's so much here."

"Yes, there is, and it was all sealed for a reason," Nate replied, staring at Jack. "Seems you don't want to look in the part where that may be explained."

"I'm sorry. Are we in some kind of hurry? You don't have to be a dick about it," Jack said, trying to make eye contact with Kendra, who had her eyes focused on the road as if she hadn't heard a word they said.

Nate leaned over to him and said, "No, Jack, it's not that I'm trying to be a dick, but Jesus, you've been hiding from this in some way or another since your parents died. It's right in front of you now. I guess I'm just wondering what you are going to do when confronted with the truth." His honesty and sincerity even got Kendra's attention. Both had their eyes on Jack, who looked up from the pages.

"You're right. I have avoided a lot, but that doesn't mean I will anymore. I'm not, and I mean not, going to rush into anything. It's been too long and it hurts too much to take lightly. We need to be to be rational. Let's put this stuff back in the box till we get to the boat and get on our way to the island. We can take it all out on the chart table and go through everything." He was calm, perhaps a little nervous.

"Fine by me," Nate said. "Looks like we're almost there anyway." He pointed to the yacht club as they turned onto Bayview Street. "You want to bring the whole thing aboard?"

"No, just the letter box. We can stash the big box in the trunk of the car," Jack replied. "When your boss finds it, he'll think we've been on a treasure hunt or something."

"You mean, we haven't?" Kendra asked.

"Very funny. Listen, Kendra. Park under that oak tree over there. It's for long term and I don't know when Dick will be back to get his car."

"I do," Nate said.

Kendra pulled into the upper part of the lot and parked where Jack had suggested. The three all reached for the door handles at the same time, racing out of the car. Nate and Jack each grabbed the larger box while Kendra popped the trunk.

"What do you mean, you do?" Jack looked inquisitively at Nate.

"I meant that I knew when he would be back. You mean, you really haven't noticed?"

"Well, you see, Agent Richardson, young Mr. Chandler here—he isn't trained to be as insightful as you. Such talent takes time," O'Neil said, appearing from under the very tree where they had parked. "Did you kids have fun?" He looked down at the box that they had dropped on the ground when he startled them.

"Oh, great time, Dick. Too bad we didn't find anything except for this big old empty box, but fun nonetheless," Jack said. "Nate and I wrestled in the dirt. We each pretended the other was you. You should have been there." Jack enjoyed the antagonizing, but the others didn't appear to find it as funny.

Kendra ducked off behind Nate.

"The funny thing, Mr. Chandler, is that I was there. In fact, I was standing right above you two while you went looking for what I wanted." O'Neil's sinister voice matched his facial expression.

"Hey, Kendra, did you miss something?" Jack said. She was supposed to be their lookout.

"I was reading. I didn't even see him arrive. I mean I saw him there, but you know, it was late by that time and I figured you guys knew."

"Which is why you didn't mention it till now?" Jack asked. He knew she was lying.

"Jack, it doesn't really matter, does it? Why don't you just give me the box and you guys can go on your way," O'Neil said, looking down at his watch and tapping the face. "You're wasting time. Don't you want to go see all your good friends?"

"Sure, Dick. Here it is. Like we said; it's empty," Jack said as he kicked the black box, creating a small cloud of dirt. "I just wanted to keep the box 'cause it's old and Masonic."

"Sir, you said you were going to back off this one and let us move in without you," Nate said. "Why can't you just trust us?"

"Nathan, it isn't a matter of trust. What I worry about is the three of you getting out there and getting into a bind. Now, if Jack here was a better liar, I wouldn't be worried, but his story about the box was pretty awful," O'Neil said, turning his back to them. "Granted, I never actually saw you open the box. Maybe you're telling the truth and I'm wrong. It's happened before. I just don't think that's the case this time. I saw Ms. Davids run down to the boat with something. I suppose I could give you the benefit of the doubt for now. So listen carefully. I will give you gentlemen three days from right now."

Jack and Nate looked at each other in shock as O'Neil turned and faced them.

Nate said, "What do you mean, three days from now?"

O'Neil laughed. "Three days to find out for yourselves what is going on out there and report back to me. If you don't have anything concrete by then, I'll get some men together and we'll go out to the island, with a—"

"For Christ's sake," Jack exclaimed, sighing. "I told you, they wouldn't let you on the island. They'd make you stay in the harbor."

"Jesus, do you always have to interrupt, Mr. Chandler?" O'Neil asked. "As I was saying, I will go with a warrant from a judge. A judge who has heard a tape of the conversation the two of you just had in the car."

Jack was enraged, but not surprised. How could they have trusted him not to bug the car? "You know, Agent O'Neil, I'll admit, I was probably out of line last night, but it just seems that you came here to push our buttons. You've tricked us into doing your work. And why? Because you can't and you know it."

"Jack, settle down. His plan sounds fair to me," Nate said.

Jack truly hated this guy, but liked his craftiness. O'Neil was growing on him. "Tricky Dick. You're swift, my man. Yeah, we'll take the deal, but how do we know we can trust you? How do we know you won't fly a damned helicopter out there today and blow our cover?"

O'Neil said, "Your cover, Mr. Chandler? They all know you are coming. Young Mrs. Reynolds is probably trying on a new dress as we speak, while her husband is hard at work."

"Easy pal, those are my friends," Jack replied with a look of disgust.

"Prove it, Jack. You see, I don't have to give you a reason to trust me. I'm the one giving you the chance." O'Neil made a good point. "So all I ask is that you prove yourself. Don't worry about me."

"All right, I'm in. Let's get the hell out of here before he changes his mind, Nate." Jack grabbed his bag from the trunk and started to walk down toward the dock where the boat he had chartered was berthed. "You coming?"

Nate gave a long, grimacing stare at O'Neil and followed Jack.

"Three days, boys, three days or your little utopia is going to be one big-time nightmare," O'Neil said, laughing as the two walked away.

Jack knew they couldn't trust him, but for some reason that only God was privy to, he had let them try it their way.

Chapter Fifteen

Kyle Foster's house sits right off Cranberry Lane at the northeastern tip of the island. Passing Kyle's land, with its pastures and small pond, Cranberry Lane turns inland, where it curves and meets with Quarry Side Road, which loops past Arlington Cooper's house heading back toward the town on the southern, mainland side of the island.

Jimmy's route out of town took him back past his own home—and the road to the Carroll Island Light—right on the outskirts of town. Past that, there wasn't much in the way of civilization. A couple of large houses with neatly trimmed lawns and a few pastures were the only things between the edge of town and Foster's place. Besides a few small fields and the gravel road, the land between town and Kyle's was heavily wooded, which made it very dark at night. There were no streetlights off of Main Street. Some people thought that Cranberry Lane actually dipped below sea level as it made its way out to Foster's perch among the rocks and ledges.

Most people who lived on an island like Carroll liked to take things a little slower. The hustle and bustle of the city never translated to island people, and it was rare to find someone driving any faster than Adam Cyr could pedal his bike. Sheriff Reynolds didn't even have a radar gun, but the reality was that regardless of the speed limit, he could tell when someone was driving in a manner that he considered to be dangerous. He gave a ticket just a month before to Tommy Carter, who was going so fast he lost control and damned near spun into a tree. Tommy's father was outraged that the sheriff was "abusing his power" by making his own laws, and asked The Lighthouse Society to mediate. Mr. Carter actually did have a point; there wasn't any law against it, he even cited Montana's driving laws in his case, but there was no way that the Society would step on the sheriff's toes in such a manner. They thought about using the case as a precedent and actually setting island speed limits, but they figured that would make the Carter boy some sort of martyr, or worse, it could make the news on the mainland if he blabbed. They couldn't afford to have any lawmakers intervening, so they told the Carters that the arrest stood and ordered him to pay the fifty-five dollars. When Buford Carter threatened to call the State Office about what he considered an abomination, he got a letter in the mail saying that his mortgage was going to go up to about twice what it was. His mortgage was with the Island Agency and he knew right away that if he backed off, he wouldn't be charged. He was furious, but the Society had him by the balls—the Society had everyone by the balls.

That was the first time anyone on the island thought Jimmy might be a member of the Society. At first, Jimmy was indifferent about the rumor, but as he thought more and more about it, it left a sour taste in his mouth. People looked at him differently, and some didn't even look at him at all. It was the first time he truly knew how the residents of Carroll felt about their leaders.

Jimmy passed the century-old willow tree that almost felt the impact of Tommy's car. There was a bend in the road and then it was pretty much straight the rest of the way to Foster's. Jimmy always took time to enjoy the scenery, the serene land he loved to call home. It didn't matter if he'd seen the same sights a thousand times; they never grew old on him.

In the distance, he could see another vehicle coming his way. Such an occasion was rare for that time of the day, or any time of the day for that matter. His attention was again caught by the static from the VHF radio mounted underneath the center console of the Jeep.

"Jimmy, Jimmy, come in, over," the static-laced voice cried from the receiver.

"Yeah, John, I'm here," Jimmy said. John Thorton was Jimmy's longtime running buddy, and his only deputy.

"You on your way to Foster's?" The deputy sounded like a far-off trucker asking for a travel advisory.

The truck approached much quicker than Jimmy had expected and showed no sign of slowing down.

"I am, but it looks like Captain Davidson's about to pass me going about sixty. I'll have to get back to you," Jimmy replied as he put the hand receiver down and flicked on the flashing blue lights, but not the siren.

"Yeah, that's why I'm…" The deputy continued his plea, but Jimmy's concentration was elsewhere. "I was calling to tell you about him… Oh, never mind." There was another click and a loud, screeching static sound, no doubt from Deputy Thorton ending his radio transmission.

As the truck neared, it slowed a little in view of the lights, and Jimmy switched the radio receiver from VHF to loudspeaker, again picking up the receiver. The truck hadn't come to a stop, but the driver swerved a couple of times as if to shake Jimmy from the road.

Jimmy picked up the radio receiver and said, "Captain Davidson, pull the truck over, sir." Despite his command, the truck continued toward him at a high rate of speed, its driver either not hearing or not paying attention. Jimmy was about to pick up the receiver again, but realized that it was an ill-fated measure. He spun the steering wheel of the Jeep ninety degrees, sending the vehicle into a sideways skid and effectively blocking the gravel road. When the Jeep came to a stop, he slid out of the door and unlatched his sidearm. The dust from the skid was so thick that he couldn't see if Davidson's truck had stopped, but realized there would have been an impact if it hadn't. Using the Jeep as cover, he again reached for the receiver, his gun in the other hand. His hat had fallen to the ground.

When the dust had cleared enough for him to see through, he could tell that the truck was stopped at a 180-degree position from its original course. He hoped that Davidson was okay, but also that he wouldn't try to drive off in the opposite direction. He had never been in a high-speed chase and was in no hurry to get into his first.

"Captain Davidson, if you can hear me, please step out of the truck with your hands in the air," Jimmy practically yelled, not realizing how loud his voice was already amplified. "Do not attempt to restart your engine." He coughed a little from the dust and held his gun out in front of him. He didn't think that Davidson was a threat, but didn't want to take any chances. Despite being a little nervous, he stood his ground behind the hood of the Jeep.

The driver's side door of the rusted pale blue Ford F-150 flung open, but Jimmy couldn't see anyone get out.

A raspy, smoke-choked voice rang out in the distance. "Sheriff, Sheriff, Jesus, don't shoot! I was looking to come find you as it is."

Oh sure you were, and you needed to go faster than hell to find someone that is about two miles away? Jimmy figured that Davidson must be drunk. He knew that people could act irrationally when drunk. Fact of the matter was that Captain Davidson was drunk most of the time.

"Listen, Sheriff, sir, Jimmy, we got to talk. You know?" The voice was still hidden, but closer now. Jimmy held his ground, partly because of his training, but mostly because of fear. Something wasn't right with this man. He wished he would just come out into the open, just so he could see him. It would relieve some of the tension.

"Listen, Brian. Until you come out into the open with your hands where I can see them, I'm not going to lower my gun." Jimmy stood firm. He wanted to call for backup, but other than John, there was none.

"I ain't hiding. I ain't got a gun either."

"Well, sir, I can't very well ascertain that," Jimmy said. "I can't see you. Now get out from behind the damned car!"

"Sure. So you can shoot me, huh?"

"Why would I shoot you, Brian? Hell, I just want to know why you came down the road at sixty plus and out of control?"

"Someone wants to kill me and the damned Society won't help," Davidson answered.

"Damn it, Brian, can we stop this crap, please? I don't know anything about the Society or what is wrong with you, but I know you're drunk. I'm not going to arrest you for a DUI, I just want you to come out so we can talk."

Captain Davidson stood up from the ground. The bulk of Jimmy's

Jeep had shielded him from any danger, but also kept him from seeing Davidson.

"Jimmy, that you?" Davidson asked, as if the conversation had just begun again.

Who else would it be? Jimmy couldn't believe what he was hearing. Only the sheriff was allowed to drive the Jeep. Davidson knew that, but this was certainly the liquor talking.

"I gotta talk to you, Jimmy." Davidson's hands were in the air, in plain sight.

Jimmy couldn't help but feel bad for the man; he was a man with a disease, a common one on the island. Maybe he had been drunk on that ferry, but drunk or not, the incident effectively ended his career. The only time he could pilot a ferry now was if another captain was on the bridge. It took all the pride away from being a captain.

Jimmy lowered his gun, switched the safety back on, and put it back in his holster. "Jesus, Brian. You scared the hell out of me," Jimmy said, relaxed and relieved. "You want to tell me what the hell is going on here, please?"

"I got this letter in the mail today." He held up a piece of white paper with something typed on it. "It says I'm going to be dead if I don't leave the island."

"Who sent you that?" Jimmy asked, sighing. "May I see it please?"

Davidson handed the letter to Jimmy. "There ain't no return address and it ain't signed, but I got a pretty good idea who sent it. I hear Jack Chandler's coming back to the island. Probably thinks I killed his parents."

Jimmy himself believed that it was Davidson who was behind the helm of the ferry, but the Society had put out a statement by Adam

Cyr claiming responsibility. Despite his intuition telling him it was a setup, Jimmy figured that it wasn't a good time to argue about it with the incoherent captain. "Yeah, Jack's coming back, but I see no cause to worry about him," he said. He wasn't so sure that was really the case, but he didn't think Jack would come all the way out here just to shoot a drunk.

"Who the hell else would it be?" Davidson mumbled. "I hear he's coming back soon, like in the next couple of days. Bit of an odd coincidence don't ya think?"

"It isn't that you don't have a good point, Brian, but I doubt Jack would send something so obvious." Jimmy thought he had made a good point, but he couldn't help but remember what they had said at the academy about reverse psychology to create a false alibi. "What were you doing out by the point anyway?"

"I went to see Foster. Figured that he was on the Society and that they would help," Davidson replied.

"What did he say?"

"Told me to take a flying leap. Said it'd suit me right to get shot."

"Sounds like Kyle Foster to me." Jimmy tried not to laugh. It was, after all, a serious situation.

"Hell, maybe he sent it to me. Maybe everyone's after me." Davidson's speech began to slur more and it was hard to understand him. "You know what he said then?"

"Nope."

"He said it wasn't his problem and he didn't know anything about The Lighthouse Society," Davidson replied. "Then he told me to get off his land and go to hell."

"That is a bit much, I suppose, but you know old Kyle; he likes his privacy. Regardless, Brian, I can't have you driving around here anymore so I'm going to take you home, okay?" Jimmy snatched the keys from Davidson's trembling left hand. "You get into the Jeep."

"You ain't gonna do nothing about this?"

"Listen, Brian. There's nothing I can do about this other than type up a report and ask Jack about it when he gets here."

"What if he denies it?"

"Well, there isn't any evidence that he sent the damned thing." Jimmy was losing patience. "So all we can do is watch out for you." He helped Captain Davidson into the Jeep, closed the door carefully, and went over to move the F-150.

Jimmy agreed it was odd for Davidson to get a letter like that, but he really couldn't believe Jack had any ill intentions. He knew Sally had spoken to Jack several times about the house being ready and all. If Jack wanted to pull off something stupid like this, he wouldn't be so vocal about coming back.

Jimmy got into the rusted-out truck and moved it off onto the soft shoulder of the road so it would be out of the way of any other traffic. He tried to lock it, but the door handle was broken. He laughed as he looked at the inspection sticker. It said 1977 on it; probably the year he bought it. It was little things like that that didn't really matter out on an island. He was surprised the truck still ran.

Who the hell would send a letter like that? he wondered. *If it wasn't Jack, who would it be?* He had to ask himself some tough questions. The letter had been postmarked in Portland a couple of days beforehand, and he didn't even know of any folks who'd gone down that way.

When Jimmy got back into the Jeep, Davidson was passed out. "Jesus, you could've killed someone," he said to the snoring captain, who smelled like a vat of whiskey. He knew Davidson wouldn't even remember the conversation, but decided that he would still go out to see Foster after driving Davidson home. Maybe he could be of some help. He folded the letter into quarters and tucked in into his pants pocket.

Chapter Sixteen

The afternoon sun was at its peak as it beat down on the cold Penobscot Bay water outside Camden Harbor. The mast of the boat was like a sundial, changing the time as the boat cut through the water under the wind's power. The gusts, which swooped down from the nearby Camden Hills, were notorious for being strong and unpredictable, yet they would assure fast passage for Jack and his friends aboard the *Island Prayer*, a thirty-five-foot sloop Jack had chartered from a local marina in Camden.

Jack scattered the pages of the minutes on the galley table, and Nate kept pace by putting them in order by date. He turned to his FBI friend, who had just donned a pair of reading glasses. "I'll be right back," Jack said.

Nate looked up curiously. "What are you doing? This is your stuff."

"Easy, killer. I know. I'm just going to give Kendra a few directions so she doesn't run us aground," Jack replied.

"All right, but hurry up," Nate said. "I don't really know what I'm looking for." He turned his attention back to the paper-covered table as Jack turned and made his way toward the steps.

Jack shielded his eyes as he climbed up out of the cabin and into the cockpit, where Kendra was standing at the helm. "Damn, it's bright," he said. "How's it going out here?"

"Good," she replied.

Jack looked down at the compass, then up toward the bow. "You know where you're going?"

"Hmm. Ah, kind of," she said. "I mean, I know where the island is." She pointed down to the chart. "We're here, right?"

"Yes, we are. Nice job," Jack said, smiling. "Thought I was going to have to come out and give you directions, but apparently I assumed too much." He climbed up out of the cockpit and around the dodger and leaned against the boom.

Kendra leaned back against the lifeline, putting her right in the path of the sun. She said, "Well, I think I got it. I'm just going to stay on this course for as long as I can. It looks like a straight shot. My dad used to take my mother and me sailing out here when I was a little girl. That's all I really remember of him, aside from him taking off."

"You never mentioned that before," Jack said. "Did your family own a boat?" He left his position at the boom and walked back toward the cockpit. He wanted to know more about her childhood, but had learned that asking such questions had always angered her. *Why would she be so inclined to open up now?*

"My dad owned a small day-sailor, nothing like this. Quite frankly, I hadn't given it any thought until I remembered how beautiful it is out here," she said as she sat down on a cushion back in the cockpit, keeping one hand on the wheel. "It's funny. There are little bits and pieces of good times we had, but whenever I think of them, they just get overshadowed by the fact he left us, alone, with nothing."

Jack sat on a cushion next to her and took her right hand, holding it in his own. He rubbed her fingers softly. "I can relate, I guess." He searched for the right things to say. Kendra had never opened up so much, even if it was just one little thing like sailing.

"Well, at least you know what happened to your parents," Kendra said. "I swear, the hardest thing is just wondering why he left. Was it something I did? Something my mother did? She never talked about it afterwards. It was almost like she was trying to protect me from something." She took the sleeve of her light blue sweater and wiped her face as a tear trickled down. "Anyway, enough of that. I wouldn't want you to think I really cared either way." She produced a seemingly fake smile, her eyes locking briefly with his.

Jack rested his chin on the palm of his hand, looked up into the dark oval lenses covering her eyes, and said, "Maybe I don't know exactly how you feel, but I do know about not having closure. Sure, I know my parents died, but given the circumstances, their bodies never being found, it never seemed to be enough to know they were dead. I've always felt like it was partly my fault, even when I wanted to blame someone else."

"Maybe you'll get your closure from this trip."

"Maybe I will," he replied, tapping his fingers on the naked fiberglass of the cockpit as he looked down at his watch. He cringed, feeling uneasy. Being so candid was foreign to him. Deep inside, he knew there was a tenderness the two once shared that he hoped moving to Carroll would rekindle.

"So anyway," she said, inhaling deeply as though some deep burden had been lifted. "Any more advice, skipper?"

"The most important thing is that the course is clear of any ledges you'd have to worry about navigating around. Once we get out past North Haven, I'll take the wheel from you."

Jack turned and smiled at her as he made his way back to the cabin door.

"Jack," she said softly, almost under her breath.

He turned. He had a foot already down one step into the cabin and his hands propped on the sides of the door. "Yes, Kendra?"

"You wear it well, you know."

Jack looked confused. "I wear what well?"

"Your fear," she replied. "You pretend to be tough, but you're as vulnerable as any of us. You may not be afraid of guns or stalking FBI agents, but you're scared. You're scared that nothing will happen and that you'll never know about your parents. You're scared you'll have to go on with a life full of unanswered questions."

"You're right, I am scared. The fact of the matter is that I'm facing my fears for the first time in my life. I may never find the answers I want, or even the ones that I don't want, but a life of regret based on doing nothing would be worse," Jack said with a determined look. He turned away from her once more. She was right, and it pained him, but he knew that his pain might have a solution. He wasn't hiding anymore. He wished she wouldn't either, but he had never felt like he could help her. Anytime he brought up her father, he got rebuffed. They were her demons. No one could slay them but her.

"How's she doing?" Nate asked as Jack rejoined him in the galley.

"A hell of a lot better than I would have thought," Jack replied. "She's got us on a course that should give us a good half hour to get through this stuff." He neglected to mention his revealing conversation with Kendra. "You found anything yet?"

"Yeah, I think so," Nate replied, scratching the side of his head. "It appears that the names are only blacked out on the cover pages of each set of minutes. Seems kind of pointless." He sighed. "You have any idea who Adam Cyr is?"

"Adam Cyr was Davidson's first mate," he said, looking puzzled. "He would have been far too young to be in the Society."

"Oh, you're right, my friend. Take a look at this." Nate's eyes widened. "It says here that they brought him in for questioning."

"The police?"

"No, The Lighthouse Society did."

Jack edged closer to him. "Well, what did they ask him?"

Nate sifted through the loose pages. "Hold on. This was just where they had written the attendance, 'Island resident Adam Cyr, blindfolded.'"

"I don't get it," Jack said with a confused, yet interested look on his face.

"Well, it would make perfect sense," Nate explained, his tone reflecting his excitement. "If these people were supposed to be anonymous, they couldn't have him see them, right?"

"Yeah, but it's a small island, man. He'd know them by their voices."

"Probably, but first of all, he would've been pretty scared, having been blindfolded," Nate said. "Second, it's doubtful he would have said anything to anyone unless he could ID them."

"Maybe Adam would talk to us?" Jack was totally unaware of how willing Adam truly was.

"You have any idea if he still lives there? This was quite a while ago."

"True. I guess we'll find out. Does it say what he was asked or what information he gave them?" Jack stretched out, making himself more comfortable.

"Hold your horses, I'm getting there." Nate flipped through the pages, skimming them briskly. "Ah ha, right here: 'Brother McKay questioned the guest.'"

"Let me have it." Jack was getting anxious.

"Fine, man. Chill." Nate handed him the small stack of pages.

Jack started sifting through the pages. "Skip that, that, nope, okay, here we go: 'Mr. Cyr, you know that we will be having some guests from law enforcement visit the island, do you not?' Brother McKay asked. 'Yes sir,' Cyr answered.'"

"Whoa, hold up. Can you skip the entire, Brother this, Cyr that? I don't need you to read it verbatim. I think we know who the people are that are talking." Nate fidgeted.

"Okay, sorry," Jack replied, shooting him a glare. He knew that Nate meant well and that he was just trying to be efficient, yet the reality of the information they uncovered was a lot for Jack to take in. He had never worked on a case before. His approach was much different. His stakes were higher. "Anyway, here's the deal, I'll just read the conversation that McKay and Cyr had."

"These guests, agents if you will, are going to ask you questions about the accident, and we just want to make sure that you have your facts straight. Do you mind if the two of us go over them?"

"Not at all, sir."

"Good. Now, Mr. Cyr, let me get this straight, you were the First Mate at the time of the accident."

"Yes sir, I was."

"However, you do have a pilot's license?"

"Yes sir, I do."

"Oh, so you must have been at the helm quite a bit?"

"Whenever Captain Davidson needed me to be, I got my own route as captain last summer. Only three days a week though."

"Well, good for you. Now tell me, who was at the helm when the ferry hit the ledge?"

"Captain Davidson was, sir."

"But you were in the cockpit with him?"

"Yes sir. I tried to relieve him of duty, but he wouldn't listen."

"Why would you relieve your superior officer of duty?"

"He was drinking, sir, heavily. I was at the top of the pilothouse stairs when Mr. Chandler came in wanting to talk to Captain Davidson. He said that he had seen the captain drinking. Captain Davidson then went down to talk to him and they got into an argument."

"Did you see this argument?"

"No I didn't, sir, but I heard a sort of scream, then Captain Davidson came back upstairs and took the helm back from me. A couple minutes later we were on the ledge."

"Have you told anyone this?"

"Not yet, sir. Listen, I tried to do the right thing, but he had the damned knife, and was drunk. Then all of a sudden we hit ground."

"Had you been drinking, Mr. Cyr?"

"No sir."

"Okay, so let me ask you again. Who was at the helm when the ferry struck the ledge?"

"Like I said, sir, Captain Davidson was at the helm."

"You don't seem to understand the importance this question

has regarding the future of our island. The authorities already know Captain Davidson was drinking."

"As I said before, sir, I have not talked to anyone about this."

"Oh, I know, Mr. Cyr, but chances are, you will, so let me ask you again, and think very hard before answering. Who was at the helm of the ferry when it struck the ledge in February of last year?"

"I was, sir…"

"Did you see or hear any argument between the captain and Mr. Chandler?"

"I heard them, sir."

"Why don't you think about that answer again, Mr. Cyr?"

"I didn't hear or see any argument, sir…"

After he finished reading from the text, Jack looked up with a blank stare.

"Jack. It's all there. All the proof we need to nail The Lighthouse Society," Nate said, jumping up from his bunk and snatching the document from Jack's hand. His laugh was sinister.

Jack sat motionless, staring down at the table. What he had suspected for so long was true. He had thought he would be thrilled to know the truth, but his reality was void of any such feeling. "Nate, this sounds like there was more to it. Something happened between my father and Davidson, a fight or something."

"Jack, this proves negligence and maybe an argument, but don't jump to any conclusions before we talk to Adam or Kyle."

"Is this enough to get us a warrant from a judge?"

"Should be more than enough, but it's your call, my friend. If you want, I can get on the horn and give O'Neil and his boys the word, but I have a feeling—"

"Not a chance in hell," Jack interrupted. "I say we finish what we started and nail these guys ourselves. Damn it, I know we can get people to help us find them, and we'll bring 'em in. We don't need that nut case on our backs."

"Well, like O'Neil said, we've got three days. After that, there won't be anything we can do. I'll have to turn this information over to him."

"Fine with me," Jack replied. "What do you say we enjoy the rest of this little cruise? When we get to the island, we'll play dumb, like we don't know anything about The Lighthouse Society. I'd be willing to bet someone will come to us in no time." Jack wasn't as excited as he acted toward Nate, but he knew full well that moping around feeling sorry for himself wouldn't do anyone any good.

"Sounds good to me." Nate peered back at Jack. "I just hope your friend Sally wasn't hiding anything and Julie Billings didn't get word back to her buddies on Carroll before she was killed." He pulled his gun from his duffle bag and popped off the clip.

"What are you doing with that?" Jack asked.

"Just cleaning it, Jack. Don't worry. In case we need it again."

"Where's mine?" Jack smiled.

"All things in due time, my friend."

Jack left his friend to his gun cleaning and went topside to see the progress Kendra had made. More time had passed than he had thought, but she hadn't requested any help. When he got to the cockpit, he found Kendra relaxed on a boat cushion. The afternoon sun gleamed down on her olive-colored legs, one of which was used— instead of a hand—to steady the helm. Her hair was pulled back and she was wearing a white baseball cap.

"I see you didn't need any help getting around North Haven." Jack was impressed.

"Yeah, well, the wind died down and I was all set," Kendra replied. "I just let out the main a little when I came around the point. I followed this old loran course set on here. Looks pretty old."

Jack was still thinking about their last conversation. He felt like he was talking to a stranger. "It's all pretty simple when you get the grasp of it. These are all his courses, though. I've never set a course down here. Any course I've needed has already been plotted."

"Not even with your father, when you were little?" Kendra asked.

"Oh no, he didn't let me or my mother touch anything. It was like a private science to him. Truthfully, it made me want to learn it more because of that. So a few years after they passed away, my grandfather took me out into Casco Bay and taught me everything I needed to know."

"Well, he must have taught you well, because I learned everything I know from watching you." She winked at him, pointed up toward the bow, and said, "Looks like we're almost there."

"You bet. Probably only about fifteen minutes till we enter the harbor." Jack spun toward the cabin. "Hey Nate, you want to come up here, please? We're almost there."

Nate's head appeared from the cabin door. He looked rather boyish with his hat on backwards and his sunglasses resting on the bridge of his nose. "That was quick," he said.

"Not really," Jack answered, shrugging his shoulders. "About two and a half hours from the yacht club to here, another ten to fifteen minutes to go." He reached his hand through the cabin door and pulled out a radio receiver from within. He squinted as he looked past the cockpit and into the small harbor. He depressed a small button on the side of the receiver and said, "Carroll Island harbormaster, this is Jack Chandler aboard the vessel *Island Prayer*, over."

"Vessel approaching Carroll Island Harbor, this is the harbormaster. Please stand by on six-eight, over," a man with a raspy voice answered.

"*Island Prayer* switching to six-eight, clear on nine, out," Jack said, turning the dial till it read sixty-eight.

"*Island Prayer*, this is the Carroll Island harbormaster. Jack, this is Carl Swanson."

"Hey, Carl, you sound very official." Jack spoke into the radio while still looking ahead into the harbor. "Hey, Carl, looks like blue lights at the dock, please advise, over." He tensed up all of a sudden, pointing the lights out to Nate and Kendra.

"Roger that, Jack. We have a bit of a situation here. I need you to pick up a mooring in the outer harbor until I can get the word from the sheriff, over."

"Will do, *Island Prayer* standing by on six-eight, over." Jack placed the receiver back on the latch and stood up. The late morning sun was right behind the island, blocking the sight of everything except for the flashing blue lights in the distance.

"Any idea what's going on, Jack?" Nate asked, hanging from the boom.

"Beats me. I'm not too sure I really want to know either. He sounded pretty shook up and said we had to wait out here."

"Want me to make the call to O'Neil?"

"No, not yet, Nate. This may just be a coincidence," Jack replied, almost stuttering. His body was trembling. He knew full well this was no coincidence.

Chapter Seventeen

Kyle Foster sat on an old wood crate in the garden next to his house. He wore a faded blue t-shirt and an old pair of cut-off jeans. Crouched over, there was a v-shaped patch of perspiration on his back.

Looking up from his small strawberry patch, which was self-contained in his garden, he could see the cloud of dust on the horizon and figured Jimmy was finally coming to see him. "Damned kids," Kyle said out loud as if there was an audience other than his dog around. He had told Jimmy to be out at his house around 10:00 a.m. and it was approaching 11:30.

The Jeep veered off Cranberry Lane, up Kyle's gravel driveway, and came to a stop a few yards from the garden. Out came Jimmy, baseball cap and sunglasses on.

Kyle liked Jimmy. Whenever he saw him, he recalled the fond memories of when Jack, Jimmy, and all the other kids came out to play in one of his fields or search for pollywogs in his pond. He couldn't relate to the generations that came after him, and rightly so; it wasn't as if he had met all that many new people while living on the island. After what he considered "the bad years" back in the 1990s,

Kyle didn't get out of the house as much. He didn't have much reason to. He continued to pick the ripest strawberries as Jimmy drew closer.

"Morning, Kyle," Jimmy said, crouching down to a squatting position.

"Thought maybe you'd forgotten." Kyle added two more berries to his half-full wicker basket.

"Well, Kyle. I kind of got caught up in some business down the road and I had to make a little detour," Jimmy said.

"Ya don't say." Kyle picked another berry, big one this time, dropped it in with the rest.

"Yeah, I ran into someone who claimed he had just been out to see you. Actually, he almost ran into me coming down the road into town."

"You'd think that out on an island like this, you'd be immune to the danger of such things as drunks getting behind the wheel." Kyle snickered. "Ah, we should have let the state troopers lock that fool up when we had the chance. It'd be a lot easier than what's coming our way." He finally turned and faced his young friend.

"I don't follow you," Jimmy said.

"Well, Jesus, if we're talking about the same person, I don't have to tell you the crap he's blathering about these days." Kyle took one of the berries out of the basket, picked off the stem, and put it in his mouth. "Damned fool thinks Jack Chandler's on his way to come kill him. So I told him he was nuts. What does he do? Says that it was probably me. Can you believe that? Me, sending him some sort of threatening letter? Bastard had Jack Daniels coming out his pores."

"If it makes you feel any better, I know it wasn't you that sent him the letter, but the fact remains, he did have a letter from someone."

Jimmy took off his hat and scratched the top of his head.

"You really think it was Jack?"

"Hell, I don't know. He was ranting and raving about Jack coming back out here to take revenge on him. Doesn't make much sense. You know?"

"Funny thing, that booze is," Kyle said. "It can make a hardened liar tell the truth." He looked up at Jimmy like he was trying to tell him something, but couldn't quite think of the words. "All these years, people have been blaming the Cyr boy for hitting that ledge. Damn shame, ya know? I could've stopped it, but we had a good thing going out here back then. I didn't like the idea of letting someone else take the blame, and I told the others, but they were set in their ways. I'll admit it seemed like an easy out at the time, but jeez, what if Jack is coming back out here to get him?" Kyle's posture straightened and it looked as though he had just taken off a heavy backpack.

Jimmy sat down on the grass next to the dark brown soil of the garden and said, "What the hell are you taking about? You been drinking too? Didn't the doctor tell you to stay away from the hooch?"

"For cryin' out loud, Jimmy. I ain't been drinking," Kyle replied with a frown. "The doctor suggested I don't drink, so I don't." He got up from the crate and started toward the house. "You coming?"

"I'm coming." Jimmy got up from the ground. "I'd kind of like it if you'd fill me in on all the crap you were just spewing."

"And I will," Kyle confirmed. "That's why I asked you to come out here. I've decided I've had it up to here with the bull crap that's been going on out here for the past sixteen years. I figured I'd fill you in on some stuff—kind of get your opinion." He moved quickly for an elderly man.

"Does this have something to do with the Society?"

Kyle turned and gave a deadly stare at Jimmy. "This has everything to do with the Society."

The two went under the covered porch of the house and out of the sun. Jimmy took a seat on the porch swing while Kyle went into the house to get some lemonade. When he returned a few minutes later, Jimmy looked half asleep on the swing.

"What do you know about The Lighthouse Society, Jimmy?" Kyle asked.

"Not much, really. Just rumors, I guess," Jimmy said, shrugging his shoulders. "I've heard that you're a member. Is that true?" He dragged his feet on the wooden floor to slow the swing.

"Oh, that's true, but don't you go telling anyone I said that. Liable to get me killed," Kyle replied with a disparaging look on his face.

"Is it true that since this town's been here, you guys have run it?" Jimmy asked, looking into Kyle's eyes. "Illegally?"

"Let's just say that what was legal back a hundred and fifty years ago might not be so today. Regardless, we tried to uphold tradition. Up until about twenty years ago or so."

"How is telling people how to live their lives considered tradition?"

"Haven't heard you complain," Kyle replied. "Hell, you probably get paid twice what a city cop gets paid."

"That's not the point, Kyle."

"You're right, it isn't, but it isn't that easy to just change things. Some people get set in their ways, won't budge if you tell 'em a bomb's falling. That's the way most of these guys have been all along. It wasn't always that bad. People like Jack's ancestors founded this place with the Society as a basis. They kept true to things for a long, long time. It just seems that people started to get the wrong sorts of motivations, like me, I guess."

"How so?"

"Honestly, I figured that if we'd let the Feds out here back in '95—like they wanted—we'd have television crews and news people out here. Not the kind of folks you want poking around and knowing our business."

"What exactly are you trying to tell me?" Jimmy took a long sip from his lemonade.

"Just telling you what you probably already know, Jimmy." Kyle drew a deep breath. "We covered the whole thing up. Hell, we ruined a young kid's life to save an island's reputation, and to save a drunk's reputation. I told them, though—I told them that Jack and his grandparents ought to know the truth. His grandparents had moved away, so the others figured they wouldn't make trouble for the island. Plus, how do you tell a mother and a father that their daughter was cheating on her husband, which is what caused all this?"

"So you blamed the accident on Adam Cyr?"

"Apparently you don't understand, Jimmy. It wasn't the accident that killed Jack's parents."

"I don't understand, Kyle."

"At first, Adam and Davidson were the only ones who knew this, but Timothy Chandler was dead before the ferry ever hit that ledge," Kyle explained.

"What do you mean?"

"The fact of the matter is that Davidson intentionally ran the ferry aground to get rid of evidence. Think about it. No one fusses when a body isn't found after such an accident around here because the ocean is so vicious. Well, Davidson knew that."

"Are you telling me that the bodies were recovered and hid to keep people from realizing the real cause of death?" Jimmy asked. "Why would Adam come forward with this and why would you believe him?"

"Because I helped bury the bodies, Jimmy." Kyle got up, turned his back to Jimmy, and began to cry. "Adam had no reason to lie, but I needed to know how the bodies got as wounded as they did. So I asked him exactly what happened on board that ferry."

"And he said what?"

"He told me that Timothy Chandler had come into the cabin at the base of the stairs to the cockpit and had demanded to talk to the captain. Adam says that he took the helm and that Davidson went down to talk to him. I guess Timothy said that, through the pilothouse window, he had seen Davidson drinking and started yelling at him about it. Eventually Timothy punched him."

"What did Davidson do then?"

"Apparently, he stabbed Timothy in the stomach. Told the Society that he didn't mean to kill him, but when he realized that Timothy was dead, he drove the ferry right up onto the rocks at a pretty good clip, ripping the hull in two."

Jimmy took a deep breath, exhaled, and said, "Okay. Let me get this straight, Kyle. The press reported the bodies were never found, but you're telling me that they were found and that you buried them?"

"Hell, Jimmy, Davidson had radioed the island before he called anyone else. He told the harbormaster the ferry had run aground before it actually had. Carl Swanson got into his Whaler and made his way over to 'The Graves.' When he got there, the damned ferry was perched right up on that ledge like it was meant to be there. What Davidson didn't know when he and Timothy got into it was that Jack and Laura were both on the car deck of the ferry and not upstairs with the other passengers," Kyle said.

"Was anyone else down there with them?"

"Apparently not. When Carl got there, he was surprised that not only was Timothy dead, but that the impact of the crash had killed Laura, too. Apparently, she landed on a piece of the torn metal from the hull."

Jimmy started to rub his head. "So what about Jack? How did he live after getting thrown into that water?"

"They found Jack right next to his mother and originally thought he was dead too, but when they dragged his body into the Whaler, they noticed he was breathing. Carl tried to wake him up, but it was no use. The doctor on the island said he'd slipped into a coma."

"Why didn't someone call the police?" Jimmy asked. "He could have killed everyone aboard."

"Because no one really knew what had happened, and the Society wanted to do its own investigation. When Carl brought the bodies back here, none of us knew that Timothy had been stabbed, or that Davidson had intentionally run the ferry aground," Kyle explained. "We assumed his wounds were from a shard of splintered metal, like Laura's. When we realized that there had been a murder, we figured that we would all go to jail as accomplices, so we just buried the bodies here on the island. The fact of the matter is that we didn't realize it had been a murder for a couple of days. Davidson had been on the mainland overnight in the hospital. By the time he was out, enough time had passed to make it look suspicious, even if it had been an accident. Ultimately, folks were glad he had stayed silent while in the hospital, but no one was pleased he tried to keep it quiet when he got back to the island."

Jimmy started biting his fingernails. "And what about Jack? You obviously didn't keep him there?"

Kyle donned a look of disgust and said, "No. After we decided to cover the thing up, we realized we had to do something with him. We couldn't just bring him to the hospital on the mainland or they would have been a lot more suspicious, and we couldn't keep him on the island either, so we had him planted on the shore near Tenant's Harbor. Apparently, Carl had been listening to the scanner and learned that they would be searching that area. So when he got the news that the authorities were headed out that way, we got him into the Whaler and Carl brought him there. He was still in a coma, but I really doubt he was on that shore too long before they found him."

Jimmy got up and began to pace. "And what would have happened if Carl had been wrong—they went looking somewhere else that day?"

"I never said I was proud of anything we did back then," Kyle said, turning away, his eyes welling up.

"How'd you get Davidson to confess to the stabbing?" Jimmy asked angrily. "Did Adam actually see him stab Timothy and come to you?"

"No. He later told us that he heard most of it, but he never actually saw Davidson stab Timothy."

"I can't imagine the Society was quick to believe him, were they?"

"Not at first, but when we had the two bodies in the boathouse, we noticed that Timothy's wounds were much cleaner than Laura's," Kyle explained. "There wasn't much doubt after that."

"Where were Davidson and Cyr during this?"

"I told you." Kyle sighed. "Davidson was at the hospital, which is how the mainland authorities found out he was drunk. Apparently he got knocked unconscious after calling for help the second time. The seas were so rough the ferry kept getting slammed against the rocks." He paused. "Adam was brought back to the island. He was hysterical and Carl thought he might just be in shock, but he wasn't. He was trying to tell us what had happened, but no one would listen to him. He was just an eighteen-year-old kid." Kyle took out a cigar and lit it, his hands perspiring. "It wasn't that the Society initially tried to cover up the accident or the murder, but by the time any of us understood what was going on, we didn't think we had any choice. Then those lies led to more lies, and it got more and more out of control until every fabric of our being became a lie."

"How did you get people to go along with it?" Jimmy inquired as if he was a skilled detective and not a twenty-eight-year-old rural sheriff.

"Easy. They didn't know either way. We knew, and Jack probably did too, but he'd been in a coma, so we figured that his credibility wouldn't hold up."

"Did anyone challenge you?"

"Not after we'd put a lien on their property or cut their lobster trap lines," Kyle replied, looking away from Jimmy.

"So you threatened people, made them afraid to question the truth?"

"I, my friend, didn't have much choice. Majority plus one has always been the rule. In the end, I voted against it all. I wanted to come clean, but those threats weren't only against the residents. Hell, if the others knew about the conversation we're having right now…"

"Did you ever think about telling Jack?"

"A couple of us did, but by the time he was old enough to comprehend, he'd apparently gone sour. The only person outside of the Society that I have talked about this with is Adam Cyr. I wanted to tell him that I was sorry. I wasn't afraid he would point me out or turn me in, it didn't really matter. I just wanted him to know that I knew I had done something wrong. Maybe I was looking for forgiveness. I don't know."

"What did he have to say about it?" Jimmy's questioning sounded routine. "I assume he was pretty pissed at you."

"Adam knew I was one of them. He didn't seem overly concerned with himself. He only wanted justice for the Chandler family. He told me that he wanted to go to Portland to find Jack, but was afraid."

"Afraid of whom, the Society?"

"Honestly, I don't know. He mentioned that Davidson and others would always follow him when he went off-island. He told me he had to break curfew just to get away from the island without someone trailing him. He was paranoid, but then again, who wouldn't be?"

"So why are you telling me all this now? Do you really think that Jack sent that letter to Davidson, or do you think it was Adam?"

"In theory, it could have been either of them or someone else completely. I doubt Adam would go to the trouble of going to Portland to send a letter, but who knows?" Kyle said, heaving a sigh of relief. "I think it's time we blow this thing wide open. Let everybody know. It's time that Adam gets justice for himself, and that Jack gets the truth."

"I can't say as though I disagree, but you could go to jail. There aren't any statutes of limitation on covering up manslaughter, or conspiracy to commit it. Perhaps if you and Adam testified, we could get some leeway for you," Jimmy explained.

Kyle chuckled. "I'm an old man, Jimmy—all but dead already. What are they going to do to an old man that's worse than having to live with such a horrible secret?"

From the porch, they heard Jimmy's radio, but neither could make out what was said. "I'd go get that, but it's probably just the deputy wondering how to fix the coffee machine again."

They both laughed before the voice came over the radio again. "What the… That sounded like he said someone was dead." Jimmy jumped up and darted toward the Jeep. "I'll give you a call later."

Kyle stood in his driveway, staring at the tornado-shaped trail of dust following Jimmy's Jeep. He had only heard a slight bit of the radio transmission that came from Jimmy's radio, but he had an ill feeling. The night before, he had heard the other members of the Society practically in hysterics over the thought of Jack's return. He knew that, despite what they may have said at the meeting, none of them really cared about the safety of Captain Davidson, or the possibility that Jack might go after him. It was about them. Like Jimmy had told him, they could all go to jail for their cover-up. That was motivation enough for irrationality.

Chapter Eighteen

Sheriff Jimmy Reynolds gripped the steering wheel of his Jeep with both hands. The narrow dirt road leading back into town was still damp underneath the sun-scorched surface, from the storm the night before. The back end of his SUV fishtailed slightly as he increased speed on the soft road. Lights on, siren blaring, this was his first real emergency since he became sheriff.

"Jimmy, Jimmy, come in, over." The voice echoed from the dashboard speaker. "Jesus, Jimmy, we got an emergency down here, over."

Jimmy took his right hand off the wheel and switched off the radio without so much as responding to his deputy's call for help. Concentrating on getting to town safely, he figured there was no use in answering the call. He had heard the word "dead" from Kyle's porch. He didn't need further confirmation. By the time he could get all the information over the radio from John, he'd be in town.

Nearing the island's only real intersection at Cranberry and Main, Jimmy could see a couple of small groups of people walking toward the town dock. He passed the same picturesque lawns he had passed by a couple of hours before. The houses showed no signs of life, and he assumed the whole town was already down at the dock. As Jimmy approached the two-story brick bank building on the corner of the intersection, he couldn't help but think that his conversation with Kyle was meant to be a prelude—a warning of what was ahead of him.

Jimmy could see the townspeople down at the end by the town dock and ferry landing. He pulled the Jeep to the side of Main Street, just outside Hamilton's Hardware, which, like everything else on a Saturday, was closed.

Illegally parked, Jimmy turned off the Jeep's engine and jumped out, leaving the door ajar. He ran toward the crowd. His adrenaline surged as he neared the curious onlookers. "Out of the way, folks. Let me through, please," he yelled.

"Oh, Sheriff, thank God you're here," Jimmy heard a voice cry, but didn't look to see who it was. His eyes focused toward the center, where he could see his deputy's hat.

Deputy Thorton turned from the scene, seeing that Jimmy was coming through the dense crowd. "Damn it, Jimmy. I tried to call. Where the hell were you?" he said, standing in front of the stretcher the body was on, blocking Jimmy's view.

"I was out at Kyle Foster's," Jimmy replied, out of breath. "I heard your call and got here as soon as I could. Who is it?"

"Well, sir, it's, ah, it's Adam Cyr," John replied, taking a deep breath.

Jimmy said, "Adam Cyr? Jesus, what the hell happened?" He had an overwhelming sense of irony, thinking about the conversation he just had with Kyle. He heaved a sigh and brushed past his deputy to get a view of the body.

Kneeling next to Adam Cyr's lifeless corpse was John Hadley, the island's doctor. Cyr's body was wrapped in what looked to be a light blue and green-striped shower curtain.

"Hello, Jimmy," the doctor said without looking up at the sheriff.

"John says it's Adam Cyr," Jimmy said, covering his nose with his left hand. He had never seen a real dead body. "Who found him, Doc?"

"Johnny Sampson was steaming toward his traps out by the southwestern bell when he saw the body tangled in someone's trap line," Dr. Hadley said, stroking his neatly trimmed goatee. "Jimmy, the body was wrapped in this shower curtain. This isn't something we put on him to cover the body. Now I admit, I did unwrap the body a little so I could identify and look for a cause of death. If he had just fallen off his boat, he would have had to have been taking a shower. If you know what I mean."

"Determined a cause of death?" Jimmy asked.

"Well, it's not like I've had the opportunity to do an autopsy. With the body wrapped like it is, I assumed that it would be a crime scene. Tried not to disturb the scene any more than I had to. However, preliminary examination of his neck and chest shows his lungs saturated, but—"

"But what, Doc?" Jimmy asked. "This is between you and me right now."

"Well, he's got a large bruised bump on the back of his head," Hadley said. "It could have come from hitting his head on the side of the boat."

"The man was wrapped in a shower curtain. If he was found that way, I find it very hard to believe it was by chance." He scribbled some notes on a pad of paper he took from a pocket inside his jacket. He wanted to make it look as though he knew what he was doing, but he realized that hypothetical situations practiced at the police academy hadn't prepared him for the real thing.

"As I said, Jimmy, I can't even conclude a primary cause of death till I can get him to the hospital in Rockland." The doctor took a deep breath and said, "However, I received a note saying that the body was to remain on the island. I don't have the equipment to do an autopsy out here for Christ's sake."

"I'm the only one here who can order a body to remain on the island." Jimmy raised his voice while grabbing the doctor by the shoulder and leading him away.

"Be that as it may, Jimmy, the note came from The Lighthouse Society. I mean, it's not like I want to undermine your authority, but damn it, I've got a mortgage."

"I don't care if you got a note from the goddamned Pope, I want you to get a proper body bag and have this body ready for transport to the mainland. I'll have my deputy over here to help you," Jimmy explained, patting Dr. Hadley on the back. He turned back toward the crowd. "John, could you come over here, please?"

"What's up?" John asked.

"The body wasn't seen by any of these people until it got on land." Jimmy leaned over to John's head and whispered, "I want you to stay with this body until I say otherwise. No one, and I mean no one, other than myself or Dr. Hadley is to have access to Adam's body."

"Well, sir, we can't just keep it out here in the sun," John pleaded.

"You're right. How 'bout you and Doc Hadley bring it over to the Village Dock Store and get it in the storage cooler," Jimmy said, shaking his head in frustration. The fact that the Society was trying to get in the way of him doing his job was upsetting.

"But Sally will—"

"I'll take care of Sally," Jimmy interrupted. "You worry about what I am asking you to do, please."

Jimmy looked up at the crowd of people gathered around whispering to each other. "Folks, can I get your attention please? I need you to go back to your homes, work, or wherever you are supposed to be right now. There is absolutely nothing you can do here. Thank you."

Doctor Hadley and John picked up opposite ends of the stretcher and headed toward the store. Jimmy followed closely.

From a little shack at the end of the dock, Carl Swanson appeared and waved at Jimmy. His eyes fixated on the two men carrying the body, Jimmy didn't see him and continued on. "Sheriff Reynolds, I need to speak with you," Swanson said.

"Can it wait, Carl? I kind of have a bit of a situation over here."

"More of a situation than you might realize, Sheriff," Swanson replied. "I need to speak with you."

Jimmy motioned to the deputy and the doctor to wait as he walked over and met Carl halfway to the dock. "What's wrong, Carl?"

"I just got a call over the radio from Jack Chandler." Carl pointed toward the outer harbor, where the thirty-five-foot navy blue sloop was moored. "He wants anchorage instructions. Told him to grab a mooring and hold on till I could get word to you. Assumed you didn't want anyone coming ashore, given the circumstances."

"Jack's here, now?" He looked over toward the body and then back out at the harbor, a confused look on his face. "Umm, tell him to take whatever mooring you see fit and ask him and his party to come ashore." Jimmy scratched his chin and rolled his eyes. "I need to secure Adam's body with the doctor and John. If Jack gets in here before I'm back, I need you to stall him. Tell him he has to sign some papers or something."

"Well, actually, Jimmy, he does," the harbormaster confirmed. "Why do you want me to stall him?"

"I will explain everything that I can, when I can, but I really have to get a hold on one situation at a time."

"Understood, Sheriff, I'll be here if you need me," Carl replied.

Jimmy nodded at Carl and walked back toward Dr. Hadley and Deputy Thorton, who looked anxious as they stood next to the body, which was resting on the frayed planks of the wood pier. Sally stood outside the store a few feet from the body, her hands at her side. She had an angry look on her face.

"Jimmy Reynolds, don't you dare think you're bringing that body in my store," she instructed.

He hadn't even asked her about using the cooler.

Jimmy approached with his hands in the air. There was nothing else he could do with the body. She had the only walk-in cooler on the island, and he had no way to get the body off the island yet. He managed a small, yet fake smile and said, "Honey, what do you want me to do, leave him out here in the sun? Believe me, with the stench, you'll have a thousand seagulls to contend with."

"It is not my problem, Jimmy. I own a damned restaurant, not a morgue. Do you realize that I can be shut down for health violations? Imagine the food I'd have to throw away just to make room for that... that body!"

"Sally, no one's going to shut you down, and as for the food, I will talk to the town council and have you fully reimbursed. Can you please cut me some slack? My hands are pretty much tied here," he pleaded.

Sally stepped back up onto the porch and walked over toward the front door of the store. She opened it and flipped the sign in the door window over so it read, "Closed, Please Call Again." "I'll tell you what. You do whatever the hell you need to do, but when I open back up, I don't want there to be any sign that this ever happened," she yelled to Jimmy as the doctor and John picked the body back up and came toward her. "And if you think I'm staying to help you move food around … well, I'm not." Sally took her apron off and threw it back into the store before storming off.

"Okay, boys, bring him on in. I'll get the cooler open and clear stuff out of the way," Jimmy ordered.

"Oh yeah, this will do the trick just fine," Dr. Hadley added as he brought his end onto the cooler. "You want to keep it here overnight, Sheriff?"

"I don't know yet. Might have to. Carl said that Jack Chandler just arrived," Jimmy said, rubbing his eyes. The slight smell started to make his eyes water.

"Heard he was coming back," the doctor said. "Didn't know it was today. A rather unfortunate time, I should think."

Jimmy looked to John and frowned. "Yes, that's true, Doc. Tell you what, if we need you this afternoon or evening, we'll give you a call. Deputy Thorton and I have some work to do right now, if you would kindly excuse us."

"Oh, not a problem," the doctor said. "I could use some rest myself. The heat out here's brutal." He walked out of the kitchen, turned back toward them, and said, "Say, Sheriff, do you have any idea about any suspects?"

"Yes, Doc. We have some suspects. We'll release all of that information later on, but certainly not before any arrests are made. Oh, and Doc, the less gossip about this, the better," he said with a wink of the eye.

"Sure thing, Jimmy. Call me at home if you need me." The doctor left the store.

John closed the door to the cooler and walked over to the counter where Jimmy had just opened a soda. "Who are the suspects, Jimmy?"

"You're kidding, right?"

"No. Is there something I should know that I don't?"

"Jesus, John, you got the same phone call from Captain Davidson that I did," Jimmy said. "Hell, you called me to let me know about it."

"You really think that Captain Davidson killed Adam?" John opened a soda Jimmy had given him. "Oh wait, you think that Kyle did it?"

"Come on, think about it. Davidson gets a letter in the mail, threatening his life, right? He was the captain of the ferry that killed Jack Chandler's parents…"

"Okay, so Jack has a motive to kill Davidson, but what does that have to do with Adam Cyr?"

"John, Adam Cyr was Davidson's first mate on the ferry. He admitted to being at the helm when it ran aground," Jimmy explained, taking his hat off and turning it around. "Did you, by chance, hear my conversation with Carl?"

"No, I was talking to the doctor about the stench."

"Anyway, we were discussing the fact that Jack had just arrived in the harbor. He's probably at the dock right now, and unfortunately, I think we have to detain him," Jimmy said with a distraught look on his face.

"Do you really think Jack would do something so obviously dumb as killing someone, then show up at his victim's homeport?"

"I wouldn't think so, but there are a couple things we need to look at," Jimmy replied. "First, we haven't seen or heard from Jack in what, sixteen years? Second, I haven't shared this with anyone else as of yet, but Adam never showed up on Vinalhaven yesterday for that scallop trip. Actually, no, I'm sorry, he did show up with Sam Robertson, but immediately took off on another boat. He was seen heading south toward Marshall Point. I don't know where he was going, but from the conversation I had with Kyle, it seemed as though Adam wanted to meet up with Jack."

"Did Kyle actually say that Adam was going down the coast?"

"No. He didn't have to. It was as though he desperately wanted to tell me, but was afraid to give away too much information."

"So what is it you're really afraid of here? Would it have been so bad if Adam had gone to meet Jack? I personally wouldn't see why he would, but at the same time, I don't see it as a determining factor either."

"Well, Jesus, John," Jimmy pleaded. "You know as well as I do that Adam's been saying that people have been following him everywhere, right? Well, what if he was followed away from Vinalhaven by someone who thought he was going to open his mouth and then decided to kill him? On the other hand, what if he did meet up with Jack, and Jack wasn't as forgiving as Adam had hoped?"

John sighed. "Yeah, but it's always been rumored that Adam was a cover for Davidson being behind the helm."

"Rumor or not, Jack wouldn't have any other way of knowing that, unless Adam told him. I'm not so sure he'd believe him. So anyway, I asked Sally if she and Jack ever discussed that stuff, and she said no. I really hope that it's just a coincidence, but he has motive written all over him right now. It's my job to find out what's going on here. Whether he's our friend or not." Jimmy got up from his stool and went over to the window that faced the dock. "They're here. Looks like Jack, his girlfriend, and some other guy. Did you hear about him bringing anyone else with him?"

"Yeah, there should be two guys with him. Sally said that he had two friends from Colorado helping him bring the boat from Portland. I don't know anything about them. According to what he told Sally, they're just here for a couple of days." John joined Jimmy by the window. "Why? Are you going to arrest them, too?"

"No, but the fact remains that we have a dead body here. I'm going to get a lot of pressure from the Society to deal with it," Jimmy said. "Now, that brings even more problems, if you think back to the two possibilities I came up with. First, if the Society did have something to do with it, we're screwed. I only know of one of the members, and that person has been accounted for—clear alibi. We don't have proof who the others are, so it would be rather hard to pin anything on them, right? As for the second theory, well, I wouldn't be able to prove that either, but if I went with an obvious motive, I'd have to suspect Jack."

"Jimmy, I fail to see how your intuition on a motive Jack may have had could outdo a claim of reasonable doubt. Police get sued all the time for making false arrests."

Jimmy bowed his head and spoke softly. "You don't seem to get it, John. The Society doesn't give a damn what I can prove. They care about containment. Now, are you going to go against a direct order from them? We'd be found floating off North Haven by the end of the week."

"What if this has nothing to do with the Society?" John asked, following Jimmy out the door.

"That would be great, but it would also lean toward the whole revenge theory. The way Kyle was going on today, I have a really bad feeling about all of this."

The two walked across the pier toward the town dock, where Carl had the three visitors tied up in paperwork.

Jack was engrossed in a conversation with the harbormaster, but Kendra and Nate saw John and Jimmy coming toward them and tried to get Jack's attention.

Jimmy was torn. He was glad to see his childhood friend had come home, but he couldn't help but feel the pressure of making the difficult decision, which would certainly make the homecoming much less sweet.

"My God. I thought your wife was lying when she said they made you sheriff," Jack said as Jimmy walked over to the group. He turned and extended his hand. "Just kidding, bro. It's good to see you."

"Hey, Jack. Good to see you, too. I wish it was under better circumstances," Jimmy said as he looked away. He was afraid to look Jack in the eye. He didn't know if he was looking at a vengeful killer or a humble friend.

"Jimmy, what the hell is going on out here?" Jack asked. "Carl said that you guys fished a body out of the water this morning."

Jimmy paused and then took a deep breath. "A local lobsterman found the body of Adam Cyr outside the harbor this morning. I'm sorry I have to ask you this, but where were you this morning, Jack?" He knew in his gut that Jack couldn't have anything to do with the death, but the pressure from above was strong. He had a family to worry about.

"We were at The Children's Chapel in Rockport. Probably got on board the boat around eleven-thirty," replied Jack. "Come on, Jimmy! Don't tell me you think…" His cheeks were bright red, his nostrils flaring.

"I assume you have someone to back that up?"

Kendra jumped in between them, gave Jimmy a stern look, and said, "Don't say a word, Jack. Sheriff, I'm an attorney and my name is Ken—"

"It's okay, Kendra. We've got nothing to hide," Jack said, turning back to Jimmy. "No. Not here, obviously, but if you let me make a call or two, I'm sure I could find someone to speak for us."

Jimmy thought for a moment, looked back toward Jack, and said, "Listen, buddy, come here a second, okay?"

"Sure," Jack said as they walked away from the others. "What's going on, Jimmy?"

"Honestly, Jack, I don't know. Now, I know damned well that you didn't do this, but there are people—"

"The Society wants answers, and you don't have them, right?" Jack interrupted.

"No, I don't. I'd swear on my life that someone connected with them had a lot to do with it, but there's no proof. We figure the only person with motive—that we know of, that is—is you. The problem is that they know that too. If someone wanted to kill Adam, they would know that they could try and pin it on you, because of the ferry connection."

"I know full well Adam wasn't at the helm," Jack said.

"That's not the point," Jimmy replied. "The point is, I'm going to get a call asking what I've come up with. You know about these guys. Now, I don't want to ask you this, but—"

"But you want to hold me in jail?" Jack chuckled.

"I know it sounds stupid, but it would make things a lot easier until we could figure something out. Plus, it might be good for your safety."

"I'll do it," Jack said. "You just act as though you are arresting me. I'll put on a little show."

Jimmy led Jack back toward the others. They both had disappointment on their faces. Jimmy knew that for his plan to work, everyone, especially people like Carl, had to believe it.

"Jack Chandler, I'm placing you under arrest for the murder of Adam Cyr. You have the right to—"

"Oh, what-the-hell-ever, Jimmy!" Jack yelled, his head hanging. His eyes looked up toward Nate. "Remember that name I told you about?"

"Sure do," Nate replied.

"Find him. He'll know the truth. If you can't find him by tonight, you'll have to call Dick," Jack explained as John applied handcuffs to him.

John led Jack away from the dock and his friends.

Jimmy stayed behind with Nate and Kendra at the dock. "I assume you're Kendra," he said. "And you are?"

"Nathan Richardson."

"Well, folks, we have a ferry leaving at six. That's the last of the day. I doubt very much that Jack will be able to even get a bail hearing from our town council till tomorrow."

"Your town council? Since when does a town council set bail?" Nate asked.

"Well, Mr. Richardson, I don't know where you're from, but things are very different out here," Jimmy said. "I can make a call for you at the station, but I don't know if any of them will be able to provide any news till tomorrow. I assume they will meet first thing, but quite frankly, we haven't had a crime out here in quite a while, and not since I have been sheriff. Regardless, Jack is my friend, too. I will make sure that everything is done fairly." Jimmy didn't really know if he could make sure of that, but he had to make it look real, and that included making Jack's friends believe it was. He didn't know who he could trust.

"Well, we'll follow you," Nate said. "We're not going anywhere till we know what is going on with Jack."

The three walked down Main Street as the Jeep, with Jack and Deputy Thorton inside, sped off ahead of them. Jimmy was silent. They all were. As they passed the town square, the blue lamp lit up.

"What's up with the blue light?" Nate asked, looking at Kendra as if she would know.

"That means curfew is in effect tonight at sundown for all residents. If you are out in public after dark, you will be arrested," Jimmy lied. He hoped that Jack might have seen it and could tell them at the station. A burst of thunder rumbled above and they all looked up. Light rain began to fall.

Chapter Nineteen

Nate and Kendra sat on an arch-shaped bench in the gazebo adjacent to the town hall. As thunder roared in the distance and rain fell around their sheltered refuge, they sat silent, like strangers in a park.

The gazebo was an attractive little building near the center of town, surrounded by expansive lawns and gardens. Someone spent a lot of time and money on the upkeep and Nate was impressed. He had read a few copies of *Down East* magazine over the years and was stuck with the preconceived notion that Maine's islands were all rundown fishing ports. He knew that it was probably a common misconception, but Carroll Island was surely an anomaly of sorts. The brick foundation of the gazebo matched the brick façade of almost all the buildings on Main Street, including the town hall, which also housed the Public Safety department, where Jack was held.

Jack hadn't mentioned his conversation with Kendra on the boat to Nate, but Nate had heard most of it from the cabin below. He knew Kendra as a bubbly, self-driven young attorney and, before then, couldn't figure out why she would agree to move to an island with Jack. The conversation he overheard gave him a fresh perspective on her. He could see that she, too, was struggling with her past, and figured that maybe she thought she could help herself by helping Jack.

"Any ideas, Kendra?" Nate asked.

"I don't even understand what's going on," she replied. "We get off the boat and all of a sudden Jack is arrested for murder. Perhaps if it was the captain of the ferry that was found dead, I could see Jack as a suspect, but I don't know who this guy is. I don't see where they got the motive. Why can't they take our word he was with us?"

"I talked to the sheriff. From what he told me, the guy whose body they found had been the first mate on the ferry. He was actually at the helm at the time of the accident. Jack never told you that?"

"No, and I doubt he knew," Kendra said. "The only person he ever talked about was Captain Davidson. I used to feel like I knew that damned guy, but he stopped talking about it years ago."

"Regardless, if it is true that this Adam Cyr guy admitted to being at the helm of the ferry, it certainly gives the sheriff cause to suspect motive. As for means, it's our word against a dead body."

"Couldn't you just call your boss and end this thing right now?"

"Jack specifically asked me not to call O'Neil. I can't think of much else we can do," Nate replied with a sigh. He had had an uncomfortable feeling about his boss' covert activities the past couple of days. He had never seen O'Neil away from the office. "I'd like to get a hold of this Kyle Foster guy, but the sheriff wouldn't give me any information on him. Not even a phone number."

"Was that who Jack was referring to, Mr. Foster, I mean?" she asked.

"Yeah, but I don't have any idea where to find him, and it doesn't seem like anyone is around that we could ask," he replied.

"I recall Jack telling me that he and the other kids used to ski on a hill at Foster's land. It looks pretty far away, but I only see one hill out here." Kendra pointed toward the northeast end of the island.

"Why didn't you mention this before, Kendra?" Nate jumped up, grabbed her arm, and said, "If we start now, we can get there by dark for sure."

* * *

Nate and Kendra walked past Hamilton's Hardware and turned left onto Cranberry Lane, which led all the way out to Kyle's on the northeastern tip of the island. They passed the little houses on the edge of the village, the tidy lawns leading to sturdy, white-stained, wood-shingled capes. They hadn't seen a single person since leaving the center of town, and the houses were all dark, desolate, like their owners were away on vacation or perhaps turned in for the night.

"It's only six-thirty and all the houses are darker than it is outside," Nate said, looking down at his watch. "Where the hell do you think everyone is?"

"Doesn't any of this bother you?" Kendra asked.

"Does what bother me?"

"I don't know. It just seems that a couple of days ago I had a pretty normal life and a normal fiancé. Then yesterday the lies started flowing like a dam had just been breached. I wonder if Jack ever really planned to move out here. Nate, I don't even know where his house is," she said, shooting him a glance, her eyes welling up.

"Some of those lies were mine."

"Yeah, but you were just doing your job. Trying to keep him out of trouble. He told me time and time again that this whole conspiracy thing was over, and then, all of a sudden, Rob is being carted off to a hospital, and two people are dead." A single tear rolled down her face, which she quickly brushed away and sniffled.

"I think you've got it wrong, Kendra. Jack fully intended to move out here with you. He dreamed of starting over out here. He dreamed of writing a book and getting it published. He wanted to do all of that with you. His approach may have been weird, but the kid's been dealt a tough hand, and he obviously didn't know how to go about things like you or I would. As for what happened yesterday, he wasn't lying. He really got an anonymous call the day before we left. I think that anyone in his position would have done the same thing and gone straight to Seguin."

Kendra stopped, grabbed onto Nate's arm, and said, "If yesterday was such an impulse response, why did the FBI send you?"

"They didn't send me. Jack called me and Rob and said you two were going to take the boat down the coast. He asked if we wanted to get away for a while. It was me that went to my superiors and told them he planned to go back to the island and that I was going with him." Nate was getting frustrated. He understood where she was coming from, but still didn't think Jack had any malicious intent.

"So what you are saying is that you still suspected he might do something rash?"

"Not at all," Nate replied. "To be honest, I was being selfish and actually using his invitation to try and further my career. Maybe that makes me the bad guy, but the fact of the matter is that I really have always believed Jack. I believed he was done crusading, but I also believed that he really felt, for a long time, there was some sort of conspiracy. So, I figured I'd try to get out on the island and prove to the Bureau that the case really could be solved after all these years.

Jack knew nothing about that until yesterday in the lighthouse. If there is anyone to be angry at, it's me, not Jack."

"I appreciate your honesty, and I want to believe both of you, but I'm scared," Kendra said, smiling softly.

He looked at her with a childlike grin and said, "You know, sunshine? I think we're all a little scared, especially the guy sitting in jail right now. Question is, is there any way to make all of this right?"

As the two approached the first bend in the road, they saw a lone driveway to their right with an iron gate crossing it, a steel chain wrapped around the opening end. A short distance beyond, they could see the 35-foot tall stone tower, painted white with its black lamp house on top. Even in the waning hours of daylight, the beam extruding from the giant bulb rotated slowly, 360 degrees. The lighthouse rose from the rocky ground, void of trees and soil too thin to support much life. Three other buildings occupied the land. There was the lighthouse with its attached keeper's house, a large carriage house over by the trees, and a medium-size water tower a stone's throw from the keeper's house. Like the tower, the two larger buildings were made of stone and painted white, symmetrical in every detail, down to the windows, showing the pitch-black atmosphere inside each.

Nate tugged at Kendra's mist-soaked sweater. "Hold up a second," he said, looking out toward the lighthouse. "Want to see what this lighthouse is about?"

"Don't you remember the last time you screwed around in a lighthouse?"

"Damn, you are moody." He shrugged, not able to understand how quickly her emotions could switch from being a caring girlfriend to being downright bitchy. "I remember quite well what happened.

It's just that I find it interesting that there happens to be a blue light outside that building over by the trees. Do you really think it is a coincidence that we've seen two blue lights in the past hour, neither of which seem to signify anything other than a so-called curfew?"

"The sign says that TRESPASSERS WILL BE PROSECUTED. That means stay out, Nate."

Their conversation was cut off by the screeching sound of rusting brakes. "What the hell?" Nate said as he jumped. The sheriff's Jeep skidded to a stop alongside of them, shelling them with tiny divots of mud. "We haven't trespassed yet, pal," Nate said as the dusty gray cloud dissipated.

The passenger side of the door flung open and Jimmy Reynolds leaned over from his seat. "Get in. Let's go. Before the two of you do anything stupid," he said.

"Stupid—like locking up an innocent man?" Kendra said.

"At least he's safe. For now, that is. Now, get in," Jimmy replied.

"He's safe from what?" Nate inquired.

Jimmy looked at both of them. "Not what, Agent Richardson, but whom, and you'll find out, but you have to come with me now. We don't have much time left."

Kendra said, "How did you—"

"Jack and I go back a long ways. He believes in me. Now it's your turn," Jimmy said, revving the engine.

"So, why isn't he in the Jeep with you?" Kendra asked as she and Nate climbed into the Jeep.

"Because Jack realizes that several people may be looking to turn him into a pale shade of blue like Adam Cyr, and it's best to stay in a safe place." Jimmy reached behind his seat and pulled out a towel. He tossed it to them. "Plus, if I let Jack go, that would tell the community that I didn't think he was the killer. I can't afford to do that right now." He looked at the two of them curiously. "Jack told me that the two of you would most likely be heading out to see Kyle Foster. It just so happens that I'm on my way there."

"So you believe that Jack didn't kill that guy?" Nate asked, drying his damp legs with the towel.

"I know Jack didn't kill him, but I had two things I needed to consider," Jimmy replied. "First, I wanted whoever did to think I thought Jack was our man. Second, I don't really know who did it, but I have a damned good idea of who's behind it. That's why we're going to see Kyle."

Nate was wary of Jimmy. He didn't know how much he could trust him. Short of calling O'Neil, Jimmy was their only shot at exposing the killer, or killers, and freeing Jack. "So then, Sheriff, are you a member of The Lighthouse Society?" Nate expected either a quick rebuttal or a possible slap in the face. He got neither.

"Off the record, there was a chance that I would have been nominated, but I have a feeling that the Society is going down sooner than anyone could have thought."

"Wait a minute. Jack and I have read the minutes and the constitution. We know that members are tapped. How would you know ahead of time?"

"Normally, one wouldn't, but Kyle wants this whole thing blown open, and he's willing to risk everything to make that happen. With that in mind, he filled me in on one of his plans, which was to step down and for me to take his place. That could still work, but for the sake of the people on this island who haven't a clue about the Society,

I'd rather get it over with sooner than later. That's where you guys come in."

"I don't follow," Nate said, looking at Kendra.

"When I was talking to Jack, he told me about your boss. O'Neil, right? He also told me that your boss would bring this place down if the three of you didn't do it your way in a few days. Well, I think the latter is the best approach. After seeing Adam's body today, I can't imagine what might happen if we wait three days."

"Well, apparently whatever interrogation technique you used was effective," Nate said. "I guess we're all on the same page. Do you and Kyle have a plan?"

"Not exactly, but with your help, we will," Jimmy replied.

"If that's the case, why did you refuse to give me Kyle's address or phone number?" Nate asked. "Why'd you want us to leave if you needed our help?

"To be honest, at first I didn't think I did want your help. But then Jack told me about you being an agent. And, I might add, Ms. Davids, these folks might need a good lawyer."

Kendra laughed nervously and said, "How can we help with something we don't even understand?"

Jimmy slowed the Jeep down and turned to them. "You asked about the blue lights. The blue lights come on when a meeting has been called by The Lighthouse Society. The Society's roots come from Masonic tradition. Whenever a Masonic lodge meeting is in progress, a blue light is illuminated outside. The Society imposed the curfew to help protect their identities. Now, the reason I think you guys can help is because you have proven to have a lot more balls than the people who live out on this island. I don't know what Kyle has planned, but the more people willing to stop the Society, the better."

* * *

Like any other night, Kyle sat in his rocking chair on the back porch when the three arrived. Shredded cornhusks and shelled pea pods were scattered around the legs of the chair. When he saw it was Jimmy's Jeep, Kyle got up from his chair and swept up most of the debris before going inside.

Nate and Kendra had heard a lot about Kyle from Jack. It wasn't until earlier that day that Jack and Nate learned he was a member of The Lighthouse Society. Nate recalled the shocked look on Jack's face when he read the name out loud. Given his age and stature on the island, Nate assumed Kyle was a member, but he couldn't quite put together this wonderful person Jack often spoke of, and a person who would help hide a crime. Nate had been in the Bureau for over five years, and finally realized why people like O'Neil told him he still had so much to learn.

"He knows we're coming," Jimmy said, entering the back screen door. Nate and Kendra looked at each other and shrugged.

Kyle sat in his chair by the door, reading the latest issue of *National Geographic*. "It's been a bit of a long day for you, hasn't it, Jimmy?" he said while flipping through the glossy pages.

"I assume you heard?" Jimmy said, taking a seat in a wicker armchair next to Kyle. "It was Adam."

"I figured as much when I heard it over your radio. When you ran off and didn't come back, I assumed you probably had a suspect. Didn't expect you'd bring strangers out here with you, though," Kyle replied, looking up from his magazine and peering into the eyes of Kendra and Nate. "You Jack's friends?"

"Yes sir," Nate said.

"I knew Jack was bringing friends. I was told it was three, though. Where's the other?"

"Our friend Rob had an accident yesterday," Kendra added.

"Accident, really? I don't buy it," Kyle said. "You don't have to tell me what happened to your friend, but I'd like to know where Jack is."

Jimmy cleared his throat. "Jack is detained, Kyle. I charged him with Adam's murder."

"That's very clever, Jimmy. McKay probably salivated when he heard. Billings, too. You know he didn't do it though, right?" Kyle lit a cigar he had sitting in an ashtray next to his chair.

"Mr. Foster, are you saying that Adam was the one who called Jack about Seguin? Was he out there yesterday?" Nate asked, sitting on the edge of his chair. "Jack had pretty much assumed it was you."

"It would have been me, but to get off this island without being noticed, you have to be young and quick," Kyle replied. "Adam might not have been the youngest, but he was as quick as anyone I ever knew. I assume you found the box then?"

"Yes, sir, we found it. Jack and I read all about the Society, including your membership," Nate said, shooting a glare over at Kyle.

Kyle laughed. "Do you really think I care if you have me arrested? I'm prepared to be arrested, but only if it means the rest of the bastards go down, too."

"I think I can offer you immunity, but you're going to have to help us nail the rest of 'em, tonight."

"Agent Richardson, can you really offer him that?" Jimmy asked. "Wouldn't he have to—"

"Inform on the others?" Nate interrupted. "Yes. He'd pretty much either have to write us a whole statement, or he could wear a wire to the Society meeting tonight."

"Nate, where did you get a wire?" Jimmy asked. "What sort of plans did you all come out here with?"

"I didn't really have any plans until we got out here. I was content to jump the gate and see if your Society boys showed up at the lighthouse. You realize that I have enough evidence in those hidden documents to lock up about six people, right?"

"So why not just do that?" Jimmy asked, grinning. "Is it because you don't think that fifteen-year-old documents would hold up in court?"

"I'll wear the damned wire." Kyle interjected, as Jimmy and Nate stared at each other from across the room.

Kyle left the room and walked into the adjacent kitchen. Looking out the window, the gray evening had turned to a hue of charcoal and it was only seven o'clock. He poured himself some iced tea and sat at the kitchen table alone. Kendra followed suit shortly after and pulled up a chair next to him. "Are you okay, sir?" she said.

"I'm fine. I'm ready to get this started. It's starting to get dark out."

"I can see that," she replied.

"That means the meeting starts in about an hour," he whispered into her ear.

"Listen, Mr. Foster—"

"It's just Kyle."

"Sorry. Kyle, I happen to be a lawyer, and Nate's right. If you agree to wear a wire, he can get you immunity from almost all charges."

Kyle laughed and said, "Almost all, huh?"

"Well, you wouldn't have to do any jail time, sir."

Kyle turned to her. "Will the rest of them go to jail?"

"Well, sir, if you can get them to admit it on tape, we'd have everything we need," Kendra said. "Could charge them with tampering with evidence, covering up a manslaughter case, conspiracy to commit murder, along with maybe murder itself."

"Hmm. Sounds pretty good," Kyle said, looking down at his tea. The humidity had melted the ice. "I'll do it for Jack."

Kendra smiled at him and got up from the table. As she walked toward the living room where Jimmy and Nate were, she turned to Kyle, who was still seated. "Thank you," she said softly.

* * *

Kyle stood in the middle of the room with a disgruntled look on his face. His arms and legs were as dark as dirt from the sun, but his torso was pasty white. The others started laughing when he took his shirt off.

"What? You ain't ever seen a farmer's tan before?" Kyle asked, frowning. "The doctor suggested I keep my shirt on while doing my gardening."

Nate and Jimmy affixed the wire to Kyle's leather belt and ran it up his stomach to below his neck. Jimmy held it in place while Nate cut short strips of medical tape with his teeth and started fastening the wire to his skin.

"Now don't make any sudden movements, Mr. Foster, or you'll feel the tape rip out your hair," Nate suggested.

Jimmy looked at Kendra, who was sitting on a couch playing with the remote receiver. "Kendra, why don't you go into the kitchen and turn that on. Just don't turn the volume up very high while we're this close," he said as Kyle put his shirt on and he stepped away to see if the wire was visible.

"I can't really see it. Is this what you'll wear, Mr. Foster?" Nate asked.

"No, I'll have a robe on over this," Kyle replied. "It's going to be damned hot in that basement, I'll tell ya."

"Okay, it's working fine," Jimmy yelled from the kitchen and then appeared through the door. "Don't worry about talking into the microphone. We have it set so it will pick up everything in about a ten-foot radius. Will that be good enough for you to get everyone in the room?"

"Oh yeah. It's a small room in the basement of the second building. You know which one it is?"

"Yes, I do. Now don't worry about anything, just go about the meeting however you guys normally do. Whenever you feel comfortable, ask if anyone knows about Cyr. Chances are, if one of them is behind it, they'll gloat over it and laugh about Jack being in jail," Jimmy said, jotting notes on a piece of paper. "When we have all that we need, we're going to bust right in and make the arrests."

"We've got guns in there," Kyle said. "However, if you come down through the bulkhead, I doubt even McKay would have time to get to one."

"Okay, hold up a minute," Nate said. "What's the deal with this McKay character anyway? Everything is McKay this, McKay that."

"Oh, nothing really, he's just an old prick like me," Kyle replied. "He and I have never really seen eye to eye. I guess when I think of all that has gone wrong with the island and the Society, he seems to be behind it. He's a sly, crafty bastard."

"Crafty or not, I recommend that when you hear us coming in, you get underneath a table or behind something," Nate said. "We have guns too, and if they start shooting…"

"I've always wanted to go undercover, like in the movies, you know?" Kyle said, walking toward the door.

"Well, this is your big chance." Jimmy smiled at him. "You better get moving if you're going to walk down there in time. Are you sure you don't want us to drive you partway?"

"Nay, I'll be fine. Plus, Cooper will be coming this way and he'll think it odd if he doesn't see me walking." Kyle opened the screen door and looked out. "That reminds me, if you're staying here, you'll have to drive the Jeep up on the lawn and behind the house. I can't imagine what Cooper would think if he saw it in the driveway right before a meeting."

As Kyle Foster made his way down the driveway, the others walked out onto the porch and watched. Nate had an anxious feeling about the night ahead. There was so much that could happen, and he hoped it would all go smoothly. He and Jack had talked so much about taking down The Lighthouse Society, and he knew that it had been such a big part of Jack's life—he felt a bit sad that Jack wouldn't get to see it all happen.

Chapter Twenty

Jack looked over at the television set through the cast-iron bars of his cell and then glanced over to Deputy Thorton. "John, is it not enough that I'm in jail? Do you need to torture me further by have this God-awful show on?" he said, sitting Indian style on a wooden cot.

"Jack, we only get two channels out here. It's either *The Insider* or *Who Wants to be a Millionaire*. I like *Millionaire*," the deputy said, turning his attention back to the game of solitaire he was playing on the computer.

"Well, seeing as you're not really watching the damned thing anyway, why don't you just turn it off and give me a book."

"You've got books. Read one of those." Deputy Thorton pointed to the small wood crate underneath Jack's cot.

"Yeah, um, the Hardy Boys were great when I was a kid, but I was thinking of something with a little more substance," Jack said, frustrated. He and Jimmy had talked about keeping him in the jail for his own safety, but the deputy had been left out of the conversation. Jack didn't understand why, as the three had all been best friends, but he tried to play along. "So John, you really think I killed Cyr?"

"That's not for me to say, Jack," the deputy replied. "All I know is that the sheriff thought there was enough evidence to hold you here, so we're holding you." He clicked on the mouse and dragged a card across the screen.

Jack looked out the window of his cell, which was in the basement of the town hall. Past the harbor anchorage he could see the orange and purple sky break through the dark gray clouds off on the horizon. He gripped the bars of the window and pulled himself up so he could position his head, trying to catch a glimpse of *Island Prayer*, moored just out of his line of sight. What he wouldn't give to be onboard, sailing away from the mess he'd gotten himself into.

The Public Safety Department consisted of three rooms: Jimmy's office, a small conference room, and the main room where the cell was located. The room looked like it had been refinished not too long ago, but the cell had been left unchanged. He remembered playing in it when he was a boy and Jimmy's dad had been sheriff. Jimmy told him that other than a few drunken fishermen, Jack was its first real occupant since those days.

"John, didn't Jimmy tell you why he was holding me in here?"

"You've been charged with first degree murder, Jack," the deputy replied, his eyes still glued to the computer screen. He let out an elongated sigh and swiveled around in his chair so that he faced Jack.

"Hey, all right, I finally got your attention," Jack said.

"Jack, shut the hell up and look up in the corner behind me," he said softly, almost whispering. "Don't stare."

Jack peered over John's shoulder and saw a surveillance camera mounted in the top right corner of the room. It looked just like the one in the conference room at the Coast Guard base.

Jack looked back down at John and whispered, "So it has both video and audio?"

"Not sure," John replied. "Better not take a chance, though."

"John, Jimmy told me I was the first person to actually be jailed here in years. So why do you guys have a surveillance camera in here?"

"It's not ours," the deputy said. "The island got a deal on it from the company that Mr. Billings works for. I guess the Society wanted it put up. This isn't the only one. There are more on the island. Jimmy said that until further notice, we need to act as though you are really a suspect."

"Well, damn, I hope no one's listening in right now then," Jack said with a smirk.

"No. Don't worry," John said. "Hear that static?"

"Yeah, so?"

"I turned the computer speaker toward the corner and switched the radio to a station that doesn't come in. If the camera picks up any audio, it will be interfered with by white noise."

Jack rolled his eyes. "Well, where did Jimmy go, anyway? Did he go with my—"

"Yes, Deputy, where did the young sheriff go?" a raspy voice cried out from around the corner of the hallway.

As the shadow of the man came into view, John jumped out of his chair and said, "Oh, Mr. Billings. How are you this evening, sir?"

"I've been better, Deputy Thorton, but the day is still young," he snickered. He was just out of sight of Jack's cell. John moved out from behind his desk and walked over to him. "So I hear you caught the bastard that killed Adam."

"Well, sir, we have Jack Chandler in custody," John said. "We've charged him with the crime, but you'd have to talk to the sheriff for the specifics."

"As I asked before, where is the sheriff?" Billings asked.

"I think he probably went home for dinner," John explained. "He usually does about this time at night. Most nights he stops back in." He looked like a deer in headlights as he spoke to the man.

"How much better can it get, Deputy Thorton?"

"I'm sorry, sir. I don't quite follow."

"Well, let's see, the sheriff's at home for dinner, Jack Chandler's locked up for doing our dirty work—"

"Your dirty work, sir?" John interrupted.

"And as I was about to say before you so rudely interrupted me, you're going to take a long nap in the mop closet."

Jack heard the muffled sound of a pistol with a silencer and saw John fall backwards freely. His head hit the tile floor and lay in a small, but expanding pool of blood. The deputy's lifeless head, void of any muscle control, turned toward Jack, his eyes still open.

Jack lay motionless on the cot. He assumed he would be next and there was nowhere to go, to hide. He sat there, eyes fixed on John's, while he heard rustling of some sort from down the hall. Suddenly John's body was dragged away.

"So I guess it's your turn, Mr. Chandler?" Billings said, still out of sight.

Jack couldn't help but wonder if news of his daughter's death on Seguin accounted for the visit. He didn't remember much about Billings, but his voice sure sounded familiar. "Show yourself, you coward!" he yelled, shaking the cell bars.

"Can't you tell I'm busy?" Billings said. "You in a hurry? All locked up in that little cell. And your friends—your friends got on your boat and left you here all alone."

"Why don't you show yourself and open this goddamned door?"

"As entertaining as the idea sounds, Mr. Chandler, I'm in a bit of a rush. You see, I have a meeting to go to. Don't you worry, though, we'll most certainly be seeing each other soon enough."

Jack saw a wet mop slap against the off-white tiles, its water diluting the dark red blood. He felt sick to his stomach. Suddenly he heard the slam of what sounded like a closet door and then Billings was gone.

* * *

Jack heard what sounded like the back door open and his heart beat faster. Was Billings back to fulfill his promise? He hoped it was Jimmy. He didn't believe Jimmy had gone home for dinner, but instead to see Kyle Foster. Maybe they'd already gotten to Jimmy.

"Hello?" Sally's voice rang in the hallway. "Jimmy, John, someone?"

"Sally, it's Jack, in here," he cried out, hoping she too didn't think he was the killer.

"My God, Jack. Where is everyone? It's not dark out yet. It isn't time for curfew, but I don't have any idea where Jimmy is," she said, almost in a panic.

"I doubt as though I'm the best person to ask," Jack said, still shaking the cell bars in frustration.

"Yeah, well, Jimmy told me he was just keeping you in here for your own protection. Then he left and wouldn't tell me where he was going." She paced back and forth, not making eye contact with him.

"Listen, Sally. John's dead."

"What do you mean, John's dead?"

"It was Mr. Billings. He came in. The two talked. Then Billings shot him. Go down the hall and open the closet door," Jack said, heaving a sigh. "Can you get the damned keys to this door while you're at it?" He heard Sally's scream from down the hall and the sound of her running back toward him.

"Jesus Christ, Jack! Did you see Mr. Billings do this?" she said, cringing.

"Well, yes and no. I saw it happen, but I never actually saw Billings. I heard him in the hall. He said he would kill me too, but then he left."

"Why would Mr. Billings kill anyone?"

"It's a long story, and I'm not too sure how much your husband told you. Actually, I don't even know how much he even knows. Julie Billings' body was found yesterday after she tried to kill my friends Nate, Rob, and me out on Seguin."

"Huh?"

Jack knew his story sounded improbable. "Yeah, I kind of thought you might react that way. We were out there looking for something, and apparently she had been sent to protect what it was we were looking for. She shot at us and we shot at her, but we only hit her in the leg. Besides, we didn't know it was her… are you following?"

"Uh, I think so," she replied.

"Okay, so we got to the mainland, because my friend Rob needed medical attention, and when the Coast Guard went to scout the island, they found her body. It had been shot at close range and I swear that we didn't do it."

"You still haven't answered my question. Why would Mr. Billings kill John? Did he kill Adam, too?"

"To be honest, I don't know who killed Adam, but I know we

won't find out anything as long as we stay here. So, do you think you could unlock me?"

"Oh yeah. Sorry." Sally inserted the bulky iron key and turned it counter clockwise. The lock echoed as it clicked open and jarred the door free. "Okay, so where the hell is my husband?"

"I don't have any idea. Billings said that my friends left the island. Do you know anything about that?"

"It wouldn't surprise me," Sally replied. "Your boat's gone."

Jack stopped short of the foyer. To his left was a small window at about eye level. "Maybe someone just moved it or something. I really can't believe Nate and Kendra would leave me here."

"I was telling the girls the other day that I thought I remembered a girl named Kendra from high school, but that I couldn't quite put my finger on who she was," she explained. "Well, I went home after that and got my yearbook out and realized that she and I were both on the cheering squad sophomore year. After I saw the picture, all this stuff came back to me about her. I remembered that she got kicked off the team for fighting because someone made fun of her family."

"And your point is?" Jack inquired.

"My point is that she never had any friends before or after that. She was a total recluse. She just doesn't seem like your type. Jack, there was something just not right about that girl. For Christ's sake, she wore all black the rest of high school. I think that's your Kendra."

"Oh Jesus, can we skip the high school melodrama for now." Jack snatched her handbag from her. "Where's your cell phone?"

"Hey," she said, slapping his arm. "I told you, cell phones are illegal out here."

Jack pushed past her and walked through the double glass doors and up the stairs. "If cell phones are so illegal, why do you keep one in your purse? Don't tell me, it's for emergency purposes only. Well, guess what, sister? This is an emergency!"

As the two walked around to the front of the building, Jack looked around and saw all the streetlights turn on automatically up and down Main Street. Darkness had fallen on the island, and they were in violation.

Jack walked across the street to the gazebo, where the ground was slightly higher. He looked down at the phone screen. "Okay, two bars should be enough," he said to himself and stepped up onto the second step, just out from underneath the gazebo's roof.

"Jack, even if you get through, you'll get—"

"Will you shut up for a minute, please? It's ringing." He waved his hand at her and concentrated on the phone.

The phone rang three times before being picked up. "Coast Guard Group, Boothbay Harbor," proclaimed a male voice on the other end.

"I'm looking for a Richard O'Neil," Jack said.

"With whom am I speaking?"

"My name is Jack Chandler, this is an emergency—"

"Holy cow, Jack. This is Commander Morelli. I've been hoping you would call. Special Agent in Charge O'Neil is…" A loud screeching noise extruded from the little phone receiver and the line went dead.

"Well, what the hell happened?" Jack said, looking around to see if anyone had heard or seen them. He stepped down from the gazebo and walked over to Sally.

"I was trying to tell you that even if you got through, you'd get cut off," Sally explained. "All lines, mobile in particular, are closely monitored at night, especially when there are meetings."

"What the hell does that mean—monitored?" Jack looked at her as though she had three heads.

"You know how when you call the island, an operator picks up and connects you?"

"Yeah."

"When there isn't an operator on duty, the whole system is computerized. During the day it's pretty easy to get away with cell phone calls because the operator is usually too busy to even pay attention to the mobile phone monitor, but when the computer takes over, it catches every call. That's why you got cut off. Once the cell signal is identified, it's cut off," Sally said. "Mr. Billings' company designed the system. Apparently they do a lot of work for the government."

"What's the name of his company?" Jack asked.

"I don't know. Some company on the mainland."

Jack scratched his head. "Let me see that phone again, please."

"Jack, I told you. It isn't going to work," she said, handing him the small, metallic-colored device.

"Not the way you're thinking, no, but I've got an idea. I just hope that number I called uses the same cell phone company as yours." Jack took the phone, dialed several digits, and held it above his head to get the best reception.

"What the hell are you doing?" she asked.

"Just a long shot." Jack turned and began to walk toward Cranberry Lane. "Let's go pay your little Society a visit."

"No, Jack, they'll kill you," she shouted, running toward him. Once she caught up, she grasped his arm, slowing him slightly.

"Well, why not? Hell, they've killed everyone else," Jack said as he stopped and looked her in the eye. "Would it be better if I just made my way to Captain Davidson's house and killed him? I might as well. Everyone out here thinks I killed Adam."

"Jack, you're being irrational."

"Look, Sally. Go home. I'm not going to stay here and argue with you. Don't you get it? My parents didn't die in an accident. Davidson killed them and the Society covered it up. Now they've had both Adam Cyr and John killed. What do you expect me to do, just wait around for my turn? I don't think so. My friends got off this damned rock while it was safe, but I got stuck here, and goddamn it, I'm going to do something before more people get killed." Jack jerked his arm free from Sally's grasp and started jogging toward Cranberry Lane. A thin cover of ground fog hovered over the turf of the village green. Above the trees, Jack could see the gleam of the lighthouse. He fixed his eye on it and didn't look back.

"Oh Jesus, Jack," Sally said as she ran after him.

"Where the hell do you think you're going?" Jack asked, practically panting.

"Same place you are," Sally replied. "To the lighthouse."

* * *

After traveling the equivalent of a few city blocks, Jack slowed to a walk. Sally jogged around him as if daring him to chase her, but he was out of breath and out of shape.

"Sally, get down. You see the headlights?"

"Of course I see the headlights, but for Christ's sake, Jack, no one can see us from that far away. Relax," she said, pulling away from him and squinting at the vehicle. "Looks like Jimmy's Jeep."

"Yeah, and he just happened to turn down my driveway," Jack

said, rolling his eyes. "Do you realize that I haven't even been to my driveway?"

"Jack, where did he go? The Jeep vanished."

"No, no, he didn't go anywhere. Jimmy's smart. He knows that he can see everything that goes on out on the point from right there in the shade of those trees. No one can see him." Jack slapped at a mosquito that buzzed around his knee. "Let's go." He took off through the thick, wet ferns. Each one he passed sprayed him with an accumulation of mist and dew. A few fireflies floated above the ground, their tails lighting up the sky for a mere second.

Jack peered around the trunk of a lofty pine, no more than fifty feet from the Jeep. "Hold up. Stay behind me and keep down," he said to Sally, who was close behind him but, nonetheless, out of breath. Jack was probably the more out of shape of the two, but he had survived the past couple of days on pure adrenaline. "Look. You see that little light? It looks like the cherry of a cigarette."

"Well, Jimmy doesn't smoke," she assured him while looking around the other side of the tree. "Someone's got to be with him."

"Yeah, but who?" Jack reached into his fleece and pulled out a revolver.

"Jack, where the hell did you get the gun?"

"I borrowed it from Deputy Thorton. It's not like he really needs it now."

"What do you need with a gun?"

"Perhaps you didn't hear me when I went over the current body count."

"I heard you loud and clear, but what does that have to do with Jimmy? You know full well that Jimmy is on your side. Hell, if he wasn't, do you really think he would be spying on the Society?"

"Who says he's spying?" Jack checked the chamber of the gun, then put the safety back on, returning it to his inside pocket. "Regardless, we're not doing anyone any good by sitting here in the woods. What do you say we find out who he's entertaining in that Jeep?" He sprinted to the next tree.

Jack crawled up onto the driveway and walked toward the Jeep as if he were surrendering, but he really believed he had nothing to lose. If Jimmy was indeed his ally, he would be happy to see Jack. If not, well, he hadn't quite thought that far ahead, but it wouldn't matter. With Kyle in the meeting, Jimmy and Sally were the only ones he figured he could count on.

The back driver's side door flung open, and a figure jumped out as though there had been a fire. "Jack, is that you?" a man said as he walked toward Jack.

"Nate, thought you took off on the boat," Jack said.

"Leave? Are you nuts? This is too good an opportunity to just get up and go," Nate replied as if he were involved in some sort of capture-the-flag game.

Jimmy and Kendra quickly ran to Nate's side, but Sally was still hiding. Jack looked around for her but didn't say anything to them. Would Jimmy be upset at her for helping him escape?

"How the hell did you get out of jail?" Jimmy asked. "What's this I heard about someone leaving the island on your chartered boat?"

"Oh, it's a long story. I don't know where to start."

"Just tell them the truth, Jack. Jimmy's a big boy, he can take it," Sally said as she came out from the canvas of the trees, brushing off her jeans.

"Tell me what, Jack?" Jimmy looked sternly at Sally. Just as Jack had thought, he didn't seem exactly glad to see her. "Then I want you to tell me what you are doing out here after curfew."

"For Christ's sake, Jimmy, if it wasn't for her, I might be dead now," Jack said, taking a deep breath. "Speaking of which, I'm afraid that I have some bad news. John's dead, Jimmy."

"What do you mean, John's dead?" Jimmy looked at Jack in disbelief.

"Just what I said, John's dead. He was shot in the head back at the station." Jack was relieved to have told him, but knew the news would devastate Jimmy. John had been his best friend his whole life.

Tears formed in Jimmy's eyes. "Who was it, Jack?"

"I think it was Mr. Billings, at least that's who John was talking to when he got shot. I have to admit I never saw the guy's face. He was around the corner, in the hall. He said that he would be back for me later. He said he had a meeting to go to. It was like he was trying to torture me, knowing that I was locked up. He's the one that said that Nate and Kendra took the boat and left the island."

"So what about the boat?" Kendra asked. "Is it gone?" She glared at Sally like the two were archrivals.

"It's not in the harbor," Jack replied.

"How did you get out of jail?" Kendra asked. "Did she get you out?"

"I was looking for Jimmy and went down to the station," Sally explained. "Jack told me what happened and sure enough, John's body had been stuffed in the mop closet." She tried to give Jimmy a hug, but he pushed her away.

"This has gone way too far. I've had it with waiting; I say we go in there right now," Jimmy said, clenching his fists.

"I know how you feel, Jimmy," Jack said. "It's like I felt today when I realized my dad had been murdered rather than accidentally killed. The fact of the matter is that we need to bring all these guys down." He spoke as though he were sincere, but he really wanted to find Davidson and rip him limb from limb. "What are you guys doing down here by my house anyway?"

"We've got a pretty good view of the lighthouse and the building they're in," Nate replied.

"So? What the hell good is that?" Jack asked.

"We got Foster to wear a wire." Nate pointed to the receiver in the Jeep, and the recorder hooked up to it. "When they've spilled all their guts, we're going in."

"When did they start?" Sally asked.

"About fifteen minutes ago. It appears that they are as freaked out as we are. I don't think they're all on the same page," Nate said, getting back into the Jeep.

"Why do you think that?" Sally asked.

"Well, all of them except for Kyle seem to speak on a regular basis, from what we've heard, but Kyle wasn't the only one who didn't know about Adam Cyr. It seems as though Henry McKay and this Billings guy are in it together. Hell, they even have Davidson there," Nate explained.

"Why do they have him there?" Sally asked.

"To protect him from Jack, I assume." Nate looked up at Jack and said, "They didn't even find out about Julie Billings' murder or our little visit to Seguin until this morning, and guess who told them?"

"Good old Mr. Billings?" Jack asked.

"Right you are," Nate replied. "This guy's one bad dude. I don't know what you think, but we might want to call O'Neil. I don't know if we can handle this ourselves."

"Yeah, well, I've already tried that route. I called the number after Sally freed me and got cut off," Jack explained.

"What did he say before you got cut off?" Nate asked.

"Nothing, he wasn't even there. I spoke to Commander Morelli for a second and then the line went dead."

"Well, boys, I hate to say it, but I doubt we can get through to them at all. The radio frequency has been jammed as well. Probably 'cause of the meeting. I assume you guys are finding out the hard way how paranoid these people are," Jimmy said, staring at Jack's fleece. "What's that, Jack?" He pointed to the butt end of the gun sticking out.

"Um, that's John's gun. I'm sorry, Jimmy, but given the circumstances, I thought it would be a good idea to take it before leaving the jail."

"You're probably right," Jimmy said. "Hell, they probably have an arsenal in there."

"So when do we go in?" Jack asked.

"As soon as we have enough to put them away for good. We can't just rely on testimony from Kyle. We need this tape and we have to hope that he gets them to admit to everything," Jimmy explained. "I want to have it on tape that they killed John."

"Actually, Jimmy, with the minutes we found today—"

"I told you," Jimmy interrupted. "I don't think those old pieces of paper will mean much when all is said and done. I want these bastards to pay for killing John!"

Chapter Twenty-One

At around 8:30, Arlington Cooper took off his reading glasses, rubbed the corner of his eyes, and closed an inch-thick file folder in front of him. He stared intently at his four colleagues, and the dark bags under his eyes accentuated his fatigue.

Kyle Foster and Henry McKay glared at each other from opposite ends of the long, rectangular table.

Cooper checked his watch one more time before passing a quick glance to Peter Jacobs, who was sitting with a pen and fresh pad of paper, eager to begin taking the meeting minutes.

"I call this special meeting of the Carroll Island Lighthouse Society to order. Are there any special announcements before we get down to the business at hand?" Cooper looked over at Kyle and said, "Yes, Brother Foster."

"Yeah, what is the business at hand?"

"Brother Foster, we will get to that. Please remember this is a time for announcements pertaining to the well-being of the Society or the island as a whole," Cooper explained.

"Okay, well, I have a question pertaining to the well-being of all of us," Kyle said. "I don't think we should talk about anything until it is addressed."

"Fair enough. What is the question?" Cooper asked.

"I would like to know why Brothers Billings and McKay brought Brian Davidson here tonight."

"That is indeed a good question," Cooper replied, nodded at Kyle, and turned his attention to the men in question. "I will ask one of you two to please speak on the reasoning for this circumstance before we continue."

"Yes, Brother Cooper," McKay responded. "We felt that with Jack Chandler back on the island, the apparent death threats to Captain Davidson, and the murder of Adam Cyr, it would be prudent, for his safety, to bring him here."

"That's nonsense, Henry," Kyle said. "You know damned well that Jack is in jail."

"Yes, Brother Foster, I am aware of that, but we don't have proof that he is the one behind the death or the threats. If it isn't him, then Davidson would not be safe," McKay explained with a grin.

"Brother McKay, do you have any idea who could be a threat to Davidson or any other island resident?" Cooper asked.

"There are many people who could be dangerous out here, lots of secrets, Brother Cooper, scary secrets. Mr. Chandler's girlfriend for instance, how much did you know about her before her arrival?" McKay asked.

"Well then, Brother McKay, since this is an openly honest Society, let me ask you a question." Kyle stood up, trembling.

"Ask away, old man," McKay said.

"Did anyone in this room have anything to do with the death of

Adam Cyr?" Kyle asked with a sharp and directive tone. He knew McKay would have to answer honestly.

"Well, Brother Foster, I suppose the answer to that would have to be yes," McKay said, turning away.

"Brother Cooper, I feel that it would be in the best interest of the Society for Brother McKay to fully disclose the events that led to the untimely death of Mr. Cyr," Kyle said.

"You mean, you don't know, Kyle?" McKay said, grinning. "Doesn't that sheriff tell you everything?"

"What Jimmy and I talk about is between the two of us. If you want to ask him questions, I suggest you call him here."

"Settle down, you two," Cooper said, banging his gavel. "Brother McKay, as I am unaware of the circumstances, I will speak on behalf of the whole Society and ask that you tell us everything you know."

McKay's grin was gone and replaced with a look of anger. "If I have no other choice, I will, but I would ask that Brother Foster also answer any questions that may pertain to the events."

"Granted, but I will let you know right now that I will have the final say as to whether or not they are relevant," Cooper explained. "No one is on trial here. We all just want to know the truth."

McKay cleared his throat and looked directly at Kyle. "Two days ago, I got word that Mr. Cyr had been seen leaving Vinalhaven. Admittedly a little suspicious, I had him followed because he was not on the boat he was scheduled to leave on. He was followed down the coast, where he was seen leaving Five Islands on a lobster boat. He didn't return to Five Islands yesterday, but we heard from a Coast Guard broadcast over the VHF that there had been an altercation on Seguin."

"Jesus, first you had him followed and then you had him killed for taking a ride on a boat?" Kyle interrupted.

"Please, Brother Foster," Cooper yelled, seemingly loosing his cool.

"The same Coast Guard broadcast reported that a boat fitting the description of Mr. Chandler's was anchored off Seguin yesterday as well," McKay said.

"Continue," Cooper said.

"The Coast Guard later found the body of Brother Billings' daughter, Julie. She had been shot twice; once in the leg, and once in the head. The latter shot killed her. It should be noted that according to another Coast Guard transmission we overheard, the shots had been apparently fired from two different guns. We also learned that while on the island, one of Mr. Chandler's crew was severely injured and ultimately airlifted while he and two friends took another boat to the Boothbay Harbor Coast Guard Station. The Coast Guard didn't think any of them had killed Julie, but that another person had been on the island," McKay explained, his hand resting on Billings' shoulder.

Billings' facial expression was cold, emotionless.

"So you made the assumption that it was Mr. Cyr?" Cooper asked.

"There was no one else, Brother Cooper," McKay said. "It should be known that because of this little visit of Jack's, we lost some very valuable items."

"Which items?" Jacobs asked.

"The sealed meeting minutes, Brother Jacobs," Billings interrupted. "The sealed minutes that Brother Foster swore to protect when you took the post as light keeper on Seguin years ago."

"And I did protect them," Kyle explained. "I hid them when I left the island. I hid them on the mainland. I also left the coordinates to their whereabouts in the lighthouse if we were to need them and I was dead." He was surprised that they knew he had left the engravings, but also knew full well that lying about leaving them would do no good. His throat began to close and his heart pounded in his chest. The damage was done, out in the open. He hoped they wouldn't call his bluff on why he left the engravings and hid the minutes.

"Why didn't you share those coordinates with us?" Cooper asked.

"I did," Kyle replied. "I told Brother Jacobs where the coordinates were marked."

McKay laughed. "Brother Cooper, may I ask a few follow-up questions?"

"This isn't a trial, McKay, but proceed," Cooper replied, "respectfully."

"Brother Jacobs, did Brother Foster reveal to you this location?"

"Yes," Jacobs replied.

"So let me get this clear," McKay said. "Brother Foster, did you tell anyone else, who has no affiliation with this group, the location of the engravings?"

Kyle hesitated, sweating, breathing deeply. He knew this would be his undoing. "I told Adam Cyr."

"Why would you divulge such information to Mr. Cyr? Were you hoping that he would do your bidding and bring the information to Mr. Chandler?" McKay paced back and forth between the members like he was in a courtroom.

Kyle got out of his chair and stood in front of Arlington Cooper. "I do not intend to answer any more of Brother McKay's questions." He feared imminent reprisal, but still had faith he might be rescued.

Cooper demanded, "Why won't you answer any more of his questions? Do you not feel that they are pertinent?"

"No, I don't. I think that Brothers McKay and Billings are trying to avert the acknowledgement of recent incidents by finding fault in others, such as myself. I admit, I have wronged this group, and I should indeed be punished for my actions, but I did not take anyone's life." Kyle stood tall. He had a renewed sense of vigor and assuredness. "I will, however, make a compromise. If Brothers McKay and Billings disclose their involvement in the murders of Timothy Chandler and Adam Cyr, I will tell this group all of my indiscretions."

"Agreed," Cooper said and pointed to Billings and McKay. "To what extent were the two of you involved in these incidents?"

"As for the deaths, I can speak for both of us in saying that neither of us killed them," McKay said.

"Did you order their deaths?" Kyle asked.

"Old man, you know as well as I do that I had nothing to do with Timothy's death, apart from our cover-up of the event as an island and as a Society," McKay replied.

"And Mr. Cyr?" Cooper asked.

"You'd have to ask Captain Davidson how he died," Billings replied.

"Are you saying that Davidson acted alone in the killing of Adam Cyr, like he had done with Timothy Chandler?" Kyle asked.

"Why don't we ask him?" Billings replied.

"Brother Billings, please go to the tower and bring the captain before us," Cooper instructed.

Robert Billings disappeared into the darkness of the stairwell while the others remained silent. Cooper leaned over and whispered for Kyle to return to his seat. Kyle felt a huge weight lifted, as he knew that he had gained the backing of Cooper and perhaps even Jacobs. He didn't, however, want to see Davidson in the Society chamber again. He knew that it was a delay tactic on McKay's and Billings' part, but didn't know why they would try and weasel themselves out of the most recent killing by putting it all on Davidson, who made up only one-third of the guilty party. He would have bet the others felt the same.

* * *

"Hey, guys, I've heard enough. I say we move now," Nate said, loading a clip into his gun and making sure the safety was on. "What do you think, Jack, ready?"

Jack sat there, silent. He didn't know what to think—what to do. Everything had all happened so fast.

"Nate's right, it's time we go. I'm worried they might do something to Kyle seeing as he's admitted to screwing them over." Jimmy looked over to the two women. "You two are staying here."

"Fine by me," Sally replied.

"That's a load of crap, Jimmy," Kendra said. "I can handle myself as well as any guy can."

"Kendra, Jimmy's right," Sally said. "Why don't you and I just sit back a ways and let them handle it?"

"Bite me, bitch," Kendra said. "I'm surprised you don't want me to get shot so you can move in on Jack."

"Whoa, whoa, hold on, Kendra. What's going on here?" Jack got between the two, fearing the worst. "What's this all about? Sally was just trying to be nice."

"It's no use," Sally interrupted. "I told you earlier that she has a mean streak in her."

"Sally, go over with Jimmy and let me handle this, please," Jack said, pushing her away.

"What? You don't think I can handle myself either, Jack?" Kendra glared at him.

"Quite frankly, I don't know what's gotten into you, but I don't want you with us when we go down there."

"Come on, Jack, admit it," Kendra said as a tear rolled down her cheek. "You've been keeping me down this whole trip. Everything's been about you and Nate. Did you ever think that maybe I should go hunt for that box at the chapel or that I could help take out Captain Davidson?"

"What are you talking about?" Jack asked. "First of all, you didn't seem to have any interest in the little treasure hunt Nate and I went on. Second, what is this crap about going after Davidson? Nate and I have never even entertained the idea."

"After everything that has happened in the last couple of days, you can actually stand there and say that you never planned on coming out here to get revenge on Davidson? Even after you found out that he had actually killed your father and sank the ferry himself?" Kendra looked up at him in amazement.

"No, Kendra, I told you before and I'll tell you again, that isn't why I'm here and never has been." Jack sighed. "I don't need revenge to live the rest of my life. I want answers and I want people to be held accountable, but what good would it do for me to come out here and kill some old drunk?"

"You're actually serious, Jack, aren't you?" Kendra had a crazed look on her face. "You self-righteous son of a bitch! Had you ever given an ounce of thought to the possibility that maybe he'd hurt other people along the way? Of course not, you only care about you, right? It's all about Jack Chandler." She snatched the revolver from Jack's hand. "Well, the hell with you guys. I'll take care of it all myself." She dashed into the woods, just out of the reach of Nate, who had tried to grab her as she ran for the trees.

"Jesus, Kendra, would you come back here?" Jack yelled. "She's absolutely friggin' hysterical, perhaps certifiably insane." He was freaked out by the outbreak he had just witnessed from the woman he planned to marry. "Guys, I don't—"

"Jack, it's not your fault, man. She flipped," Nate said. "Someone was bound to sooner or later. It's been pretty rough the past couple of days."

"Yeah, but the things she said," Jack said. "She was talking about things that neither you nor I have ever spoken about."

"About Davidson, you mean?" Jimmy asked, holding Sally's arm.

"Yeah, she seems to think that I really planned on coming out here to kill him, and she's pissed that I never intended to do so."

"Jack, we can't worry about Kendra right now," Nate said. "We need to bust up the party at the lighthouse and do it before they hurt Kyle."

"Do you have enough to go on?" Jack asked.

Nate said, "These guys will all die in jail."

"What about Kyle?" Jimmy intervened.

"Relax. Kyle will be fine. I promise," Nate said as he donned his navy blue FBI pullover. "Oh, and if you're worried about Kendra, the lighthouse is really the only place she'd go if she is looking for Davidson. Chances are, she's off hiding in the woods waiting for one of us to come get her."

"You want me to go look for her?" Sally asked.

"No, Sally," Jack replied. "It's far too dangerous. We don't know what state of mind she's in, and she has a gun. I appreciate your offer, but it would be best for you to just stay back out of the way of everything."

"Sally, Jack's right," Jimmy said. "You just stay here in the Jeep and listen for anything to come over the radio. Try and reach the Coast Guard if you can. Tell them we have a serious situation."

"Jimmy, the signal's jammed," Sally said. "Has been all night."

"I know that, honey, but let's just hope," Jimmy replied and kissed her on the forehead.

Nate, Jack, and Jimmy scurried into the woods, leaving Sally all by herself at the Jeep.

"Hold up, guys. What do we do when we get to the house?" Jack asked. "How do we get in there without being seen?"

"Kyle unlocked the door to the bulkhead. We're going to have to be really quiet, but we should be able to surprise them," Jimmy responded.

"Obviously you guys have thought this out, but what happens next?" Jack asked. "I don't suppose you think they'll just agree to surrender?"

"Guns, Jack. We have guns," Nate said, grinning.

Jack rolled his eyes and said, "Yes, I understand that, thanks, but we don't have backup. Are we just going to point guns at them and ask them to walk nicely to the town dock and then sit there while we try to get help?"

"Oh no, we're going hogtie them," Jimmy said.

"Excuse me?" Jack's eyes widened.

"I've got those plastic fence ties. Tighten those things on their wrists and ankles. You know behind their backs, hurts like a bitch."

The three came to the clearing in the woods. Lying in the wet underbrush, they were about five feet from the bulkhead. The door was slightly ajar and inside was darker than the night.

"Jack, you stay behind us and keep down," Nate said, waving his gun.

"Okay, just give the word," Jack responded, his teeth chattering slightly.

* * *

The outer door of the water tower creaked like it hadn't been opened in some time. The structure was just as Kyle had described. Its thin, wooden, eight-foot walls served to protect the bulkhead, a concrete-reinforced stone structure with two rusted iron doors on top.

"Was there another house or building here before?" Nate asked, peering at the ominous entrance to the ground.

"Not for as long as I've lived here," Jimmy said, looking at Jack, who nodded in agreement.

"It's got to be fifteen or so feet to the building," Nate said. "Kind of a weird place for a bulkhead, you think?"

"Purposely built, I would assume. You have to remember that The Lighthouse Society has been here as long as there have been inhabitants, and it's been secret the whole time," Jack said, looking curiously at the doors. He backed away from the double doors and contemplated the situation. Where had Kendra run off to? Was she okay? He wondered what dangerous situation might face them on the other side of the heavy iron partitions. But he also knew that he had come a long way and that a successful mission by the three could change the face of Carroll Island forever. Would his father have approved of what he was doing? Jack ultimately wondered if they had waited too long and Kyle was dead.

Nate pushed the two out of the way and grabbed one of the rust-covered handles. He pulled upwards ever so slightly, looking back at the others. "Ah, to hell with it." He jerked the handle, and the door popped open with a piercing sound that echoed in the tower. Nate stood there looking into the dark, cavernous tunnel. It was pitch black and smelled of must and mold.

"Can you see anything?" Jimmy asked, peering over Nate's shoulder.

"Well, it's dark down there," Nate whispered. "I can tell you that, but then again, you'd know that if you had the balls to go in."

"Why are you whispering?" Jack asked and crawled to the edge of the door.

"Because I don't want anyone down there to hear me," Nate replied. "What are you doing on your hands and knees?" He looked down and made eye contact with Jack, who was practically under him.

"Okay, first of all, you just opened a door that probably hasn't been opened in over a century. If they didn't hear that, they won't hear us talking up here," Jack said. "Second, I'm on the ground because I don't have a gun. I feel safer down here."

"The two of you are like an old married couple," Jimmy quipped.

Jack rose gingerly to his feet and stepped through the doorway. "Someone's gotta go first—might as well be the guy without the gun." He slowly descended a couple of steps and turned. "Nate, give me your lighter."

"How about a flashlight?" Jimmy asked.

"No, too much light. If there are cracks in the foundation, it will seep through." Jack took the lighter from Nate's hand.

"How much difference could that really make?" Nate said.

"A lot, given the fact their meeting room is only lit by candles," Jack said. His tone reflected a renewed sense of assurance. His adrenaline flowed and he descended with an awkward eagerness. He wasn't in law enforcement like his two colleagues, but had learned that neither of them really had much of a leg up when it came to actual hostile situations, something that was comforting and scary at the same time. Comforting because it was good for his self-esteem, scary because it meant that between the three of them, none had experience in such situations.

Jack got to the bottom of the staircase and onto level ground. He could only see a few feet in front of him, and the tunnel walls were only about four feet apart. He brushed his hand along the wall, which, like the doorway foundation, was constructed of stone with concrete-filled cracks. The wall was damp and cold. He took a few more steps and decided to wait for his friends, who were still negotiating the stairs.

"Kyle said it was just a wood door," Jimmy said. "Probably pretty old and brittle."

"What, I'm just supposed to kick it open and say hi?" Jack gave them both a dumbfounded look. "I don't think so. I don't want to be the first guy to get shot. You guys at least get paid to do this."

As the flame from the lighter Jack was holding flickered out, they could see a thin band of light directly in front of them, about five feet away.

"Come on, guys, this is ridiculous," Jimmy said. He brushed between Jack and Nate and ran at the door, cannon-balling himself right at the middle of it. The door split open like a pea pod, clouding the air with a moldy dust.

"Jack, get down," Nate said, charging ahead and jumping over Jimmy, who was on the ground. He extended his gun. "Everybody freeze, FBI."

The room was small and looked like any other old basement. Four men sat with stunned looks on their faces as Nate ran into the room waving his gun.

A single candle was placed in front of each of them and they sat motionless. A fifth candle sat atop a three-foot-long pole mounted into the ground, but the chair behind it was empty.

"What in God's name is the meaning of this?" Arlington Cooper said as he stood up and squinted. "Is that you, Jimmy?"

"I said freeze, goddamn it," Nate yelled. "That means don't move! Now sit down!" He pushed Cooper back into his armchair. "The party's over. You're all under arrest."

"For what?" Jacobs asked.

"Jimmy, you want to list off all the counts or should I?" Nate turned as Jimmy and Jack came to his side.

Jimmy's hand shook as he reached into his pocket and took out an index card with fuzzy writing on it. "Hmm. Well, Agent Richardson, it's a pretty long list, but let's start off with obstruction of justice in a capital investigation and conspiracy to cover up murder."

"Are you mad?" Cooper responded. "This is private property."

"Well, I guess we should add trespassing to the list," Jack said excitedly, pulling out a folded stack of paper from his fleece pocket. "You're damned right it's private property, and it was deeded to me— Jack Chandler—upon the death of my father."

"Nice. Where did you get that?" Nate asked.

"It was in the box with the minutes," Jack replied.

"Minutes?" Cooper asked. "Are you saying that your evidence is based on old meeting minutes? What minutes?"

Jack handed him one of the documents he had kept in his pocket. "Jesus, Jack, what are you doing?" Jimmy asked.

"Showing him the proof."

Cooper held the paper over the flame of his candle and laughed. "Thanks, Jack."

"So it's Arlington Cooper, right?"

"Indeed it is, Mr. Chandler."

"Mr. Cooper, why would you burn a document if it wasn't true?" Jack asked, staring at the aging man. "Then it must all be true, right?"

"True, untrue, we'll never know. Will we?" Cooper said.

"Well, we might not ever have another copy of today's weather report, but as for probable cause, I think you just proved at least that much." Jack reached into his other pocket and pulled out another set of papers. "As for the minutes, I think we'll keep them."

A haunting laugh came from the corner of the room. There sat Kyle Foster, the flickering light of his candle casting a shadow over his face. He coughed a couple of times, leaned forward, and extinguished the wick of his candle with his fingers.

"Foster, Jesus, what are you doing?" McKay shouted from right next to him.

"I'm doing what I should have done a long time ago," Kyle responded and stood up. "Gentlemen, per our bylaws, business can't be done without five members—"

"Brother Foster, sit down!" Cooper ordered.

"I quit, Cooper," Kyle said, walking over toward Nate and the other two. "I quit. You're going to jail, and eventually to hell. Maybe I'll see you there."

"They have no real proof, Foster," McKay said. "Who's going to let a decade-and-a-half-old set of meeting minutes into a trial? No one will believe them."

Kyle laughed as he looked McKay in the eyes. "Even if they didn't believe them, they'd believe me."

"Nonsense, they wouldn't believe you over the four of us," Jacobs intervened.

"You're right. Those aren't good odds, are they?" Kyle said, looking back over at Jimmy, who nodded with a smile. "But the odds favor the wild card."

"The wild card, Foster?" McKay chuckled.

Kyle ripped open his button-down shirt, exposing the wire he wore. "It's all on here, gentlemen."

Jack looked around the room and realized that something was missing. "Five candles, four of them," he uttered softly. *Where is the fifth member?*

Jimmy officially read Cooper, McKay, and Jacobs their rights. They had acted like they would put up a fight, but in the end, they were probably all too tired from hiding so many secrets and carrying such a heavy burden.

"I can assure you your rights will be respected in this case," Jimmy said, leading them toward the stairs. "I hardly think any of you gave much thought to any of their rights before killing Adam or John."

"You have no proof we had anything to do with that. It was all Billings," Jacobs said.

"Billings? Damn, Jack. Where is he?" Jimmy looked around frantically.

"When we heard you coming, we sent him to get help," McKay said.

"That's bull," Kyle replied. "They sent him to the lighthouse to get Davidson."

"All right, let's get these men down to the jail so we can call for some backup. We'll need to reel Kendra in somehow as well," Nate said as he paused and looked toward the staircase. "You hear that?"

"What is that?" Jack asked.

The loud blast of a gunshot echoed into the basement of the building. Jack began to climb the stairs, but was quickly pulled back by Nate as a body tumbled toward them, its lifeless limbs bouncing off the wood steps, each impact splashing blood from the fatal gunshot wound to the head.

"Holy crap, it's Davidson," Jimmy said, looking at the head of the man, which was mangled from the close proximity of the shot.

Nate ran past the body and up the stairs, slowing as he got to the top, his gun extended out in front of him. Jack was right behind him.

"Jack, get back. She has a gun," Nate said.

At the top of the stairs, they followed a short corridor to the side door of the building and paused.

"Yes, Jack, come help your little friend."

Jack recognized the voice as the same from the jail.

"Aren't you two going to come out and join us?"

"It's O'Neil," Nate whispered to Jack.

"It's the same man that threatened to kill me in the jail," Jack responded, not able to keep his voice down.

The two inched closer to the door and saw the man with his gun pointed at Kendra's head.

"Shouldn't someone arrest this woman for shooting the captain, or are you glad she did it, Mr. Chandler?" Special Agent in Charge Richard O'Neil and Robert Billings were one and the same. Jack had fleeting thoughts of all the evidence he had missed, the voices, surveillance cameras, and even the phony telephone number he called with Morelli on the other end. Did that mean Morelli was in on it too?

"I didn't shoot him, Jack. O'Neil did," Kendra pleaded.

"Agent Richardson, I came out here to help you, and you have the audacity to point your gun at me?" O'Neil said.

"You came to help us, or kill us?" Jack asked.

"Well, I really hadn't thought that far ahead, but I'll have to kill you if you don't let me get away."

"Not a chance," Nate said. "Damn, I had a gut feeling from the beginning about you."

"Okay, well, you won't mind if I shoot Kendra, will you?" O'Neil asked. "She shot her father and then tried to shoot me, but I wrestled the gun away from her."

"Her father?" Jack's jaw dropped.

"It's time to wake up, Mr. Chandler. Davids, Davidson—both from Rockland. Let's see. Kendra's father left her when she was young and she never forgave him. She knew that you could get her out here, so she hooked up with you. It's sad really. You being used so much," O'Neil said with an insidious laugh.

"No, I don't believe it," Jack yelled as Jimmy brought the others out to the porch. "Kendra, tell me he's lying."

"I didn't kill him, Jack," Kendra said.

"That's not what I asked."

"Yes, okay, my real last name was Davidson. I changed it in middle school, but I didn't come back here to kill him. It just happened."

"Just happened?" Jack said. "There have been far too many coincidences the past couple days."

"I didn't kill him, Jack…" Kendra said as a shot rang off in the distance. The left side of O'Neil's chest exploded from the shot.

"Down. Everybody down on the ground! Special Agent Scott Morelli, Federal Bureau of Investigation," Morelli said, walking from behind a shadow.

"Commander Morelli?" Jack looked up at him.

"Yeah, I got your text message. I've been following Agent O'Neil for a while now; he's under investigation for fraud, embezzlement, and money laundering. I didn't have a warrant and needed probable cause. I'm sorry I lied to you before."

"How did you know to come out here?" Jack asked.

"It wasn't till our cut-off phone call and your text message that I was sure he was in on this," Morelli said. "I tried to get back to you about your girlfriend here, but I guess I was a little late."

"Yeah, well, I don't know who this woman is," Jack said and turned his back toward her.

"I didn't kill him, Jack," Kendra said. "Here, look in the chamber. All the bullets are still inside."

"That has nothing to do with me, Kendra, Ms. Davids, Davidson, whatever your name is," Jack said.

"Put the gun down, Ms. Davidson," Morelli commanded.

"It's still all about you. You can just walk away from here and forget this all happened, right?" she said as she cocked the gun.

Jimmy saw her raise the loaded Smith & Wesson, lunged forward, and tackled Jack out of her path. Much like a Secret Service agent protecting a vacationing president, Jimmy took a bullet for his friend. Kendra shot him squarely in the abdomen.

Nate had seen her cock the revolver as well, but was not as quick on the draw; his one shot failed to reach her before she shot at Jack. Seeing that the impact of his shot had knocked her to the ground, he quickly rushed over and kicked the gun from her blood-soaked hand. The shot had hit her in the shoulder, entering and exiting slightly above the collarbone.

* * *

The large white and orange Coast Guard helicopter reminded Jack of the one that had rescued Rob the day before. Its rotors spun rapidly as it got ready to take off. Commander Morelli and the pilot had covered Jimmy's body with a black sheet. He stood and watched in shock as Sally screamed and begged the lifeless body to come back to her. Jimmy had given his life to save Jack, and he felt hollow inside.

Jack embraced Sally as she came over to him, sobbing as he stood stone-faced. Perhaps the emotion of the situation hadn't hit yet. His quest for truth was over, but it hadn't been what he had envisioned.

Jack looked back toward Agent Morelli, who was taking a statement from Nate. The two must have seen Jack staring in their direction and saluted him. He raised his right hand and saluted back, not sure of its full implication, but aware of their bond.

As Jack and Sally walked onto the gravel driveway toward the road, he glanced over to Kendra, who was handcuffed to a gurney.

"You can't leave me now, Jack," Kendra sobbed.

"I can't really leave someone I never even knew, can I?" Jack replied coldly.

Chapter Twenty-Two

Although the driving rain had stopped and the ceiling of thick, dark cumulonimbus clouds began to lift from the surface of chilly Penobscot Bay, three-foot whitecaps continued to pound down on Kendra's head with unrelenting consistency. The fog smothered her like a gray blanket. Her thrashing arms and legs had been treading the murky water for nearly a half an hour and were weary. Her toes curled inward from the raw exposure to the sixty-degree water, and she clenched her hands in fists to ward off muscle cramps.

In that seemingly never-ending half hour, she had yet to see a single soul. No Coast Guard rescue boats, no lobsterman catching up from a slow day hampered by the inclement weather, not even a curious seal had popped his head out of the water to survey the ocean surface. Only miles and miles of choppy water and the occasional multicolored lobster buoy. The little cone-shaped markers offered little solace and not nearly enough buoyancy to support her small frame.

The ever-present clang of navigational bells had provided her false hope. Each time she swam in the direction of the distinct and almost haunting sound, it seemed to just get farther and farther away. Perhaps it was a sound her tired brain was manifesting, playing tricks on her.

And when she saw the first of two dim lights barely shine through the thick fog cover, she thought those, too, must be in her head. They continued to pulse, appearing to get brighter as she drifted with the current of the water. Each light shone through the clouds about every thirty seconds, and Kendra was certain they had to be from Owl's Head Lighthouse to the south and Rockland Breakwater Lighthouse, which appeared closer to her.

If only I can make it to the breakwater, she thought, timing each deep breath so she didn't ingest a mouthful of seawater. That would surely drown her. Drown her when it appeared she was so close to safety. *Keep fighting, girl. It's your only chance.*

As the distance between bobbing lobster buoys got shorter and shorter, Kendra knew she was near the half-mile-long granite jetty. The light emanating from the end of the breakwater became brighter still, illuminating the water around her. She anticipated colliding with one of the thousands of giant granite blocks making up the breakwater, yet each long-reaching stroke grasped nothing more than an armful of water.

Kendra longed to plant her feet on terra firma. What she would do after that, she hadn't a clue.

Her right shoulder was perfectly numb now. The pain from the gunshot wound was masked by the cold saltwater.

For the first time since she was a young girl, she longed for the comfort of her mother's arms. Yet she knew full well that if she survived, if she made landfall at all, her mother would not be waiting. Kendra hoped no one would be searching or waiting for her. There wasn't a person on earth she could trust now. No one.

Chapter Twenty-Three

When Jack awoke the next morning, he hesitated before opening his eyes. The thin walls of his room revealed the absence of rain outside. He knew he would have heard it; the pitter-patter had been like a soundtrack to him the past couple of days. Sun, then rain, then sun, then more rain; all the while, a constant foreboding wind had churned the sea around him and his friends.

The walls were an off-white color. They were pale and blank, much like how Jack felt. The light in the room was dim and low. It seemed like any other Sunday, and Sunday was Jack's least favorite day. Nothing good ever happened on Sundays. For years Jack woke up on Sundays with his head pounding and his memory all but empty. It was an all-too-familiar feeling, the feeling of a wasted weekend. As he lay there in the stiff barracks-style bed, with its tight, thin sheets, he wondered what was next. He was confused, lost, and hurt. For all intents and purposes, everything was blurry.

Jack reached his sweaty hands over the side of the bed and grasped the rounded metal frame below the mattress. He garnered just enough strength to sit up and swing his feet over the side of the bed, and they landed on his damp and soiled clothes. He kicked the clothes aside. The linoleum-tiled floor was cold against his skin.

A small stream of light came in from a single, narrow window near the foot of the bed. Jack shielded his eyes as he approached it. He looked down at his watch and saw that the hands were still. They read 10:49 a.m.

The night before seemed very distant to Jack. He had gone through the weekend on full adrenaline, and then after the Coast Guard showed up and brought him back to Rockland, he crashed. He barely even remembered going to bed or eating.

As he looked out of his second-floor room at the Rockland Coast Guard Station, he smiled as he saw a couple of small sailboats go by with happy families aboard. He realized that although his life had turned upside down in the last forty-eight hours, the lives of others had gone on. He knew that it would take time for him to fully comprehend some of the frightening realizations he had come to know while on the island, but that someday things would be okay. He knew that even for troubled people like Kendra and the Society members, who lived their lives through the deception of others, life would indeed go on. While they were probably headed down the road to the new prison in Warren, Jack knew the people of Carroll Island were finally free to live their lives however they chose.

Jack could hear footsteps in the hall outside and knew that someone was coming for him. He dreaded having to tell such an improbable story to a panel of stiff, white-shirted drones, yet he also knew Nate would be there to fill in any holes. As he waited and listened to the steps draw closer, he wondered how Sally was doing and if they would make her talk about the terrible ordeal that claimed the life of her husband, who had given his life for Jack.

He turned as he heard three distinct knocks on the door of his room.

"Are you awake, Jack?" Nate asked from the other side of the door.

Jack walked toward the windowless door and said, "Well, cop, if I wasn't, I would be now. Why didn't you just come in?"

Jack opened the door and saw his friend standing before him. Nate was wearing a gray sweat suit with big blue letters on the front that read "FBI." He smirked at his friend.

"How ya feeling, buddy?" Nate asked as though nothing had happened, but Jack knew he was just trying to be comforting.

"Tired," Jack replied.

"I can definitely understand that," Nate said. "Unfortunately, we have to do the whole debriefing thing. I realize it's a pain, but rules are rules. Hell, they wanted to do it first thing this morning, but Morelli convinced them we needed the extra rest."

Jack walked out into the long, empty corridor, which had at set of double doors at each end. The surroundings were unfamiliar to him; such a feeling was par for the course these days. Nate was leaning against the opposite wall as if the wall kept him from falling to the ground.

"How's Sally?" Jack asked.

"She's doing okay," Nate replied. "They brought her up to County General, where she would be a little more comfortable."

"Well, I don't know how much good I'll be with a bunch of questions, but I'll do my best," Jack said. He realized that the topic of Sally would inevitably lead to talking about Jimmy, and that made him uncomfortable.

"Oh, don't worry about it, man, Commander Morelli and I will be doing most of the talking," Nate explained. "The reports have all been filed, but there is going to be a special investigation into how former Special Agent in Charge O'Neil, or as we also came to know him, Billings, was able to breach the system so effectively."

"And what about Kyle?"

"Believe it or not, Kyle got up at six and has already left to go back to the island," Nate said with a smile. "Granted, they'll need to have some further discussion with him and he will have to testify, but he's not being charged."

"Oh, that's good. I assumed he'd get some fraud charges or something just for being a part of the Society and all for so many years."

"Well, that would usually be the case, but there are certainly special circumstances which allow us to leave him out of any further charges the Society members will face," Nate explained. "So anyway, grab a shower and meet me in the conference room."

"And where's the conference room?" Jack asked. "I don't have a clue where I am."

"Sorry," Nate replied. "Down the hall, through the doors, and to the left." He turned and began walking down the hall when he suddenly stopped and looked back at Jack. He took a deep breath and was about to speak.

"There's something you're not telling me, isn't there?" Jack said. "Something about Sally?"

"No, Jack. Not Sally," Nate replied. "It's Kendra—"

"On her way to rotting in jail, I hope."

"There's been another accident, Jack."

"What kind of accident?"

"Kendra was lost overboard last night on the return trip from the island. The seas were rough, and we were tossed by a rogue wave."

"Did you find her?" Jack asked. "Is she dead?"

"Helicopters are still searching the coastal area, but it doesn't look good. You'll know as soon as we do." Nate heaved a sigh as he ran his fingers through his hair. "I'm sorry, Jack."

"Any chance she got away?"

"In those waters? Not likely."

* * *

Jack entered the conference room, where five men sat at a horseshoe-shaped table. He walked in slowly as his nerves got the best of him. He looked toward the men, but realized they were too caught up in whatever conversation they were engaged in to notice him there.

He cleared his throat and smiled as the men stopped talking and looked his way.

"Hi, Jack," Nate said. He was now sporting a pale blue oxford and a red tie.

Jack smiled at him, but said nothing. He recognized Agent Morelli and Nate, but had never seen the other three men, who looked to be in their late forties to early fifties. One of them was in a formal US Coast Guard suit while the other two had what appeared to be matching two-piece black suits. They reminded him of O'Neil, which made him nervous.

"Well, good morning, Mr. Chandler," the man in the middle said as he rose to his feet. "I'm Deputy Director Benjamin Chambers with the Federal Bureau of Investigation. To my right is Commander Joshua Vassar of the Coast Guard, and here on the other side of me is my right-hand man, Special Agent Brandon Knowles." The two rose to their feet and extended their hands to Jack. He put on a half smile and shook. "You know Agents Richardson and Morelli, correct?"

"Yes, sir," Jack replied. He walked over toward Nate and took a seat. When he was properly seated, Chambers sat back down and looked toward him. Jack's mind must have drifted a bit before he caught on to the introductions.

"Listen, Jack. I know what you're probably thinking about us; I would also be a little skeptical after being lied to and fooled. I just want to assure you that here, today, everyone is really who they claim to be," Nate explained. "In reference to Agent Morelli over here, I have to say that I didn't even know he was FBI, but the fact of the matter is that he was undercover as a Coast Guard commander." Nate looked over to the senior officer and said, "Sorry, sir, I just thought it would be easier if I stepped in there."

Chambers raised his left eyebrow and said, "Not a problem, Richardson, but in the future, let us handle this inquiry." He removed a pen from his inside jacket pocket and tapped it against the table. He turned to Jack. "Well, Mr. Chandler—"

"Jack, thanks," he interrupted.

"All right, Jack, I just want to thank you for being with us this morning. I understand that you are probably going through some difficult things, emotionally and all, and with that in mind, we will keep this as short as possible. Quite frankly, you, Agent Richardson, and Agent Morelli all did such a good job documenting everything, we won't need much out of any of you." He looked to the table and opened a manila folder, which was filled with pictures and documents with red-inked stamps that read CONFIDENTIAL. "This is more of an informational session than anything else."

"How did you guys know about Billings or O'Neil?" Jack asked, glaring at the others. "If you knew this guy was out there and a part of The Lighthouse Society, why didn't you go after him earlier? A few lives could have been saved if he hadn't been on the loose."

Chambers cleared his throat and said, "That's a fair, yet difficult question to answer, Jack. To be honest, we suspected he had a connection with Carroll Island, but he'd always covered his tracks really well. We couldn't prove his involvement with the Society, and we couldn't prove that he and Robert Billings were one and the same. O'Neil was an expert. He was a former Marine and CIA operative. He probably has more aliases than we will ever know about."

"With all due respect, that doesn't answer my question, sir," Jack replied. "You must have had something on the guy."

"Yes, Jack, we did," Chambers said. "Agent Morelli had been investigating Agent O'Neil on some very serious internal *and* external issues."

"What issues?"

"I'm sure you will understand that we cannot disclose those to you or any other member of the public," Chambers insisted. "Your friend Agent Richardson hasn't even been fully briefed on the investigation. I can assure you, though, our investigation of Agent O'Neil dealt specifically with Bureau matters. If it weren't for you and Agent Richardson, we'd never have known of his full involvement on Carroll. We couldn't get a warrant to go out there, and that's where you were particularly helpful."

Jack was growing increasingly agitated at the run-around he getting, yet realized he shouldn't have expected anything different. He stood up from his chair. "Director Chambers, it doesn't seem as if you really need me here at all. If you don't mind, I need to make arrangements to get on with the rest of my life..."

"That's exactly why we wanted to speak with you today," Chambers said. "Jack, I've spoken with Agents Morelli and Richardson about the events of the past weekend, and they felt that you could be a very good asset for the Bureau to have."

Jack chuckled. "You know what the problem would be with me doing something like that?"

"No, I don't."

"Orders," Jack replied. "I'll admit, it's a fairly enticing offer, but just ask these two. I'm horrible with orders."

"It's a great opportunity, Jack," Nate said. "We could really be a great team."

Jack shrugged his shoulders and smiled as he walked toward the door. He reached for the knob, turned to the others, and said, "Perhaps someday, Nate. If you will all excuse me, I have a funeral to plan. Sixteen years is long enough. My parents deserve a proper burial."

THE END

ABOUT THE AUTHOR

Jerry Graffam was born and raised on the rugged coast of Maine and began sailing with his family at an early age. After spending his teenage years living in London, England, Jerry returned to the U.S. and enrolled at Babson College where he studied business menagement. Three semesters and numerous short stories later, Jerry decided that financial accounting was far too monotonous for his tastes and he transferred to the University of Maine to study English.

After graduating from the University of Southern Maine in 2003 with a degree in English Literature, Jerry decided to forgo the life of corporate America and concentrate his time learning the craft of the novel. Fortunate to study with the likes of Dennis Lehane and Tom Perotta at the Stone Coast Writer's Conference for two straight summers, Jerry completed his first novel, The Lighthouse Society.

Jerry lives in greater Portland, Maine, with his wife and their 13-year-old cat, Fatty. Jerry spends his weeks working in risk management for a disability insurance carrier and spends most non-working days skiing or sailing.